I0744619

Published by: Cinnabar Moth Publishing LLC
Santa Fe, New Mexico

Cover Design by: Ira Geneve

ISBN-13: 978-1-953971-91-3
Library of Congress Control Number: 2023939996

The Order of the Banshee

ROBYN SINGER

Dedicated to my Goblin Gal

CHAPTER 1: YAEL

For the bulk of my career as a thief, I'd been a solo operator. I'd had engineers to keep me flying and Jellz to arrange jobs for me, but I'd done all the stealing on my own. Now, however, I had a crack team of experts working alongside me.

Or at least, I would have, if I hadn't ended up responsible for a bunch of kids.

"Dr. Gor'Nx, so nice to finally meet you," a bespectacled scientist greeted me as he shook my hand.

The facial prosthetics I was wearing to impersonate Ralack Gor'Nx, disgusting eugenicist, had taken me forever to put on right. Fortunately, the stuff was far easier to take off.

"You as well, Dr. Horowitz," I replied. "These are my assistant and bodyguard."

Layla and Shun, standing right behind me, nodded. They were both only seventeen, and they certainly looked it out of costume, but the prosthetics made them appear double their true ages. Both of them taller than me, Layla had light skin and short, straight, dark hair, while Shun was closer to Aarif in skin tone, had two braids running down her back, and was even more muscular than me.

Dr. Horowitz nodded back at them. "Shall we get straight to business?"

I smirked like the real-life supervillain I was impersonating. "Lead the way."

Dr. Horowitz turned around, and we followed him through the halls of the Cykebian Center for Genetic Development. "Ralack" was here to aid in their ongoing quest to make all Cykebian babies be born with enhancements. Of course, said process would also kill any fetuses that lacked enhancements.

That wasn't why we were here though. The work these people did was awful, but normally it wouldn't be any of my business. A client wanted a flash drive with information that wasn't kept on any computer, though, so here we were.

Surrounding us were humanoid robots with weapons. Along with the developments in genetic enhancements over the last five years, cybernetics had also come a long way. That meant not only was everyone who worked here about as strong as me, if not stronger, but they were guarded by even stronger machines.

We took an elevator up to the top floor of the complex and arrived in a black and silver office with Cykebian flags and an ornately framed picture of the emperor who'd legalized genetic enhancements hung up on the wall. Seated at the desk was the man in charge of the facility, Nathaniel Horn. The duke of Siswiol, he was fat as a pig and dressed in an aqua jumpsuit with white gloves, black boots, and a cravat, with a monocle on his face.

Nathaniel was as bad as Cykebian nobles got. On top of the work he did here, he was also known for beating his wife and was a proud advocate for the reinstatement of slavery. There was no question he spent his weekends torturing commoners.

He sort of reminded me of General Galopire of the Sunrisers. They were both bastards who were as ugly on the outside as they were on the inside, and yet they thought they were the gods' gift to the universe. Credit where it was due to Moli's dad, he'd at least tried to kick Galopire out of the Sunrisers when he'd been caught extorting the people living on his land, but, of course, the rest of the generals stood by the bastard. The only major difference I could think of was, from what I'd heard, Galopire was actually against the R&D of genetic engineering. He saw it as a waste of money.

"Yael, I'm in their systems," Marcos said to me over my com device, bringing me back to reality. *"Plan 'My Wife's Boobs are the Best" is ready to go on your call."*

"Yes, yes, that's all well and good," Griffin groaned. *"Now can you please tell me what my role in this mission is? Surely you can't expect me to just wait in the ship and do nothing for the third time in a row. I deserve some action!"*

"Marcos, please shut him up," Shun said under her breath. *"You don't have the authority to tell them what to—"*

Griffin was cut off as he was tazed by Marcos. I respected his desire to not be a traditional noble and instead become "a gentleman thief," but he could be as annoying as any other of his people. If not for Moli's built-up tolerance and ability to handle guys like him, I probably would have shot him into space years ago.

"You okay, Griff?" Layla asked softly. *"I'm... gonna kill you... Platyperson."* Marcos snickered. *"You can try, Posh Boy."*

I forced myself to smile and nod as Nathaniel stood up, and he and Dr. Horowitz continued to speak, pretending to pay attention. I'd barely been able to listen to other, boring people when it was just Aarif in my ear. With a whole school chatting around me, it was basically impossible.

"So, what do you think?" Nathaniel asked.

"Umm," I hummed. I'd heard only about five or six words total, so I turned to Layla. "I'm interested in my assistant's opinion on the matter."

"Me?" Layla bounced on her feat. "Oh, okay. Well, um, I think that the recent tests seem to have exceeded our expectations, and that we're ready to move on to experimenting on organic subject matter. However, Dr. Gor'Nx will need to overlook all the primary data herself to be sure."

I nodded. "I couldn't have expressed my thoughts on the matter better."

Layla may not have wanted to be here, but she was as sharp as her great-grandma, and far better than me at dealing with others. Apart from her lack of a desire to be a thief, she reminded me a lot of when P'Ken was a kid.

Nathaniel led us all downstairs to one of their numerous cold and sterile laboratories. In the presence of the duke, the scientists at work lowered their heads. He approached a safe and opened it with a 35-digit pin, followed by a finger scan and a retinal scan. Looking inside, the sole contents of the safe were what we were here for.

"Thank you, your lordship," I said, reaching out my hand. "I'll review the data and return the drive to you at my soonest convenience."

Nathaniel sneered. "Doctor, you know as well as I do I can't allow this data to leave this facility. You must review it here."

I smirked. "I was really hoping you'd say that."

Making a fitting sound effect with my mouth, I kicked the

drive out of Nathaniel's hand, leaped into the air, and caught it.

The duke and Dr. Horowitz scoffed. "What is the meaning of this?" I licked my lips. "Ladies… faces off."

Shun, Layla, and I stuck our fingers in our ears and twisted them around. Moments later, the prosthetics we were wearing disintegrated. Upon seeing who they were dealing with, the duke and Horowitz backed up in horror as other scientists shrieked.

"Super Soldier, Shun Segisteel. Bounty: 82,000,000 gidgits."

"The Prodigal Daughter, Layla N'Gwa. Bounty: 100,000,000 gidgits."

"And the second most wanted thief in the universe. Evil Incarnate, Yael Pavnick. Bounty: 290,000,000 gidgits."

"You know, I think the emperor may have been thinking with a little bit of bias when she named me that," I laughed. "So how's this gonna go?"

Nathaniel's face warped, his fear morphing into a wide grin. "You've made a big mistake coming here. But I must thank you for giving me the opportunity to be the one to lead your capture."

"Really?" I raised an eyebrow. "All the geniuses and generals and armies I've beaten without breaking a sweat, and you think you're the one that's got my number? You and the other losers that work here?"

Nathaniel breathed heavily as he nodded. "Everyone who works in this building has been genetically enhanced by proper, Cykebian science, as opposed to the grimy criminals who worked on you." He turned his head to Shun. "You may be stronger than all of us, but you still can't compete with our numbers." His eyes turned to Layla. "And you even brought a weak link."

"Of course I did," I cheered. "If you knew how much Madame N'gwa was paying me to teach her, you'd get it." I cracked my fingers. "But seriously, I'm supposed to be scared of a bunch of scientists and secretaries? Come on, man. I may not be able to take you all down in one punch, but I'm still feeling pretty good about my odds."

The duke took a step back, grinding his teeth. "Your lordship?" Dr. Horowitz whimpered.

"BWAHAHAHAHA!" Nathaniel's eyes bulged from his head. "I think someone is overestimating herself. I know all about you. You play tricks on people to get them to do what you want."

I shrugged. "Not my fault most people are dummies."

"Well alas for you, I'm not like most people. You knew coming here how strongly I believed in the superiority of those enhanced by the empire, and you're trying to goad me into proving it by taking you on directly, instead of calling our proper security. Well, that's not going to work." Nathaniel put his fingers to his ear. "All Cykerdroids to Laboratory ZX-Alpha. Voice command: Lasagna."

Dr. Horowitz pointed at us, his hand shaking. "You see. You have no chance of escaping.

Su...surrender now!"

I clicked my tongue. "Cykerdroids. I've read a lot about them. As intelligent and disciplined as a seasoned soldier, and virtually indestructible. They're impressive. Layla, Shun, do you think you could take more than maybe one of them?"

"Of course not," Layla answered. "No," Shun followed, succinctly.

"And I agree! Those things would kick my ass."

Nathaniel laughed again. "So you admit it then? This

is checkmate?"

"Oh. I never said that."

The doors to the lab slid open, and in rushed over a dozen Cykerdroids. Mostly black with bits of silver, they were each over a head taller than me, and their blasters, which were capable of taking out entire armies, were pointed at my head.

"Drop the bravado. It's over. Emperor Kaybell will make your execution the most grand in history, and I will be rewarded most handsomely."

I raised a finger. "Ooooooooor, and hear me out… voice override: Moli's boobs."

In an instant, the Cykerdroids all turned their blasters away from me, and onto Nathaniel, Horowitz, and the other scientists.

"Cykerdroids! What are you doing?!" Veins popped out of Nathaniel's forehead and his head shook in place. "How? How did you do this?!"

I covered half my face with my hand as I laughed hysterically. "Too easy." I lowered my hand and rolled my shoulders back. "Okay, so you clearly know a thing or two about me. This should include the fact that I know my way around writing code. And, with some help, it wasn't too difficult to hack into the network the Cykerdroids are all linked up to. Of course, you have security measures in place for such an occurrence, but those can also be temporarily disabled without notice. And with my dude on the outside, we were able to line up the timing perfectly." I took a few steps toward the duke. "You were right. I do trick people into doing what I want. But you thought I wanted a fight? No! Shun and I are awesome, but we could have still easily lost. I had to make sure that you gathered all the Cykerdroids here, so that they could escort us out, and we wouldn't have to deal with any others on the way."

Nathaniel screamed at the top of his lungs, his rage palpable, as he fell to his knees and buried his face in his hands.

"Cykerdroids, let's move out!" I ordered. "Protect myself and the two women next to me at all costs."

Guided by the killer robots, with the flash drive still in my possession, we made our way out of the building I'd only momentarily considered setting ablaze.

"You really are as scary as my g-gma," Layla commented.

"*Please, without me, this plan wouldn't have worked at all,*" Marcos replied.

"*I'd still like to know why I wasn't included!*" Griffin shouted. "*Shun didn't even do anything!*"

"She was back up," I said. "In case we did have to fight, she's the only one who can keep up with me. Plus, her face is already known. It's best we keep you a secret until the time is right."

"*Hmph! I deserve a bounty and a cool nickname.*"

"*Permission to taze him again?*"

"Please," Shun said.

"No!" Layla followed.

I shook my head, giggling. "We'll be back at *Ricochet* in a few minutes. Let's go home."

———

I never thought I'd own a planet, and technically I still didn't, but for all intents and purposes, I may as well have. Three years after I joined The Order of the Banshee, Madame N'gwa asked me to train her daughter and make her more enthused about the family business. Naturally, I agreed to the job.

Not long after, Jellz retired, and while I no longer needed a manager, I did still need a superior programmer, so I picked up Marcos. However, instead of gidgits, they wanted training.

And just when I thought *Ricochet* couldn't get even more cramped, Griffin tracked me down and begged me to take him on as a disciple. I put him through some fake tests that I assumed he'd fail miserably, but when he actually managed to pass them all, I had no choice but to let the doofus in.

At that point, since I refused to get a new ship, we needed a new place to call home. We found MCV-2, an uninhabited but terraformed planet, and had a big-ass castle built on it. I'd wanted something smaller and simpler, but I was outvoted. And not long after the castle was completed, Shun found her way to us as well.

This wasn't exactly the situation I'd ever pictured myself in, and the kids' voices sometimes grated my ears like cheese, but we had a good thing going on for the time being. Before I was 40, they'd all move out and become independent thieves, and my wife and I could get back to flying around space and going on non-stop adventures.

BARK! BARK!

Along with the greatest dog in every reality of the multiverse, of course.

"Hi, Juri!" Layla cheered as we stepped off the ship. "How's the best girl doing today?"

"Well, it's bath day, so neither of us is at 100%" Aarif said, coming down the stairs, covered in scratch marks.

"For the millionth time, hire a professional groomer," Griffin said, the blonde dressed similarly to the duke and even paler than usual.

"And for the billionth time, if anyone but me tries to

bathe Juri, people will die."

"Dumbass," Marcos snorted, hovering past Griffin in their chair and, like usual, wearing a platypus hoodie.

Unlike the others, Shun remained silent. It was easy to see how well she'd been trained by the Utozin military with how she could make herself almost invisible.

"There's my girl!"

My heart raced as Moli ran into the shuttle bay, dressed head-to-toe in leather like she was most days, and jumped over the railings above us, into my arms.

"Mmm, I missed you," I moaned as we made out for the first time in two days.

"I missed you more," Moli replied, doing my second favorite thing she could do with her tongue.

"Hey, hey," I said, pulling away for a second. "We should probably all scatter and do this in our room. Before—"

"Yael!"

Ah, crap, I thought, going as pale as Griffin.

Slamming her bejeweled walking stick against the metal platform, P'Ken glared down at all of us. Her eyes were ice cold and sent a chill through the entire room. It hadn't taken long for her to become a brilliant thief, but when we opened the school, she'd fallen back into the element she was raised in. She went off on adventures both alongside me and on her own, but she also taught the kids, organized their curriculum, and handled all of our home's upkeep.

In some ways, having a trained headmistress to run things for me was immensely helpful. But also, she hadn't been trained to be a *kind* headmistress. When she wasn't in teacher mode and emulating her mother, we got along as well as we used to. But when she was…

"Oh, hey, P'Ken," I swallowed. "How were things while we were gone?"

P'Ken slowly and gracefully descended down the staircase. Despite only being 21, she moved with a far older presence. Upon reaching the bottom, she slammed her stick down three more times in quick succession. Without hesitation, Layla, Shun, and Griffin lined up and stood at attention, and Marcos rushed to hover over next to them.

"P'Ken, they just got home," Aarif said. "Is this really necessary?"

P'Ken didn't stop walking and whacked Aarif with her stick on her way over to me.

"I am not happy with how your most recent mission went," she said, freezing my soul. "I'll discuss the children's failings with them first because it's imperative they don't get any wrong ideas stuck in their heads, but you and I will be having a long conversation about this. Understood?"

Knees shaking under me, I nodded.

"Good. You may leave, then."

"Thanks the gods," I sighed.

P'Ken spun spun around on her heels. "I am immensely disappointed in all of you. For starters, Layla. Do you really think Madame N'gwa would be happy knowing…?"

As P'Ken continued, I took Moli's hand and led us up the stairs. Both of us giggled along the way as I imagined tearing my girl's clothes off and seeing the glorious boobs I'd named my most recent plan after.

"Don't forget me!"

Aarif and Juri came running after us, not wanting to be

alone with P'Ken. Layla was already in tears, and if the usual pattern held, Griffin would be crying soon too and Marcos would be getting repeatedly whacked for talking back.

"We could try stopping her one of these days," Moli whispered.

"Counterpoint: she's very, very scary."

Moli and I went upstairs to our room, and while we ripped our clothes off, I took all of our toys out of one of my drawers. Wild, crazy, and often drunken and messy sex with Molina was one of the highlights of my life, alongside talking to her, holding her close after sex, and stealing shit. I'd been so stupid to abandon her for a decade, and it was strange looking back that, for a brief time, we'd been enemies.

But that was all in the past. We were happily married, and to make things even better, I still had my two best friends, my amazing doggo, a job I loved, and all the money in the world. I'd even achieved practically all my dreams as a thief, with my bounty now only below my mentor and hero's.

I had everything. And yet I'd never been more miserable.

CHAPTER 2: MOLINA

Yael was never peaceful in her sleep. Sometimes it was adorable, as she'd blurt out lines from her ridiculous dreams and punch and kick the air. Other times, it was annoying as hell, as she'd sleepwalk, go to the fridge, and stuff food in my mouth. And usually it was weird food she and Aarif liked that I wouldn't touch. But sometimes, it wasn't adorable or annoying. Sometimes it was scary.

"Ahh!" Yael shrieked, shaking her knees. "Ahhh!"

"Yael, baby, wake up" I said, getting on top of her and resting my hands on her face. "Wake up!"

Yael's eyes jolted open, and she tried to throw me off her. That had happened a few times before, but I'd learned how to grab onto her so I stayed in place. As Yael panted, she wrapped her arms around my waist and squeezed me like one of the stuffed animals she'd had as a kid.

"It's okay," I whispered. "It's okay. You're home. You aren't back there."

Yael's warm breath continued to blow against my ear. "It hurts. It shouldn't, but it does. Every other week... I'm on the

Noriker. And every time I close my eyes, I see that bitch." Yael roared, slamming her fists down on the bed, shaking the entire room. "I could have killed her. Instead, she's the fucking emperor."

As I crawled back over to Yael's side and wrapped my arms around her, I swallowed my guilt. While in part we hadn't been in a good position to kill Kaybell five years ago given Yael was dying of radiation poisoning and bleeding out, I was the real reason she was still alive. Even after the horrific torture she'd put Yael through, and the heinous crimes she'd confessed to, I'd still cared about her.

I didn't think I still cared about her after all this time, especially when she was responsible for my wife's continued suffering, but I wasn't sure how I'd act if I saw her again. I'd made the choice to leave her behind, and I didn't regret that at all, but she'd still been my best friend for a decade. Those had been happy times.

"Yes, she's the emperor," I said calmly. "It would be great if we could do something about that, but we should take solace that her rule hasn't been much different from her father's."

Yael shook her head, her whole body moving with it. "She may not be acting like one out in the open, but we know what kind of monster she is. If P'Ken or any of the kids or I are ever caught, she won't hesitate to torture us to death as slowly as possible." Yael turned onto her side, her frightened eyes meeting mine. "A couple sessions did this to me. And she'd put us through so much more. I can't go back."

"And you never will," I replied immediately, tightening my grip. "It's been three years since she took the throne. If she was going to find us, she would have by now."

"But if I ever screw up, even slightly, on a mission—"

"Then she still won't nab you. You'll come up with a backup plan like you always do.

P'Ken is more than capable of taking care of herself these days, and the kids know to always do what you say. Kay may have every possible resource at her disposal, but you're the smartest woman in the universe. You always win."

I breathed an internal sigh of relief as that got Yael to smirk. "You're describing Madame N'gwa, not me."

"You're basically her apprentice, so I'd say it's apt."

Yael nuzzled her chest against mine, her smirk turning flirtatious. "If she ever does capture me or one of the others, can I count on my brave and noble swordswoman to come to the rescue?"

I smirked back at my brilliant wife and decided the best answer I could give wasn't a vocal one. I crawled under the covers and worked my way down.

"Ooooooh, my god," Yael giggled. "Really? Now?"

"It always makes you feel better."

***

"Good morning, everyone," I said, walking into my classroom.

Aarif, P'Ken, and I had each gotten to design our individual classrooms. As the kids' engineering teacher, Aarif's was more of a workshop than anything else. P'Ken, in charge of their general education, based her room off of those found at St. Shiala's School for Girls, creating a cold and harsh environment that matched her teaching style.

With the job of passing on my Sunriser training and everything I'd learned from my years of experience to them, I'd considered basing my classroom off of those at the Sunriser academy. In the end though, I wasn't P'Ken. I couldn't mix my past and my present. Captain Molina Langstone of the Sunrisers was gone, and in her place was Molina Pavnick-Langstone, educator of the next generation of thieves.

Ultimately, I'd created a more casual environment. The windows let in plenty of sun and air, the walls and furniture were a calming eggshell color, and the kids had plenty of room to walk around and stretch their legs.

"I hope you all slept off yesterday's mission."

Griffin scoffed. "Some of us didn't need to. You'd put me in the field, wouldn't you, Professor?"

"I—"

"Of course she would, but only because you play swords with her," Marcos cut me off.

"We share a common fondness for an unappreciated craft, but that doesn't mean she has a personal bias!"

"Oh yeah, I'm sure you spent plenty of time studying swords before you came here." "Professor, are you going to let them insult you like th—?"

"Oh my gods, both of you shut up!" Layla cried. "I love you guys, but it is way too early for this."

I sat down at my desk, taking note of the bags under Layla's eyes. "You *didn't* sleep well, did you?"

Layla shook her head. "Despite what Professor Amatyn said, none of us really did much on the mission, so I still had plenty of energy. Was up all night working on my newest sculpture."

"Oh? What is it?"

Layla grinned from ear to ear. "It's my interpretation of an Utozin Spider Shark. After Shun showed me one, I couldn't stop thinking about it."

I raised an eyebrow at the one student who'd been staying silent. "You're into marine life?" Shun kept as quiet as she'd been since I entered, simply responding with a shrug. "Right, well, I think that's pretty cool."

"Cool enough to convince Yael to let me submit it to interplanetary glassblowing competitions? I have a list of them and a fake identity all prepared!"

"Don't get ahead of yourself," Griffin said. "She first needs to speak to Yael about the great disrespect I'm being paid."

"If we're all making requests, I could use a new hover chair," Marcos said. "This one is starting to go."

I clicked my tongue and sighed. "Okay, Marcos, we'll definitely get you a new chair. But as for you two, you should know by now that no one can change Yael's mind about stuff like this. Layla, she lets you continue to practice glassblowing as a hobby because she's awesome, but your great-grandmother would take you away from us if she caught wind we were letting you compete. And Griffin, I believe you're ready for action in the field, but clearly Yael isn't convinced yet."

Layla and Griffin crossed their arms and turned their heads to opposite sides of the room, away from me. They weren't going to be listening to today's lesson at all.

"Not to step out of line, oh who am I kidding, I love stepping out of line, but aren't you her wife and partner?" Marcos asked. "Weren't you the one who actually made it as a Sunriser? Why don't you have more of a say in these matters?"

I groaned as I squeezed my forehead. "Yael and I are partners in life. But when it comes to the school and the business, she's the Banshee, she's the one with the expertise, and what she says goes."

Marcos laughed and shook their head. "And you're okay with this situation? You don't find it… demeaning?"

I lashed out my arm like a whip and pointed at the door. "Marcos, go see P'Ken for a disciplinary session immediately."

Marcos continued to chuckle as they hovered out of the room.

I stood back up and turned on the board behind me. "Anyone else have something to say, or are you ready to get started? Shun?"

Our strongest student shrugged again, while Layla and Griffin looked back at me only momentarily to sneer. I'd once commanded the respect of thousands, and now I couldn't even get four teenagers to respect me.

It was gonna be one of those days.

———

"Blaaaaaaah," I moaned like Yael, sitting down in the teacher's lounge with my coffee. "This morning was ridiculous."

"I did my best to reprimand Marcos, but you should have sent the others to me as well," P'Ken said, standing over me, tapping her stick against her hand. "You'd think after all this time, they'd know better than to disrespect their teacher."

Aarif sipped his coffee and set his mug down on the table. "Marcos was definitely out of line, and I'm with Yael about Griffin not being ready, but I'd think you of all people would sympathize with Layla. You ran away from finishing school to become a thief, just like she wants to run away from thief school to become a glassblower."

P'Ken pursed her lips together and sat down with us.

"She does have my sympathy. But I was only able to run away because of Yael's arrival, and her ability to protect me from the

bounty hunters Mother sent. There's no one who'd be able to keep her out of Madame N'gwa's reach. All we can do is fulfill our contract, make her a top-notch thief, and hope she eventually gets to live the life she wants."

I shook my head and stared down into my caffeinated brown sludge. I hadn't sent Layla to P'Ken because I agreed with Aarif, and I knew she deserved better. I didn't blame Yael for taking her on as an apprentice. She was still eager to please her hero and if she didn't train her, someone else would have, but we were still keeping her from living her dream.

I wasn't sure why everyone else thought so little of Griffin. I did spend more time with him than the others, as he made a far more useful sword training partner than Yael, but the impression I got was that Aarif and P'Ken thought he was too immature, which was ridiculous considering who they worked for. As for Yael, I hated assuming this of her, but I couldn't shake the feeling she was prejudiced against him for being a noble.

As for Marcos, the things they'd said weren't exactly original thoughts. They were things I'd thought about ever since I first set foot on *Ricochet*. That didn't mean I liked hearing them out loud.

"Do you guys think there's more I could be doing?" I asked.

"Don't let what Marcos said get to you," Aarif said, sipping his coffee. "You know how much of a shit-stirrer they are."

"Yeah, but even still, there may be some truth to their words. P'Ken, do you think I could handle solo jobs like you?"

P'Ken snorted. "I'm sorry, I'm sorry. But no. I was at

Yael's side constantly for three years and I picked up all her tricks. You'd just be starting out."

"I have all the same training Yael did when she started her career."

"Which means you're qualified for the types of jobs she was taking at the start. A world of difference from Banshee-level assignments." I buried my face in my coffee mug, not wanting the others to see the anxiety creeping up it. "And no offense, but you probably couldn't even handle the relatively easy stuff. Yael had her genetic enhancements and is, well, her. It's nothing to be ashamed of, but she's on a different level from all of us."

The coffee went down my throat like a lump of coal as I set my mug back down. I'd learned a long time ago that comparing myself to Yael, or anyone else, was a mistake. And even in spite of all the ways she was better than me, Yael still saw me as her equal. But P'Ken wasn't wrong. When it came to being a thief, she was special in ways I simply wasn't. And while I'd helped with plenty of heists, I'd never trained like P'Ken. Having my new wife as a teacher would have been far too weird.

"You see, you stay stuff like that, but then you talk to Yael like she's a little girl in need of a spanking," Aarif said to P'Ken.

"I have nothing but love and respect for our fearless leader," P'Ken replied. "That doesn't mean she isn't often an idiot in need of discipline."

Aarif rolled his eyes and turned his attention to his tablet.

"So I can't be a thief," I thought out loud. "But I know I could still be more than a thief's wife, an assistant thief, and a teacher of other thieves. I mean, the kids won't even be here much longer."

"What else do you think you'd want to be?" P'Ken asked.

"I have no idea," I answered, cracking a small smile. "I thought when I left the Sunrisers, I'd be free to do anything. That a whole new world of possibilities was opening up. And I have seen and experienced so many incredible things. But when it comes to how I want to spend my life, it seems like being a Sunriser was all I was good for."

"And if we're being honest, you weren't even particularly good at *that* job."

I glared at the woman eleven years my junior. "Was that really necessary to say?" "I'm just saying, we beat you fairly easily."

"You didn't even do much!"

P'Ken belted out a haughty laugh, and as I continued to glare at her, I joined in. It sucked to hear, but she wasn't wrong. I'd sucked more as a Sunriser captain than probably anyone else in history. Maybe I would have had a successful career if I'd never crossed paths with Yael, but that wasn't an alternate reality I wanted to think about.

"Um," Aarif hummed, his face having fallen. "Molina, I think...I think you should see this."

I furrowed my brow as I grabbed his tablet from him. Immediately catching my eyes was a photo of Father in his full dress uniform. My eyes made their way up to the headline of the news article it was a part of, and as soon as they did, my heart fell down my chest.

"Drenian Langstone, Supreme General of the Sunrisers, dies at 71."

CHAPTER 3: YAEL

"I don't understand how this could happen," Moli said, resting her head on my lap. "He was still so young."

Seated on our bed, I gently stroked her amber hair. "Death is something we can't ever predict. Even if you're young and doing everything possible to keep yourself healthy, something, or someone, could end it all in an instant."

Moli nuzzled her head against my legs. "It's not fair. He was a great man. He was everything a Sunriser *should* be."

I couldn't fathom what Molina was going through; both of my parents were still alive and happily running their pickle business. But her pain was my pain. And even beyond that, despite not having seen him since I was a teenager, I still had fond memories of Drenian. Regardless of what I may have thought of the Sunrisers as a whole, he'd always been good to me.

"The Sunrisers and the universe as a whole will be worse off without him."

Moli sat up straight and directed her watery eyes at mine. "We have more money than we know what to do with. Promise me we'll donate a large portion of it to fighting this illness? I don't want anyone else to go through this."

"Of course. Whatever you want." I curled my lips ever so slightly. "Remember the first time you guys had me over for dinner? He was so excited to meet the best friend you wouldn't shut up about, only to be left deeply confused as I ranked all the food we ate, jumped around his house like a goblin, and talked for 20 minutes straight about all the board games we'd been playing."

Moli smiled back at me. "It may not have been the strongest first impression, but he was still impressed enough by your knowledge and dedication to the Sunrisers that he took you with us to an amusement park the next week."

"Where the unflappable general got sick on a roller coaster."

Molina giggled with me, only for a new wave of tears to stream down her face.

"I should have been with him more," she said. "I shouldn't have stayed so distant these past few years."

"You would have had to lie to him about your entire life. He was better off not knowing what you're doing."

Moli lowered and shook her head. "Well, I'm gonna have to go back to Cykeb now, at least. I need to be there for his funeral. I owe that to him."

I tugged at my hair and bit my lip. "You definitely need to go… but you know I won't be able to go with you, right? Even if I wore prosthetics, the security they'll have for something like this will be advanced enough to detect me."

Keeping her head down, Moli cringed. "I know. It'd be so amazingly helpful if you could come with me, but… these are the results of your choices."

Maybe I was hearing things that weren't there, and now

definitely wasn't the time to bring it up, but that sounded like an attack. Where was that coming from?

"Where is this coming from?"

Dammit! I thought as I said that aloud.

Moli, still crying, looked back up at me. "I know how much being a thief means to you, and I'd never ask you to stop. But being who you are means having to give certain things up." Moli wiped her tears on her sleeve. "I gave up my entire life for you, thinking I'd be able to build a new one. But five years later, and you're still all I have. And when your job keeps you from being with me… I have nothing."

"I don't understand," I said, my hands shaking. "I thought you were happy here."

"I am happy! So long as I'm with you, I'll always be happy. And I like teaching and I like sometimes helping you with heists." Snot escaped her nose as her cheeks grew puffy. "But you're always going away on jobs, and even when we're together, happiness doesn't equate to satisfaction."

Fucking Hell. I was supposed to be one of the smartest women in the universe, and yet I'd been so busy dealing with my own shit, I hadn't noticed my Moli was having a midlife crisis.

"I'm so sorry," I said, putting my shaky hands on her face. "What do you think you need?"

"That's the problem. I have no idea. And now with Father gone, I'm more confused than ever."

There had to be something I could say or do to fix this, but nothing was coming to me. I could do thirty-two digit multiplication in my head in under a minute, but my stupid brain wouldn't tell me what I needed to do to help my wife when she needed me most.

"I'm glad you're telling me all this. I don't know how long you've been keeping it bottled up. But you're dealing with something else right now. Maybe you should go to the funeral and give yourself time to mourn, and then when we get back, we can figure something out."

As much as what I was saying was selfishly motivated, since I needed more time to think about this, it probably was also the best move. Trying to take on all this at once would be too much.

Moli nodded. "Okay. Sounds like a plan."

"I always have one." Except when I didn't. "And hey, even if I can't come, you still shouldn't go alone. Marcos and Griffin don't have bounties on them, so they can go with you."

"Are you sure it's okay to take them away from their studies?"

"Of course. This is the least they can do for their awesome teacher." Moli sniffled and rested her forehead against mine. "I love you, Yael."

"I love you too," I said, taking her hands. "And I promise, we're going to figure things out. Together."

———

Aarif, P'Ken, Layla, and Shun stood alongside me on the roof of the school as we waved goodbye to Moli, Griffin, and Marcos. Not wanting to waste any time, they'd decided to leave right after dinner, so we were standing underneath the starry night sky.

Thankfully, these days, we had not one ship, but three. While I only flew on *Ricochet* and P'Ken primarily made use of the enormous *Cascade*, Moli and the others were flying off in

Miracle, our fastest, sleekest, and most modern ship.

Once *Miracle* was out of sight, people started going back inside. Shun was the first to leave, wanting to get to her third workout of the day. P'Ken left a little later, going to pack for her upcoming heist on Chog-Chog. Aarif stuck around for a while, but he eventually had to go feed Juri.

With them all gone, that left only Layla and me. "Why aren't you going back in?" I asked.

"Why aren't you?"

I popped my lips. "Uhhhh, I really don't want to bother you with the details, but basically, I've not been the best wife I could be, and I had no idea until last night."

"I'm sorry. But you know she loves you no matter what, right?"

I laughed and bobbed my head up and down. "Yeah. Yeah, sure."

I slapped Layla on the back, but I accidentally applied too much strength, and nearly sent her flying off the edge of the roof. Fortunately, as she gasped and her life probably flashed before her eyes, I grabbed her wrist and pulled her back on.

"Gods!" Layla exhaled, coughing.

"Sorry about that. But it's your turn now."

Continuing to pant, Layla kicked her foot back and forth across the roof. "I need to get out of here, Yael."

I shook my head. "We've been over this a million times. I'm all about freedom and people living their dreams, but until I'm more powerful than Madame N'gwa, which probably won't be until she dies, she has control of your life. And, to a lesser extent, mine."

"But it's not fair! She never put this on my parents or

their parents, but I'm the one she rips away from her friends, family, and school? It's bullshit!"

"You say this every couple months. And while I continue to agree with you, neither of us is in a position to change anything."

Layla crossed her arms and turned away from me. "Have you actually tried talking to G-gma about this?"

"Of course I ha—"

"And actually made it clear you disagree with what she's doing?"

I groaned as I scratched the back of my neck. "We aren't equals. I'm not in a position to talk back to her."

"You're a Banshee, one of her sisters, you have the second-highest bounty among all thieves, and she trusted you enough to train me. You've earned her respect, and she should listen to what you have to say."

She was saying all of this like I hadn't considered it before. I understood her perspective perfectly, and I got where she was coming from, but clearly I hadn't been transparent about why, on the surface, I'd been acting like Madame N'gwa's bitch.

"Who's your biggest inspiration as a glassblower?" I asked. "Your hero."

Layla looked at me curiously. "Remnick Thuly, inventor of the freezerburn technique."

"Okay, cool, and if you saw him doing something you thought was amoral, would you have the nerve to tell him that to his face?"

"I'm… I'm not sure," she said. "He's the reason I became a glassblower."

"And Madame N'gwa is the reason I became a thief. Her

respect means everything to me." Layla lowered her head, and I put a hand on her shoulder. "I'm sorry."

I may have been a criminal, but I hated playing the bad guy. I didn't have any delusions that I was a hero like I'd dreamed of being when I was growing up, but I still prided myself on being better than the likes of Kaybell, Nathaniel, and Galopire. Were my heart not already broken from what Moli had told me, the defeated look on Layla's face would be breaking it now.

Several times over the past year, I actually had called Madame N'gwa with the intention of asking her to let Layla go back to her home and art school. In the end though, I'd always chickened out.

"I get it." She looked up at me and smiled. "Can I at least show you my Utozin Spider Shark? I think it came out really well!"

I smiled back at her. "I'm excited to see it."

I should have known today would be a bad day. Days where I was woken up by nightmares weren't universally atrocious, but they typically weren't great. Even still, today was something of a new low. Between my conversations with Molina and Layla, I'd hardly had time to think about the emptiness inside me. I could have seen a therapist, but after so many years of shouting my problems at Aarif, the habit was hard to break.

"Tell me how to not feel like shiiiiiiiit," I moaned, draping myself over my platonic life partner like a sloth.

Aarif sighed and set his wrench down. I'd interrupted him during his workshop time, and he did not appreciate being interrupted during his workshop time, but dammit, I needed him, and I'd paid for his fancy-schmancy workshop. Of course, I was happy to do so. Aarif had been keeping up with the advancements in cybernetics over the past few years, both for fun and to make upgrades to Juri, but also so he could set up a killer defense system around the school.

From our stationary position, we could outfight a Parallax-class ship.

"Okay, okay," he said. "The first thing you can do is help Layla. I know it's hard, but if you really care about her, you need to stand up to Madame N'gwa."

"I can't do that," I moaned. "She trusted me, and I'd be letting her down."

"Do you really want the approval of someone who'd do this to her grandkid?"

The answer was "Yes" because it was still Madame freaking N'gwa, but I got what Aarif was saying. I couldn't face her in person, no way in Hell was that happening, but maybe, if I was subtle and careful with my words, I could convince my hero to be who I knew she was.

"Let's see what else," Aarif continued. "Um, I'm not sure it's a great idea, but you could give Griffin a shot in the field when he gets back."

"Griffin? What does he have to do with anything?"

Aarif shrugged. "He's Molina's favorite, and it'd probably mean a lot to her to see him given a chance to succeed. Plus, he'd send more positive energy your way."

Griffin wasn't completely talentless. He wouldn't be here if I thought he was. But I remained hesitant to bring him with me on a job. He wasn't super smart like Layla and Marcos or super strong like Shun, and he wasn't even as good with a sword as Moli.

He was an average noble who got bored of his life. Still, if it would make Moli feel even a little better, I'd take a chance on him.

"Any other ideas to help Moli or is that all you've got?"

Aarif pulled away from me and looked me in the eyes. In response, my eyes wandered over to his tattoo of a rat eating a grape. Losing Kidney had been a real tragedy.

"Take a break from work," Aarif said. "Stop stealing, stop teaching, just stop, and help her through her crisis. Emotionally support Molina, and help her find what she's looking for. And most importantly, even if you're not interested in whatever her passion ends up being, you act like you are."

"Everything you're saying is hard and annoying."

"That's how you know I'm right." Aarif rolled his shoulders. "You don't need to beat yourself up over missing the signs. Focus on what you can do now."

"Blaaaaaaah. I hate you." I stood up, shook my arms and flapped my hands. "Well, thanks. I guess I'll try those things."

Aarif narrowed his eyes. "Is that all you want to talk about?"

"What else is there?" I nervously giggled. "My nightmares? I think we've established by now I can't do shit about them."

"Come on, Yael. You can fool the others, but not me. You haven't had your usual energy in a long time. Maybe Molina isn't the only one questioning her life."

"I don't know what you're talking about," I said as I flailed my head around. "I've got everything and everyone I want and need. Once things with Layla and Molina are fixed, everything will be perfect."

Aarif stood up. "You don't need to tell me what's wrong. But just like you knew you could come to me about everything else, you can come to me whenever you're ready to get real."

I bit my lip hard enough to make it bleed a little. "Thanks, man. Maybe, uh, maybe another time. I'm gonna go watch some wrestling with P'Ken. You wanna join us?"

Aarif smirked. "See, now that depends on if you two will be replicating all the moves you see on me."

I snickered. "It wouldn't be like old times if we didn't."

CHAPTER 4: MOLINA

"Father, why do people become criminals?"

Father looked up from his steak at me and across the dining room table as he chewed on his dinner. After swallowing, he dabbed at the sauce on his face with a napkin before answering.

"There are too many reasons to count," he said. "Why?"

I looked down, away from his harsh eyes, and rolled my brussels sprouts around with my fork. "The Sunrisers only exist because people do bad things. Why can't everyone just move to the Cykebian Empire? All their needs would be met, and they wouldn't have to hurt anyone."

Father sipped his wine, which was almost as red as his steak. "No one sees themselves as the villain. No one performs actions they don't view as just. The man we consider a violent radical sees himself as a freedom fighter. The petty dictator sees himself as entitled to power. Even the man who steals a loaf of bread to feed his family would rather risk prison time than live among what he views as a corrupt society."

I shook my head. "But why would anyone see the Cykebian Empire as corrupt? It's a utopia."

"That's true now, but it hasn't always been. The empire has a dark history. Its founder sought to conquer the entire universe and force everyone in it to worship him as a god, the nobility for centuries partook in torturing commoners as a past-time, and for many, the fact that the monarchy and aristocracy are still in place at all are signs that nothing has changed. Misguided as they may be, I can see where they're coming from. Getting to where I am as a commoner has been far from easy."

Everything Father was saying was so sad. The fact that people threw their lives away as criminals because they didn't understand how things worked was horrible. It meant no matter what the Sunrisers did, there would always be more people causing trouble and harming others.

"The fact you've become supreme general at all proves them wrong," I said. "Maybe when I become supreme general too, it'll help open some eyes?"

Father chuckled as he took another bite of steak. "Perhaps."

I sighed. "Of course, that'll only happen if I can beat Yael. She's so much better than me at everything!"

Father waved his finger at me as he chewed. "It's true that physically and academically, she's always outperformed you, as well as everyone else in your class. But you're still smarter than most others your age, and while you may lack in certain areas compared to Yael, you more than make up for it in manners and decorum. In an institution like the Sunrisers, you can't underestimate how important those are."

I smiled weakly. He had no idea how hard it was for me to act perfect all the time, and not like Yael. I hadn't told him about the diagnosis I'd received, and I never would.

"I understand, Father."

"Good." He grinned. "I believe in you, Molina. You're going to be the greatest Sunriser in history. And with the power of supreme general, you'll be able to change the universe."

As I smiled back at Father, the world around me faded away. My eyes flickered as my warm, childhood home was replaced with the cold metal of *Miracle*, and my endlessly supportive father was replaced by two bickering teenagers.

"You think you know anything about decoupage?" Griffin growled. "You can't even pronounce it correctly."

"I know I can replicate it on my computer in half the time it would take to do it by hand," Marcos smirked.

"No, no you couldn't! It would lack the same impact! The gravitas!"

"Someone's just cranky cause one of their special skills is worthless."

"Guys!" I shouted, sitting up in my chair and rolling my shoulders back. "We're almost at Cykeb. Do you think we could please complete this voyage in silence?"

Griffin and Marcos continued to stare each other down, before ultimately humphing and turning away from one another. For what it was worth, I agreed that decoupage was a beautiful art that couldn't be replicated by computers. But had I said that, Marcos probably would have just called me biased again. I got that they were a programming prodigy, but the ego on them was even bigger than Yael's when she was their age.

Hopefully, they'd both stay quiet for the next hour. If they didn't keep their mouths shut during the funeral, I wouldn't need P'Ken to discipline them.

———

On the surface, Cykeb hadn't changed at all over the past five years. Enormous, chrome skyscrapers covered the vast majority of the fully developed planet, and environmentally safe cars filled the clear blue skies. On the streets below, families and couples of all races, genders, and sexualities leisurely walked to one of the hundreds of businesses and restaurants in the area, everything they could ever want or need within walking distance and easily affordable. There was no one living on the streets. Poverty here had long ago been eradicated.

It was paradise. Or at least, that was what I'd always believed. Little did I know, the tradition of nobles kidnapping commoners and torturing them to death had continued into the modern day. I'd made sure to question Griffin about his views on the custom before he became Yael's student, but as I learned, his noble family held such little power and importance, they'd never been brought into the sadistic fold. He was as disgusted by the prospect as I was.

Our destination was Hxoart, and Todd's Funeral Home. Typically, they only provided their services to nobles or other exceptionally rich people, but Father wasn't like other commoners. He'd been the supreme general of the Sunrisers for over two decades. He deserved the best.

On most days, I dressed head to toe in leather. I knew Yael found it sexy, and I quite liked it. Today, however, Griffin, Marcos, and I were in matching black-and-orange suits. It was more difficult than it should have been getting Marcos to not wear their platypus hoodie.

We landed *Miracle* at a docking station—unlike *Ricochet*, it wasn't small enough to leave in a parking lot—and took a city-car to the funeral home. Griffin looked in awe at his surroundings, fully taken in by their seeming magnificence, while Marcos couldn't have cared less where we were.

When we arrived at the funeral home, there was a large group gathered outside, all of them either in black-and-orange formalwear or Sunriser dress uniforms. I'd expected people to come up to me and give their condolences, but that didn't happen. They all just continued to focus on their current conversations. Really, I should have seen that coming. I was the dishonorably discharged embarrassment of the family, after all.

"When I die, I want hundreds of women crying at my funeral and leaving flowers on my casket," Griffin said, "their hopes dashed of ever being with the universe's greatest and most handsome gentleman thief."

Marcos snorted. "You'll be lucky if you don't get yourself killed before your own flower's taken."

"I am not a vir—!"

I elbowed Griffin in the gut to shut him up before he could completely embarrass me. Marcos covered their mouth and laughed. Gods, Shun and Layla would have been easier to handle.

"Molina?"

Crap. Knew this was coming.

From the mob of mourners, Morphea emerged, dabbing at her tear-filled face with a handkerchief. She was in her dress uniform, the five earrings she wore in each ear as the supreme general's adjutant all attached to each other, and she'd dyed her bright-pink hair partially black.

My little sister and I had never gotten along. Since we were kids, we'd been in brutal competition for Father's love and affection. She'd been insulting and belittling me for almost as long as she could talk, and my Autistic ass was never able to come up with any good comebacks. Yael and Kaybell had always protected me from her, but they weren't here now, and I wasn't about to let my students fight my battle for me. I was going to stand up to her. Even if she found a way to blame Father's death on me, I wouldn't back down.

"I'm so glad you're here."

Morphea wrapped her arms around me, and not that I didn't love Yael's bear hugs, but it was nice receiving a familial, soft but firm hug again after so long. It almost distracted me from how weird it was this was happening.

"You... are?"

Morphea pulled back, keeping her hands on my shoulders. "Of course. It's been years and I wasn't sure you'd come."

"And you were hoping I would? Don't you hate me?"

Morphea sniffled as her eyes got even puffier. "No. No, of course not. I've never hated you."

I raised an eyebrow. "You could have fooled me."

"We were in competition. My cruelty toward you was smack talk between sisters, nothing more. Your friends always gave as good as you got." She paused as a heavy lump went down her throat. "But now, we're living completely separate lives. And we're the only family we have left."

Morphea resumed dabbing at her tears as I considered telling her that wasn't entirely true, but now wasn't the time for her to learn she had a family she didn't know about. Everything she was saying was a difficult pill to swallow, but if she really wanted to bury the hatchet and start new, I wasn't going to be the immature one.

"Okay," I said, nodding. "I'm glad I'm welcome here."

She nodded back at me. "Are you going to introduce me

to your friends?"

"Oh," I said, looking back at Griffin and Marcos, who were standing and sitting behind me, respectively. "These are my students. I'm training them to apply for the Sunriser academy."

"A pleasure to meet you, Commander," Griffin said with a small bow. "Sup?" Marcos followed with a small wave.

Morphea managed to barely smile through her tears and nod at each of them. "I never imagined you would become a teacher."

"Those who can't do, right?"

My sister giggled as she hooked one of her arms around mine. "Let's go inside. The service will be starting soon."

Morphea led us all inside and I recognized many of the people present. As was only appropriate, the vast majority of the Sunrisers' senior officers were present, including General Asparago and the council members who'd dishonorably discharged me. But that wasn't all.

There were kings, presidents, and several of the richest people in the universe in attendance. All here to pay their respects.

Statues of fifteen of the major gods were built into the sides of the walls of the chapel, a black-and-silver glass mural made up the ceiling, and at the far end of the room was Father's body, placed in an ivory casket.

"He's really gone," I said, looking down at him. I'd promised myself I wouldn't cry today, but his lifeless form didn't give me a choice. "This shouldn't have happened."

"There was nothing you, or anyone else, could have done," Morphea said, holding me. "By the time he was diagnosed, it was too late."

Putting our heads together, Morphea and I cried. And we

continued to cry over our late father's body until we were told by the minister to sit down.

"Today, we are gathered here to honor the life of one of the greatest men to ever live.

Drenian Langstone was not only one of the most accomplished Sunrisers of all time, but a proud husband and father. His beloved wife, Genni, tragically passed away shortly after giving birth to their second child, and they are now reunited in Heaven. His two daughters, Molina and Morphea, he could not have been more proud of, and they are here with us today. Also with us are…"

As the minister continued to speak, I couldn't stop crying. Now that I'd started again, it was impossible. This was exactly what I'd wanted to prevent.

Morphea had somewhat composed herself, but she still wasn't in much better shape than I was. Griffin and Marcos looked bored out of their minds, though. I couldn't blame them. They didn't know Father and were only here as emotional support, but it was still distracting.

Once the minister was finished with his opening, he went on to recite prayers from the Roquell. Father had never been particularly religious, he was always too busy working to pray, but we were all technically Roquellites, so it was appropriate.

After around half an hour, the prayers were finished. That meant it was time for me to go up and give the eulogy, and try not to humiliate myself in front of the people who already didn't buy that Father had been proud of me.

"At this time, we will move on to eulogies," the minister said. "However, before Molina and Morphea speak, we have a special guest who specifically requested to speak first."

What was he talking about? There weren't supposed to be any surprises today. I was barely keeping it together as things were. Who could have even made such a request to speak before the departed's family?

"Everyone, please rise," the minister continued, "and bow before the royal family!" A chill brushed past my brain and heart as both collapsed in on themselves.

"No."

The Cykebian national anthem came from just outside the chapel as, one by one, four palanquins were brought in, each carried by four muscular manservants, and each the unique hair color of the monsters inside them.

Prince Megz, the twin princesses Wink and Jolla, and Emperor Kaybell Kose Bythora stepped out onto the altar, and the entire room, including my students, bowed before them. The minister stepped out of the way, and Kay took the podium. As soon as she did, she was sure to glare right at me before looking back up.

I was a dead woman. That had to be why she was here. She knew I wouldn't be able to not attend the funeral, and now was her chance to catch me and torture me as revenge for abandoning her, and make me tell her where to find Yael. I'd known her setting a trap for me was a possibility, but I hadn't expected her to come herself, bring her younger siblings, *or* hijack the proceedings.

"Loyal subjects of the Holy Cykebian Empire, and guests from across the stars, thank you so much for your presence," Kaybell began. "I am here today not only to pay my respects to a man who will go down in history as a legend, but to someone I considered a mentor and, despite our age difference, a friend."

Kay was as beautiful as ever. She'd cut her long vermillion hair and had what was left neatly coiffed, her skin was still like porcelain, and while everyone present may have been dressed formally, compared to the tunics, capes, and boots she and her siblings were dressed in, we may as well have been wearing rags.

"Coming from humble beginnings, Drenian Langstone proved that anyone can achieve anything, provided they have the skill and drive necessary to succeed. He was truly exemplary of the Cykebian dream."

I wished Yael was here. She'd already have a clever plan for how to get out of this, but I was clueless. With Kay here, there must have been heavy levels of security both inside the funeral home and out. Marcos's hacking and Griffin's sleight of hand tricks weren't going to do us any good in this scenario.

"During the decade I spent as a Sunriser, Drenian taught me so much of what allowed me to rise to the rank of commander as quickly as I did. He was always willing to make time for my questions, not because I was his princess or because I was best friends with one of his daughters, but because he respected me. And that respect was mutual. He was not an easygoing man, nor one who was easy to get along with, but he was wiser than perhaps even my own late father, and he always did what needed to be done, regardless of how he personally felt. To speak on behalf of those I served with, he was an inspiration to us all."

I was running out of time. I needed to get my head on straight and focus on forming a plan. I couldn't think about potentially ruining my father's funeral or how messed up it was that he died before me or what Kay would do when she got her hands on me. I needed to think.

"Molina, Morphea, our relationships aren't what they once were," she continued, looking back down at me, "but I hope you know I'm speaking the truth when I wish you both my deepest condolences, and that the Cykebian Empire will do whatever it can to help you both through this difficult time." Her eyes widened, and memories of how she'd violated me rushed to the front of my mind. "Your family means so much to me."

My arms and legs tensed up as my heart seized. There was too much happening. Too much to worry about. I couldn't make a shitty plan, let alone one that would actually work. There was no hope for me. The best I could do was save the kids.

"Griffin, take Marcos, get back to *Miracle*, and go home," I whispered in his ear as Kaybell continued to speak.

"What are you talking about?" Griffin whispered back.

"I don't have time to explain. Just do as I said. Now!"

Griffin hesitated, uncertainty written all over him. We'd told the kids not to trust the monarchy, but neither Yael nor myself had ever felt comfortable sharing our exact experience with Kaybell with them.

"Okay," he eventually said. "But whatever you're planning, stay safe."

Griffin stood up, took hold of Marcos's chair, and pushed them down the aisle. Marcos hated being pushed, but this was faster, and right now, they just seemed to be content with the fact they were leaving.

"And now, I hand the podium over to my longtime friend and former partner in protecting the universe, Molina Langstone."

Kaybell was finished speaking, but I wasn't prepared to start. I couldn't give my eulogy with her here.

Shaking, I rose to my feet. I stuck my hand in the flame, and looked directly into Kay's eyes.

"If it's alright with everyone, I'd like to take a minute to compose myself before I speak," I croaked. "Would you please join me in the hall, your majesty?"

Whatever Kaybell wanted to do to me, if I gave myself up right away, she wouldn't have a chance to give the order for her men to go after the strangers I'd shown up with.

Kaybell grinned. "I'd be more than happy to."

CHAPTER 5: YAEL

"Yael, you must get up and shower," P'Ken declared, standing right over me, both hands on her stick.

"Seriously, you're starting to stink pretty bad," Aarif followed, standing right next to her.

"Waaaaaaaah!" I cried, curled up in a ball in my bed. "I miss my Moli!"

The past few days had been absolutely miserable. For security reasons, I couldn't contact Molina while she was on Cykeb, and living in the school without her around was too weird. As much as I'd been staying in bed, I couldn't even sleep in such a big one without her. My only comforts had come from my endless supply of beer, instant ramen, and gummies. The bottles, cups, and bags they'd come in all over my bed and floor.

"She'll be back soon. And then you can make up for lost time."

"For now, however, you promised Shun you'd spar with her today, and a thief of your distinction shouldn't be gaining a reputation as a *lying* thief."

"Come on, let's get ready for the day."

I groaned for an extended period, rubbing my temples. "You're not my parents."

"Obviously not," P'Ken rolled her eyes. "My child will never be allowed to make their room a pigsty."

Aarif plopped down next to me, shaking the mattress. "We may not be your parents, but we are your family. We want to help you."

I shook my head. "You can't."

"If you'd talk to us, you might be surprised," P'Ken said. "Aarif told me he already gave you some advice, but he also mentioned you keeping things bottled up."

P'Ken slammed her stick against the bed frame. "What could you possibly not trust us with?"

Dammit. It wasn't a matter of not trusting them. It was a matter of protecting them. If they knew the thoughts that had been going through my head the past few months, and especially the past few days, we'd all be in danger.

"Please leave me alone," I said, flipping myself over. "I'll be sure to get up in time for my sparring session with Shun."

P'Ken sighed, while Aarif stood back up. They were mad. Or, if they wanted to be my parents, maybe disappointed was the better word. That was fine. So long as they still believed in me.

"Do you remember that heist we pulled on Hissafsif?" Aarif asked. "It was one of the first jobs we did as a four-man squad."

Normally I probably would, but I was so drunk, everything beyond the past half-hour was a blur.

"Oh, yes, that was a fun one," P'Ken said, perking up. "The first time I got to use my cane-whip. What a disaster that was."

"Molina was still green, too," Aarif said. "Girl had no idea what she was supposed to be doing. Fortunately, you ladies had me to get you through it all."

P'Ken scoffed. "Please, you were freaking out that the two of us weren't ready for such a major bank robbery and wanted to abort."

"Yeah, okay, I wasn't holding up too well under pressure either. But Yael, you *actually* got us through it all. Not just with your wicked smarts, but by distracting us with jokes and rants, and making sure we were having too much of a good time to worry about botching the heist and getting caught."

"I was on the verge of having a panic attack when you pulled out that banana peel and purposely tripped on it. Why did you even have that on you?"

I chuckled through my tears and into my mattress. "You can't pull off a bank robbery without snacks, Aarif had insisted I take at least one healthy item, and I was too lazy to throw away the peel. And slipping on it prompted my rant about how healthy food was a menace to society."

My friends laughed. "Yeah, sounds about right."

"The school is fulfilling, but we had a lot more fun back then," P'Ken said. "I look forward to when we can get back to that."

I dragged my nails through the sheets and clenched my fists as laughter and tears continued to escape me. "Yeah. Everything will be better then."

Just as I was about to ask them to leave again, an alarm went off. "What the Heeeeeeell?" I moaned, forcing myself to sit up.

"Someone just entered the planet's atmosphere," Aarif

said. "Molina and the others aren't due back for another few days."

"Either we have yet another aspiring pupil, or the Sunrisers have finally tracked us down," P'Ken said. "Yael, are you up to handling this, or do I need to take command?"

I wasn't in top form at all. My head was splitting, I was wasted, and I was depressed to my core. But I couldn't say that. They needed their fearless leader.

"I'm on it!" I shouted, jumping out of bed and donning a fake grin. "Aarif, find Juri and Layla and get them to *Ricochet*. Man the defense system manually from there, and make sure they stay safe. P'Ken, you go with them, call Shun, and tell her to meet me outside."

Without hesitation, they nodded and went to do exactly as I said. They trusted me completely. I couldn't ever let them down.

I couldn't ever let Kaybell get her damn hands on them.

I ran down the multitude of rounding flights of stairs, using them as a potential warmup in case things got ugly, and made it to the front door. As I stepped outside, Shun appeared behind me without making a sound. She was also here in case things got ugly.

As we stepped out onto the rocky surface, we looked up at the pink sky to see a small craft, only large enough to hold one person, approaching the planet's surface. I didn't recognize the ship model, meaning it was either brand new or a piece of crap.

"Stay back," I said, as the ship landed around a dozen yards away. "Don't act unless I tell you to."

Shun nodded.

The roof of the pod-like ship opened up, and out stepped someone a foot shorter than me, dressed in a sharp gray mask, and a shiny black bodysuit, hiding their face.

"Howdy!" I shouted, waving at the stranger as I walked up to them. "How can we help you? I'm afraid if you're looking for someone to teach you the ways of the thief, I'm not looking for any more students right now."

The stranger didn't move or respond. They just continued to stand in place.

"I'm sorry, are you deaf?" I asked genuinely, signing with my hands. "I know three different forms of sign language if that'll help."

They still didn't speak, nor did they sign.

"Look, I have a long day of drinking and crying to get back to, and despite the smile on my face, my head is still spinning, so I'd really appreciate it if you could tell me why you're here."

Their head finally moved slightly, tilting an inch to the left.

"Yael Pavnick," they said in a robotic, distorted voice. "You must die for your sins."

The moment they finished speaking, two razor-bladed katars popped out of their arms. I was dealing with either an android or a cyborg.

"Listen, we don't want any trouble. Tell me what you think I did and, if I really did screw you over somehow, I'll compensate you monetarily."

In response to my plea for peace, the stranger clanged their katars together, electrifying them both.

"I don't think we're getting out of here without a fight," Shun said.

"Seems like it."

The stranger dashed at me, moving like a jaguar. They swung their blades wildly, but not quick enough to slash me, as I danced around each of their strikes. They managed to get a few strands of my hair, but that was all. It wasn't easy to dodge everything, but their movements were closer to a crude imitation of Moli with her sword than the real deal.

Eventually, I found the holes in their form, and through them, my opening to attack. I wasn't strong enough to take down modern cyborgs and androids in one punch, but I could still put a solid dent in them.

As they continued to flail their blades around, I pulled my fist back and punched them as hard as I could in the gut.

"Motherfuck!" I shouted as I tripped over myself. Not only had I not managed to injure my opponent from the look of things, but I was pretty sure I'd broken my hand.

What was this thing?

"Look out!" Shun tackled me out of the way before I could be decapitated in my dazed state. "Let me give this a try."

Shun stood back up as she dusted herself off. Even after seeing how badly I'd failed, she didn't seem afraid or perturbed to take on our mystery opponent. She lacked my years of experience, my knowledge of multiple combat styles, and my general skill level, but she more than made up for those factors in other ways.

The Utozion Authority was the second largest empire in the universe, and the only one which came even close to being as powerful as the Cykebian Empire. While Kaybell ruled over 56% of the universe, the council that led the authority controlled 22%. In their quest to gain more power, they conscripted kids into their military at a young age.

Shun had been one of those kids, and so despite only being seventeen, she had twelve years of formal combat training behind her. Not only that, but the enhancements she'd gotten before showing up at our doorstep put mine to shame. From the tests we'd done, in terms of raw strength, she was twice as strong as me.

I could buy that some scientist I'd stolen from had invented an android capable of not being phased by my blows, but if Shun met a similar result, then we were in deep shit.

Shun roared as she charged as our assailant, taking the offensive. As she unleashed a flurry of punches and kicks, the two moved so fast my eyes could barely keep up with them. Even after a full minute, Shun wasn't slowing down at all, but her opponent was still able to block or dodge everything she threw at her.

Still, she didn't stop. Not even as her opponent slashed her across the chest. "Shun!" I screamed, getting back on my feet.

"I'm fine!" she shouted back, continuing to attack.

That was very clearly a lie. She may not have been showing any sign of acknowledging it, but the cut on her was large, deep, and serious.

I may not have been able to hurt our enemy directly, but I could still help. I circled around the battlefield while the two continued to fight and got behind the machine. Best case scenario, I'd be able to put them in a hold. Worst case scenario, they were here for me, and they'd turn their attention to me, giving Shun a chance to take them down.

Our opponent spun around in a circle, swinging their blades all around them, and forcing Shun and I to jump back. Worst case scenario it was.

I charged at them again, and while I had their attention, Shun leaped into the air once more and delivered a hard-hitting spin kick to the back of their head. Finally, that managed to stun our opponent for a second, and Shun took advantage of that.

Using the moves I'd taught her over the past year, and shouting
the whole time, Shun grabbed our enemy and performed a piledriver on them, smashing them into the hard ground. Then, still
not done, she went straight into a Canadian destroyer, flipping
them over herself and slamming them down into the ground
once more.

Our enemy was down, and hopefully out, because Shun
wasn't standing back up either.

She was drenched in her own blood, and she was coughing up even more. "Come on, let's get you to P'Ken," I said,
helping her stand up.

"Is it… is it dead?"

I looked down at our assailant. They weren't moving
at all. If they were an android, they were dead. If they were a
cyborg, they were unconscious. Either way, right now, the kid
needed medical attention, and that was my priority.

"Aarif, I think the situation is handled, but just to be safe,
arm all defense systems," I said, pressing against my ear. "P'Ken,
be ready with the med-kit. Shun is—"

I was cut off by my own screams as a laser went straight
through my shoulder. Our enemy had raised their arm, and smoke
was coming out of its palm. Then, they raised their other arm.

"Run!" Shun shouted, taking my hand and speeding
off as she coughed up more blood. "Aarif, all weapons go!" I
screamed as we ran serpentine to avoid the rapid-fire lasers.

"We need immediate pickup!"

Even the most powerful lasers I'd ever faced had only
managed to leave mild burns on me. What the Hell was going on
here? How could such a massive leap in technology have come
out of nowhere?

This had to be Kaybell. She was the only one with the resources capable of even potentially putting together a weapon like this. She'd found us, and with Moli away on Cykeb, she'd sent her new toy to kill me.

Oh fuck. Were Moli and the others in danger too?

From the ground, over fifteen laser cannons emerged and fired at our opponent. At the same time, they were hit by five ice missiles, two flamethrowers, and our most powerful defense of all, our satellite beam. Everything else could take out a Parallax-class ship, but the satellite Aarif and I had built was capable of wasting an entire continent. As the ground-based attacks hit them, they were also struck by an enormous green beam from the heavens.

None of it left a scratch on them.

"No," I breathed.

There was smoke and dust everywhere, and the satellite beam had formed an enormous crater, but they were still standing, firing away at us.

At that moment, Shun tripped over themselves, more blood flooding out of their chest, and we both went down to the ground.

Our opponent ceased firing their lasers and began walking toward us. We were completely defenseless and at their mercy.

"Aarif, nothing worked!" I shouted, panting. "We need you now!"

"Yael Pavnick, you must die for your sins," the android repeated.

They picked me up by my collar and, with their freehand, smashed their fist into my face. Everything had been spinning before, but now I could barely see at all, and my ears were ringing. I hadn't been hit this hard since I'd fought Kaybell, and she didn't have anything on her creation.

They giggled. And it sounded familiar. With how distorted their voice was, I couldn't place it, but I knew I'd heard that same laughter somewhere a long time ago.

They hit me again. And again. And again. I wasn't sure how I was staying conscious, and I wasn't sure I wanted to be. I just knew this thing had cracked my skull half-way open. It would have been nice if Shun had gotten up again to help me out, but it seemed like she'd finally passed out.

The machine threw me down on the ground, right next to my unconscious student. They then levitated up into the air, showing that on top of everything else, they could fly too. In their hands, they charged up lasers, and considering what the uncharged lasers could do, this was it.

Or at least, it would have been, if they'd actually gotten to fire them, Aarif ramming *Ricochet* straight into them before they could. The machine was sent flying through the sky, possibly miles away from us, as P'Ken and Layla rushed off the ship to grab us and bring us aboard.

"Yael, are you okay?" P'Ken asked, her voice the softest I'd heard it in a while.

I tried to answer, but I couldn't speak or move my head. I closed my eyes and let the darkness take me.

CHAPTER 6: MOLINA

I couldn't stop shaking and I couldn't look her in the eyes. We were all alone in the hallway outside the chapel, and with her genetic enhancements, it would only take her an instant to knock me out or kill me if she wanted to. I was completely at her mercy.

Kaybell was standing across from me with her hands clasped in front of her, smiling like nothing was wrong. And that only made her scarier. She'd gotten up on that podium without a care, as if she wasn't the last person I wanted to see here. I may not have had nightmares about her like Yael, but now that I was in her presence again, I couldn't stop thinking about the way she'd forced herself on me.

But no matter what she did to me, I wasn't going to give up my family. I would take their location to my grave.

"I don't want to presume to know what you're feeling, but I may have an idea," Kaybell said. "When my father passed away, I was so confused. I was excited to take hold of my birthright and become emperor, but that didn't change how utterly broken I was. He'd never been a warm or supportive man, not like Drenian, but I still loved him. And with him gone, I lost a part of myself."

The heartbreak in her voice was genuine, but that didn't surprise me. She'd loved me, too.

"What do you want, Kay?" I asked, forcing myself to look at her directly despite how much it hurt.

"To pay my respects and support you. What else?" As I continued to glare at her, she lowered her head and laughed. "Oh. I see. You're afraid of me. Because I'm a monster."

"You said it, not me."

Kaybell picked her head back up as her smile disappeared. Her vermillion eyes watered and her perfect posture broke down.

"When my father died, my heart broke. But losing him wasn't nearly as painful as losing you. Not one day has gone by these past five years where I haven't thought about what I said and did to drive you away." Tears left her eyes, ruining her mascara. "And you were right. I was a monster. An evil, despicable monster. But I swear to you on my father's grave, I am not that person anymore."

I crossed my arms. "Why should I believe you?"

Kaybell choked up. "I apologized back then for what I'd done directly to you. I knew right away that I'd fucked up by kissing you against your will and trying to kill Yael, and those sins have haunted my dreams. And you were ready to forgive me for those misdeeds. But I couldn't get past my views of the universe or my belief in the traditions I'd always partaken in." Kaybell reached into her pocket and took out a handkerchief to dry her tears. "When I took the throne, I knew I had a responsibility to be better. The crown no longer supports or engages in the kidnapping and torturing of peasants, and in fact cracks down hard on those who continue to do so on their own."

My stomach churned and my heart pounded. She may have been lying, but what if she wasn't? I'd doubted that she would ever change, but what if she really had? What if she'd truly slain her demons, and all that was left inside her were the parts of her which had made her my best friend?

"Do you have proof of this?" I asked. "Records?"

Kaybell nodded. "Additionally, I'm sure wherever you've been, you've taken notice of the large movement among nobles to re-institute slavery. Not only has this been in response to my changes, but if I was still the same person I was, I would have gone along with their requests ages ago."

That... made sense.

"You... you really don't torture people anymore?"

"I'm disgusted by the fact I ever did." A half smile formed through her tears. "The nobility aren't the only ones who've given me a difficult time about it. Mother won't even speak to me, and my sisters constantly beg me to let them do it one more time, but I've remained stalwart in my stance."

My arms shook, my body screaming at me to hug her. She'd traumatized Yael, and for that reason alone, things could never go back to the way they were. But dammit, I'd never stopped caring about her, and anything else I'd told myself was a lie. More than anything else in this moment, I wanted to clear all doubts from my mind and hold her in my arms.

"I want to believe you so badly," I said as I broke down into tears as well.

"Then believe me. I have never lied to you, Molina. I may have hidden parts of myself or my true feelings, but I have never deceived you." Kaybell took my hands. Her palms were cold and clammy, but they made me warm. "I would speak to Drenian on occasion, and one time, I thought to ask him why he picked you for captain over me. As it turned out, you were right. It was entirely because of my biased views."

Father had asked some strange questions during my interview back then. Was this why he'd asked them? To make sure Kay hadn't influenced me?

"I always thought there was no one in the universe except you worthy of being with Princess Kaybell Kose Bythora, daughter of Stephen and descendant of Leon, first emperor of Cykeb and founder of the Sunrisers, future ruler of The Holy Cykebian Empire. But I have worked tirelessly to make *myself* worthy of *you*."

In the Sunriser Academy, we'd been trained to read people. To look for signs of deceit. A proper Sunriser could spot the slightest hint of a falsehood through someone's nose. And I wasn't seeing anything like that on Kaybell's face or body. She was right; she'd never lied to me.

"Kay…"

"I know you've probably been with Yael all this time. And that's fine. I'm willing to do whatever it takes to make amends with her too, because I know how important she is to you." Kaybell stepped closer to me. "But I've never stopped loving you. And all I want is to have you back in my life."

The lump in my throat weighed a ton. Yael would never forgive her. That wasn't going to happen, no matter what. But even though I'd been skeptical about Kay changing, I still believed in redemption and rehabilitation.

Yael wouldn't like what I was about to do, but dammit,

I'd given up my whole life for her. I deserved to take one piece of it back.

"I love you, too," I said, hugging her with all my strength. Kay hugged me back, not using anywhere close to her full strength. For a decade of my life, her hugs had gotten me through my hardest times. And now, she was here for me again, when the love of my life couldn't be.

The hug lasted a long time. I wasn't sure how long, but I savored every moment of it. "Um, we should probably head back inside," I said, pulling back. "Everyone's waiting for us."

"They can wait a little longer for their emperor."

I raised an eyebrow at her.

"What? I'm still me at my core."

We laughed together. Then Kaybell's smile disappeared again. "More seriously, there is one more thing we should discuss now."

"What?"

Kaybell sighed. "I came here primarily to pay my respects, as well as with the hope that you would be here, and I could tell you everything I just did. But there's something else.

Something else no one in that chapel but my siblings know about." "You're scaring me, Kay."

Kaybell finally fixed her posture and hardened her face. "I read the autopsy report on Drenian. And neither myself nor the coroner believe he died of natural causes."

I tripped backward, stumbling on my feet. "What did you say?"

"He was *poisoned*, Molina. Someone killed him."

My face grew hotter as I clenched my fists. "You covered this up."

"I did. Because he was supreme general of the Sunrisers, and if this got out, it would spread mistrust and conspiracy theories throughout the entire organization. After all, there are many people who will potentially benefit from his death."

"You have people investigating this, though. Right?!"

Kaybell shook her head. "No. I don't. Because I want to give you the opportunity to do so."

I shook my head. "No. No, I can't. I'm nothing."

"Whatever you've been doing with yourself, you're still the best Sunriser I've ever met. You deserve the chance to catch your father's killer, and no one is more qualified to do so."

For a few moments, all I could do was breathe heavily and pant. This was too much to take in at once.

"You'll... you'll give me the full resources of the empire to work with?"

"I will aid you in whatever capacity you'd like, whether you want me to simply provide resources, or work with you directly. It's entirely up to you. If you'd like, we can also call Yael, who I promise to not have arrested. She *is* smarter than both of us."

I bit my lip, drawing a little blood. "No. No, let's do this ourselves. You and me. Like old times."

I hugged Kay once again, and she embraced me.

"Come over to the palace for dinner tonight," she said directly into my ear. "We can begin the investigation in the morning, but for now, I'd like to catch up. And I'm very interested in meeting your new friends."

I nodded continuously. "Yeah. Yeah, I'd like that."

CHAPTER 7: YAEL

Dammit. Dammit. Dammit. Dammit.

As my eyes popped open and I escaped the darkness, that was my only thought. I wasn't supposed to ever lose again, but that was exactly what had happened. If not for Aarif's timely arrival, I would have been dead. Shun would have been dead.

I slammed my fists down on my mattress. They were supposed to be able to count on me.

If I couldn't protect my family from anything and everything, then what good was I?

Moving my hand over to my shoulder, it had been fully patched up and only stung a little. The fact that there now existed handheld lasers capable of putting holes straight through me was terrifying. The rest of the universe was advancing so quickly, but I'd stayed the same. The same enhancements that had once made me invincible in a fight had become completely obsolete.

My head still ached and my bedroom was blurry. I wasn't bleeding and the cracks had seemingly been mended, but it would be a while till I was at 100% again. P'Ken really had become a solid medic. I didn't know what I'd do without her.

I pushed my covers off and swung my legs over the side of the bed. More rest probably would have been a good idea, but I couldn't afford to waste any time. I needed an update from my crew on where we currently stood. Hell, I wasn't even sure how long I'd been out for.

My legs wobbled as I pressed my feet against the floor. Pushing myself up was an embarrassingly difficult task that required quite a bit of my strength. It might have been humiliating if someone saw me like this, but I was already a failure in the eyes of those on board with me. At least Moli wasn't here.

I stomped my foot down like I would when it fell asleep. *Moli!*

I needed to get in touch with her ASAP. I needed to make sure she was okay and warn her about what was going on. Of course, I wasn't sure exactly what was happening, but we were clearly all in danger.

Shuffling over to my desk, I grabbed two of my fidgets. One was a fake banana I could peel and unpeel as many times as I wanted, while the other was a soft, gel-like ball I rolled around my hand and massaged.

We'd thrown every weapon at our disposal at that android or cyborg, short of Juri, but considering the satellite beam couldn't even scratch them, she wouldn't have made a difference. There was nothing else we could have done.

This was easily the #1 most screwed we'd ever been. Even when Kaybell had captured Aarif, P'Ken, and I, Molina was still in a position of power to do something about it. Now, we had no such luck.

I wished I could go back in time to when the #3 most screwed I'd ever been was #1.

Nearly being burnt at the stake by a people who believed I was a witch was nothing compared to this.

I peeled and unpeeled the banana dozens, maybe hundreds, of times, with my thumb, as I rolled the ball around enough that I got it to light up. I kept going and going and going, and I didn't want to stop.

But I had to. There was work to be done.

I put down my fidgets and wobbled out of my room. Looking down from the railing at the main area below, Aarif, P'Ken, Layla, and Juri were gathered together. They hadn't noticed me yet, so I forced a big grin onto my face and shook myself to get my blood pumping. I needed to make it seem like that loss had just been a bump in the road.

"Howdy, everyone!" I cheered.

"Yael!" three of them called out, relieved to see me standing.

BARK! BARK! Juri followed, also happy to see me and probably hoping I had food for her.

"What, you thought I was down for the count?" I asked as I carefully made my way down the stairs. "Please, that was maybe the fifth worst head trauma I've ever experienced." Big fat lie. "How long was I out?"

"About a day," Layla answered. "We were really worried."

"Thanks, but not needed. I always get back up." Layla didn't seem to be perked up at all by my remark, her face remaining sullen. "How's Shun doing?"

"She lost a lot of blood," P'Ken answered. "She'll live, but she needs a few more days before she's getting out of bed."

Aarif and I wrapped our arms around each other. "Thanks for the save, brother."

"You know I've got you."

I turned to P'Ken as I let go of Aarif. "Thank you for saving us both."

"I'd say you've saved me enough times that it's only fair," she replied with a smirk. "I only wish I had enhancements as well so I could have helped in the fight. The whole process just seems so… icky."

"It's fine, P'Ken," I assured her honestly. "Believe me, one more fighter wouldn't have made a difference." I exhaled and slapped my cheeks. "Is that thing following us?"

Aarif nodded as Juri nuzzled her head against my leg. "*Ricochet* is faster than their little ship, but they have some method of tracking us, and I haven't been able to figure out how."

"*Cascade*'s weapons would have been able to blow them away and leave them drifting in deep space, but by the time we got it in the air, you and Shun would have been dead," P'Ken explained.

"I see," I said, lowering my head to hide my disappearing smile as I pet Juri's head.

"Emperor Kaybell has to be behind this, right?" Layla asked. "You've mentioned she has a grudge against you before, and she's one of the only people with the resources necessary to have made such a powerful android or cyborg."

I shook my head. "Good guess, but no. I was thinking that myself in the heat of the moment, but it doesn't add up. Kaybell is a sadist, and I stole the love of her life away from her. The laser that went through my shoulder was meant to go through my head, and while beating me to death wouldn't have been quick, it wouldn't have been particularly slow, either. No, that thing is coming after us to kill me, not torture me. This is someone else. Maybe I pissed off some higher-ups in the Utozin Authority. I don't know."

The room went silent. As Juri ran back over to Aarif, I tugged on my hair. It was so quiet, I could hear Shun moaning from her room.

"So, uh…" Layla started, eyes laser focused on me. "What's the plan?"

Shit, shit, shit. I'd hoped everyone would wait a little while to ask that.

I picked my head up and slammed my fist into my free hand. "Ah, yes! The plan! The cunning plan that will get us out of this mess and save our skins. Well, the way I see it, we can… we can… um…"

"Yael?" P'Ken asked.

I wasn't keeping it together. I wasn't even sure I was still smiling. It didn't feel like it. I didn't want to be straight with them, but my friends weren't stupid. They could easily see that something was wrong.

"Yael, what's the problem?" Aarif asked. "Your head still hurting?"

"Gaaaaaaaaaaaaah!" I screamed into my hands, before uncovering my face and pointing at my head, jabbing my finger into the side of it. "Guys, you don't get it. There is nothing scarier to a genius than something they can't understand. And I have no idea how something like this exists. I have no idea where it came from, and I have no idea how to stop it. It's unbeatable in a fight, and since I have no information on it and it won't talk, I can't outsmart it." I tugged on my hair again, this time nearly hard enough to yank it out. "I'm sorry, guys. I have no plan."

Layla looked like she was about to cry as P'Ken aggressively stuck the floor with her stick. I'd let them down. It was possible I'd never be able to earn their unwavering trust back.

"Um, I might have an idea then."

We all looked to Aarif. "You're really out here trying to take my big damn hero role from me, huh?"

Aarif laughed. "It's only an idea. And you're still the big damn hero. It's just not your day."

P'Ken and Layla put on small smiles and nodded in agreement. Bullshit. "What's your idea?" I asked.

"Well, everyone on this ship thinks you're the smartest woman in the universe," he began. "But anytime we call you that, you're sure to point out there's at least one woman who's definitely smarter."

Layla's eyes popped open wide. "Oh no. Please tell me you're not suggesting what I think you are."

"Sorry. But if Yael can't figure out how to beat this thing, maybe Madame N'gwa can."

"Not a bad idea at all, Aarif," P'Ken said, tapping his shoulder with her stick.

"Um, I disagree!" Layla shouted. "If she helps us out, I'll actually owe her something.

Things have been bad enough without her having anything over my head."

Everyone looked to me to make the decision, Juri included. Even if they no longer believed I could always protect them, I at least still seemed to command respect as the captain here. They still trusted me to make the calls.

"I'm not hearing any better ideas," I said, causing Layla to groan. "Layla, with me in the cockpit. You guys stay here."

I didn't like this any more than Layla did. Having to call

my hero to come bail me out was thoroughly humiliating. I was going to lose all the respect she'd built up for me at once. But Aarif was right that she might be the only person capable of figuring out how we all got out of this alive.

Layla and I walked up the steps, entered the cockpit, and I video-called the greatest thief in the universe. After about a minute, she picked up.

"Yael, Layla, what a wonderful surprise," the frail old woman said with a grin, decorated by her signature bells and fingerless white gloves. "Dear, how are your studies progressing?"

Layla huffed as she crossed her arms and turned her head away from her great-grandmother.

"Her studies are going excellently," I said, shifting around in my seat. "I think she'll be ready to start her solo career in the next year."

"Marvelous." Madame N'gwa turned to Layla. "Please don't look so cross with me, Layla. Are you still being a child about this?"

This wasn't what we needed to be talking about right now. Not when every moment we didn't do anything was a moment we were in danger. I needed to wrap this up quickly and get to the point, but I also didn't want to piss off Layla further.

"Um, Madame N'gwa, perhaps we could discuss Layla's training at another time. I think she has some valid concerns and—"

"I won't let you control my life forever!" Layla cut me off, turning back to the hologram of her ancestor.

Madame N'gwa sighed. "For what I'm sure won't be the last time, I'm simply guiding you toward the path of freedom. You'd never truly live as a candlemaker."

"Glassblower!"

"Either way."

"Madame, we're in danger," I blurted out, needing to get to the point.

"Danger?" Madame N'gwa questioned. "And you can't take care of it yourself? I must say, that's rather disappointing."

Aaaaaand, there was the knife through my heart.

"An android or cyborg on an entirely different level from any I've ever heard of is chasing after us," I explained, trying not to cry. "I couldn't do anything to it in our fight, and our defense systems couldn't do anything either. It's seemingly unstoppable, I don't have a clue where it could have come from, and all it'll say is, "Yael Pavnick, you must die for your sins" so I can't talk to it." I sighed, my face burning. "Please tell me what to do."

I wasn't entirely sure what I was expecting to happen. Would she immediately think of something I hadn't and make me look like a complete idiot? Would she insult me again? Or would she give me another chance and tell me to figure it out myself?

There were many options I considered, but I didn't anticipate what actually happened: she laughed in my face.

"Oh, Yael, I was wondering when something like this would happen."

I lowered my bushy eyebrows. "What are you talking about?"

Madame N'gwa smirked. "You are by far the most physically capable woman to ever join our ranks. You're more than smart enough to rank among us as well, but for most of us, our wits are all we have. As such, when faced with a purely physical problem, we tend to be at a disadvantage. Or at least, we would be, if we hadn't come up with a solution for this."

"And I'm just hearing about this solution now?"

She laughed again. "You are our sister, and we love you, but there are still many of us who believe you're too young to be a *true* Banshee. However, given the circumstances, and in light of the favor you've been doing me, I'd say you've earned your chance."

"My chance at what?"

A grin spread across Madame N'gwa's face. "Yael Pavnick, please join myself and the rest of your sisters at the highest point of Defnuct-7. It's time for your *real* initiation to The Order of the Banshee."

CHAPTER 8: MOLINA

The Cykebian Royal Palace was as grand as I remembered it. The largest structure on the planet sat at the center of a seventeen square-kilometer estate, which was equally marvelous.

Primarily painted and decorated in black, silver, and, since Kaybell's coronation, vermillion, every amenity imaginable was available inside the palace, so that the emperor theoretically never needed to leave. Throughout the interior and exterior, there were swimming pools, light-squash courts, exercise and entertainment facilities, libraries, movie theaters, and ship-bays.

Over 1,000 people directly worked on the estate. There were maids, laundresses, butlers, chefs, and other types of servants, along with the royal court and countless security guards.

Between the highly trained personnel, who at this point all had enhancements, and defense systems that put the ones we had back home to shame, even Yael wouldn't be able to rob this place.

The dining room the seven of us were seated in was as elegant as the rest of the palace. The long table we were all seated at, with my students and I on one side, Kaybell's siblings on the other, and Kaybell at the head, was made from some of

the finest wood in the universe. A diamond chandelier hung over
our heads, the chairs we were in were practically thrones, and
there were a number of uniformed servants standing to the side,
ready to do whatever we requested.

We'd planned on dining in the same outfits we'd worn
to the funeral, but Kaybell had insisted we change. I'd borrowed
one of her burnt-orange dresses, Griffin had borrowed a tunic
and cape from Prince Megz, and Marcos had mixed and matched
different pieces from the royal family's wardrobes.

"So Molina, what *have* you been doing with yourself all
these years?" Megz asked.

The lie I'd made up earlier was good enough for Morphea, and it was good enough for Kay. I didn't like lying to her,
especially since she was the one working to regain my trust, but I
couldn't risk sharing the truth.

"I've been helping teenagers like Griffin and Marcos
prepare for entrance to the Sunriser academy," I said. "Griffin
is well-rounded, while Marcos is one of the best programmers
you'll ever meet."

"Really?" Kay asked with interest. "You know, our father
sometimes spoke about a hacker who did some rather dirty work
for him. A non-binary child prodigy. That wouldn't happen to be
you, would it?"

Marcos shrugged. "Possibly. My parents worked me to
the bone for so many clients, I didn't really keep track of who I
was doing what for."

Kaybell seemed to accept that as an answer and resumed
eating her soup. It was probably for the best we kept the nature
of their work secret.

"And what of Yael?" Kay asked. "I'm well aware she

hasn't slowed down her illegal activity at all, but is she teaching as well?"

"Yes," I answered truthfully. "She has her own band of thieves she's training, but she does help me with my students."

Kaybell laughed. "You know, if you were anyone else, I'd have you all arrested just for being associated with her."

"I gathered. You did brand her Evil Incarnate."

"An embarrassing decision fueled by jealousy. And yet another thing I'm sorry about."

Once I was sure, truly sure, that Kay had evolved into the benevolent emperor she claimed to be, I would tell her the full truth about everything. I'd let her know that I was a thief, and that I only taught Sunriser tactics to make kids into better criminals. If she wanted to be my best friend again, she'd overlook all of that, as I'd overlooked her prejudiced views for so many years.

"It isn't entirely fair that you get special privileges," Jolla said, glaring at me with her aqua eyes.

"After all, you took away our privileges," Wink followed, also staring at me with her purple eyes.

"Ignore them," Kay said, not even looking up from her soup. "They're just upset because they're not allowed to whip servants to death anymore."

"It was what we did to relax and unwind," the twin 18-year-olds replied in unison.

Wink and Jolla had given me bad vibes since they were four. They'd always seemed creepy and disturbed. At meals, they'd stare at me silently with eyes to kill as they cut into their food with their knives, and while I was sleeping, they'd rip heads off their dolls and leave them in my bed. Looking back, they'd probably been disgusted that Kaybell had chosen a commoner as a best friend.

"Some of us are glad you changed our sister's view of the universe," Megz said. "Personally, I always found the idea of torture revolting."

"Mm!" Griffin sounded, swallowing as he set his spoon down. "I am delighted to hear you say so. You've always been an inspiration to me, my prince, and I too was disgusted when I learned of the practice."

"What family did you say you come from again?"

"House Cirico, my prince."

Megz pressed his lips together and squinted. "No, I don't believe I've heard of you. Have any of you?"

There was a brief silence, but it was broken quickly by the twins' snickering. "New money," they said together.

Griffin hunched over and frowned, looking like he was gonna cry into his soup.

Marcos burst out laughing. "You know, I can't say I'm a fan of whipping people to death for sport, but I do support bullying Posh Boy." They raised their wine glass. "New money!"

"New Money!" the twins cheered, raising their glasses as well. As they all laughed, Griffin actually did cry into his soup.

I patted him on the back as I leaned over toward Marcos. "Cut it out. Right now."

"He's a big boy," Marcos whispered back.

Honestly, if it were up to me, we never would have taken on Marcos as a pupil. They may have possessed more natural talent than Griffin, and we may have been in need of a new hacker following Jellz's retirement, but they'd always had the same horrible attitude. The Sunriser academy would have beaten that out of them.

"What about all of you?" I asked, trying to change the

subject. "What have you all been doing?"

The princesses were evidently disinterested in telling me about their activities, sighing as they sipped their wine.

"Kaybell gave me command over the military," the 22 year-old, raven-haired prince said. "Much as she's had to deal with the collection of nobles who are unhappy with her social policies, I'm in charge of keeping the elderly generals who want to complete our conquest of the universe through brute force in line."

"Of course, brute force may soon acquire 22% of the universe, whether we like it or not," Kaybell said.

"What are you talking about?" I asked.

Kay shook her head. "My spies informed us years ago that the Utozin Authority has been preparing for war. I've tried reaching out to them to prevent the conflict, but their council seems intent on "liberating" all Cykebian territory, no matter what. That's part of why I've pushed development of superior cybernetics so hard and legalized genetic enhancements. They wouldn't engage in what seems like a losing battle unless they had a plan, and we have to be ready for anything."

"We'll slaughter them all," Jolla said, licking her lips.

I held my leg so it wouldn't shake. A war between the Cykebain Empire and the Utozin Authority would shake the foundation of the universe. Countless lives would be lost, and whoever came out victorious would be capable of conquering the remainder of the universe in no time at all, with no one able to stand in their way. And while they may not have had any barbaric traditions of torture or a founder with a god complex, the standard of living across the board on Utozex worlds was far lower.

This wasn't any of my business. There would always be

people to steal from. But I still cared about what happened to the people of the universe I'd sworn to protect.

"When do you think the war will begin?" I asked.

"I keep saying *we* should be the ones to start it," Wink replied. "Make the first strike."

"And as I keep saying, we're not going to be the aggressors," Megz said. "We could potentially need the support of the unaligned planets."

"Agreed," Kaybell said. "The war could start any day, but trust me, I've made sure we're ready to win it." She grinned. "Who's ready for the next course? I gave Toshiki Kubota a call and had him prepare a sashimi platter for us."

I couldn't help but smile back at Kay. On such short notice, she'd gotten my favorite chef to come and prepare my favorite meal. Yael may have been rich, but the power that came from being emperor was like magic.

"Some sashimi sounds good right now," Griffin sighed, still depressed.

Kay snapped her fingers and the servants got to work taking our bowls away, refilling our glasses, and hustling to the kitchen to get our raw fish.

"And of course, there's been more to my life than just work," Kay said, continuing to smirk. "I've also taken up some new hobbies. Such as swordplay."

My eyes widened. "No. You didn't."

"I did. I've been training several hours a day for years, and I believe I've gotten quite good. After dinner, I'd like to test my skills against the master."

She'd actually learned to sword fight for me. Yael had always been willing to help me practice, but she'd never trained herself. Griffin had checked with one of his contacts before we'd come here and, indeed, the crown had put a stop to nobles torturing commoners. She'd turned her society upside down, changed her entire worldview, and dedicated a great deal of her limited free time to swordplay. She was doing everything she could to support me in my time of need, and she was giving me the chance to catch my father's killer. It was all for me.

I moved my hand from my shaking leg to my rapidly beating heart. "You're on."

————

Sleeping in the same guest room I had through my 20s was like stepping back into a past life. Everything was as elegant and plush as I remembered, the pillows still had my initials monogrammed on them, and the closet was still filled with robes that fit me perfectly.

Hanging out with Yael all the time as a kid, I'd never really gotten a chance to be a girly girl. Through our sleepovers, Kaybell had introduced me to the world of makeovers, spa days, and pampering. I still enjoyed nights like those with P'Ken and Griffin on occasion, but it wasn't the same.

The next morning, Marcos went back to *Ricochet*, while Griffin was invited to spend the day with Megz. Kay and I, with the minimal amount of entourage she was required to travel with, took a ship to Zenith Command to begin our investigation.

There were a dozen missed calls on my watch from Yael, but I wasn't ready to speak to her. As much as I missed her, if I did, I could give in to what everyone else expected me to do. There was one person who knew Father better than anyone else, and who had the most to potentially gain from his death. And as much as it sucked to think about given recent events, that person was my sister.

"I must say, I didn't think I'd ever see you two working together again," Acting Supreme General Morphea said, seated at Father's desk. "To what do I owe this visit?" She softly laughed. "I think we're beyond our old repartee at this point."

Kay probably would have said something cruel or sarcastic in response to that, but we'd already gone over the gameplan for today. She knew that Morphea and I had made up, and that we were going to act completely professionally.

"Too true," Kaybell said. "Alas, we have something tragic to report that we ask you keep confidential."

Morphea raised one of her recently threaded eyebrows. "I'm not sure if I can handle any more bad news right now, but whatever it is, I promise to keep it between us."

I nodded, taking a deep breath. Saying what had happened out loud still wasn't easy. "We don't believe Father died of natural causes. Based on the autopsy, we believe he was poisoned."

Before I was even finished speaking, Morphea slammed her hands down on her desk, and her eyes sharpened. "*What?*"

"All jokes I've ever made about your intelligence aside, I'm sure you can understand why I elected to keep this need-to-know," Kaybell said.

Morphea dragged her nails across her desk, scratching it and chipping the paint off her nails. Her lower lip trembled as her foot tapped against the floor over and over again. We couldn't rule anything out yet, but this reaction didn't seem fake at all. She was as hurt by this revelation as I'd been.

"Yes, I understand," she said, her breath heavy. "I'd ask if you have any suspects, but I'm one of them, aren't I?" Our silence told her where we stood. "Very well. But before you ask your questions, may I ask why you're involved in this investigation, Molina? You're a civilian."

I clasped my hands behind my back. "Kaybell asked that I assist her. We make a good team."

Kay smirked as Morphea sighed. "Very well."

Kaybell elevated her head. "Were you and your father getting along?"

Morphea smirked back at Kaybell as she wiped away a fresh tear. "You two aren't the only good team. We worked in perfect unison, and I can't remember us having a major disagreement in the past year."

"And before this past year?"

"A small fight over the promotion of General Milsp. Father believed he deserved it, while I argued his old-fashioned attitude around women should have disqualified him."

That was peculiar. Father wasn't usually the type to support those with improper conduct, but at the same time, I was unfamiliar with Milsp and his record.

"Speaking of deserving things, do you believe you *deserve* to inherit your father's position?" Kay asked. "It's what you've always been after, yes?"

Morphea sweated as she shook in her seat. Those may have been signs of guilt, but it could also just as easily have been the combination of shock, stress, and depression getting to her.

"Yes, I do. And yes, it is. I was at Father's side for nearly a decade, learning from him every step of the way. I was patiently waiting for him to retire, and just because there's a murderer now in the equation doesn't mean I'm not still his clear heir apparent."

She wasn't wrong. Throughout my entire career as a Sunriser, Morphea was the only officer I viewed as true competition. There may have been a plethora of elderly generals, all of whom would have had equal motivation to remove Father from the picture, but we always knew in our hearts it would be one of us.

"As the person closest to him, can you think of anyone in particular who'd want to kill him?" I asked.

"You know as well as I do Father had many enemies. They came with the job. There are hundreds of powerful criminals who wanted revenge on him. Likewise, many of the generals had frequent disagreements with his decisions. If you'd like, I can get files for you on the former group and arrange sit-downs with you with the latter."

"That would be most helpful," Kay said. "Thank you."

Morphea hardened her face. "I want this bastard caught at any cost. I'll do whatever else you ask to help with the investigation." She breathed. "If that's all, Your Grace, I'd like a moment alone with my sister if you wouldn't mind."

"Of course."

Kaybell turned around, hand on my shoulder, and strutted out of Morphea's office, followed by the guards who'd come in with us. In the past, I would have found an excuse for Kay to stay and help me with Morphea, but I had to put in the effort if this new chapter in our relationship was going to be a good one.

"Are you okay?" I asked.

Morphea wrinkled her nose. "No, I am very much not okay. And neither are you."

"I mean, yeah, I took the news pretty hard. But we're going to figure this—"

"That's not what I'm talking about," she cut me off.

"You're in danger."

"How so?"

"Please, Molina. We both know what the royal family is really like."

I unclenched my hands and hung my arms at my side. "I do. Don't know when you found out. Either way, they've changed."

Morphea snorted. "I don't believe Kaybell's performance for a second, but that may be the years of built-up hatred for her speaking. Even if she really has changed, though, her sisters make no secret about being monsters." She paused and looked down at her desk. "And if you asked me to name one person who I think killed Father, it would be Prince Megz."

"Megz?"

"You sound surprised. Come on, sis, I know you're smarter than this. His dashing prince persona is all an act."

"And how exactly do you know that?"

Morphea looked back up at me, pain in her eyes. "Because I *dated* him. Very briefly. We met at a party and, initially, he swept me off my feet. He seemed like the kindest man in the universe. I thought I was going to have it all, as both supreme general and a princess." She put her hand to her cheek. "Then we went to bed together. And he... he hurt me."

I clenched my fists. "What?"

"He did stop when I asked. Eventually. But while we were going, he could only get turned on by hurting me. He punched me in the face, twisted my arm... went far too fast."

"Oh my god. Morphea..."

"I broke up with him, and he understood, but he asked that I not make his sexual habits public. For the sake of my position, and, embarrassingly, because I was scared, I agreed. However, when Father saw something was wrong with me the next morning, I told him. And he was furious. He went straight to the palace and assaulted Megz. The guards stopped him from going any further, and Kaybell got everything settled peacefully, but I know Megz wanted revenge. Wink and Jolla believe that assaulting a royal should be punishable with the execution of one's entire family. As if it's akin to striking a god. And I'd bet Megz thinks the same way."

Megz had always been the Bythora I'd interacted with the least, but even based just on last night, I never would have guessed any of what she was saying was in him. It was possible Morphea was lying, and she carried a personal grudge against Megz where she was in the wrong, but for right now, I had to believe her. She was the victimized party, and she wanted Father's killer caught as much as I did.

"Thank you for telling me all that. I'll look into him. And I'll be careful."

Morphea nodded. "Even the greatest human civilization to ever exist is still a kingdom of beasts. Don't let yourself be fed upon."

CHAPTER 9: YAEL

For so long, my dream had been to make it into the Order of the Banshee. After finally getting in, landing the girl of my dreams at around the same time, and surpassing most of my heroes, I wasn't sure what was left for me.

But now, I was being told that I hadn't actually become a Banshee. That there was still some secret test I hadn't passed, and completing it would allow me to beat the most deadly fighter in the universe.

I'd been in a slump lately, and getting my ass handed to me and my heart filled with fear hadn't helped. Now, however? Now I was pumped.

"Beans, beans, they're good for your heart, my apprentice likes them and makes cool art!"

Aarif and P'Ken laughed at my silly rhyme, and even Layla couldn't help but crack a smile, spitting out some of the water she was taking her estrogen with. Shun remained stone-faced as she took her own estrogen pill, but that was to be expected. Juri seemed to like it, though.

I needed to win back my crew's confidence, and the least

I could do to accomplish that was keep them laughing. Even if on the inside I was dying over the fact that Moli wasn't answering my calls. It took a few hours to finagle a way to make sure the call couldn't be tracked, and so far that had been for nothing. She could take care of herself just fine, so I wasn't worried about her, but I *was* worried about how angry she must have been at me.

"We should be arriving on Defnuct-7 in a few hours," Aarif said. "What do you think they're gonna have you do?"

"No doubt it'll be something that pushes even your brain to its limits," P'Ken suggested.

"I'm not sure how solving puzzles will let you beat something that walked off the satellite beam without a scratch," Shun said.

I rested my elbows on the table. "Whatever the test is, Madame N'gwa says passing it will get the job done, and I have no reason to not believe her."

"God, if you love her so much, why don't you go down on her?" Layla mocked, still upset we were going to see her g-gma.

"Because I'm married, and she's probably really wrinkly down there. And now you're all going to think about that." Everyone else groaned while I laughed. "Eat your beans."

Aarif shook his head to try and get the nasty thought out. "I wish I could go with you guys."

"Sorry," I said, eating a spoonful of my own beans. "They only actually invited me and Layla. It took major convincing for the Banshees to even allow P'Ken and Shun to come to the meeting, and they definitely weren't about to let a man in on this."

Aarif picked up Juri while I chugged my second beer of the morning back. "Yeah, well, at least I'll have my *best* girl to keep me company." He kissed her head. "I'll also make sure the shuttle crafts I installed a few months ago are ready to go. Leaving *Ricochet* behind is obviously a last resort, but we may have to be ready to fly off in different directions if that thing catches us before we're ready."

The beer went down the wrong pipe. Yes, theoretically, abandoning *Ricochet* could potentially be the most strategic move in a certain situation. But at the same time, like Hell was I ever abandoning my baby.

"Speaking of, Shun, do you think the Utozin military could have built it?" P'Ken asked.

Shun shook her head. "Not a chance. I know everything they were capable of two years ago, and there's no way they could have made such great advancements in that time."

"Well, there goes that idea," Aarif said, slapping the table.

Assuming Shun was right, then it had to be someone extremely powerful within the Cykebian Empire who wasn't Kaybell. There wasn't too long a list of people who fit that description who'd I'd also pissed off, and if I ended up not able to take on the machine in our next fight, the plan would be to hunt them all down until I found the right one.

Given the timing, it was possible this was a secret project Nathaniel and Horowitz had been working on, and this was both a test drive for it and a way of getting revenge. The two of them possessed next to no knowledge of cybernetics, but it could have been a collaboration.

I was really just making guesses. For all I knew, General Galopire could have been behind this. He'd always hated Moli's dad, and even though he hadn't succeeded in kicking him out of the Sunrisers, he'd still been able to force him to work from home and not from Zenith Command, humiliating him. He could have used his endless funds as a duke to create a machine that could kick my ass and kill Molina as a way to get back at Drenian. Of course if that guess was right, with Drenian dead now, he'd probably be shaking his fist that he was too late.

Layla twirled her spoon around her beans. "How do you think the others are doing?"

I sighed as I leaned back in my chair. "They're safe, and right now, that's all I care about."

"Yeah," Aarif followed. "Molina and Griffin are probably showing Marcos all the best sights, and the kids are hopefully encouraging Molina to pamper herself to help distract from the pain."

"Do you ever think about visiting your parents?" Layla asked. "You never really talk about them."

I stood up, walked over to the fridge and grabbed another beer. I wasn't finished with my current one, but I wanted to be ready.

"My parents are well taken care of, but I'm not confident even all the gidgits I send them would keep them from turning me in if I visited them." I sat back down. "Our lives are fine, separate."

Faster than even I could react, Juri leaped off of Aarif's lap, grabbed my new beer bottle in her mouth, and ran off.

"Dammit, Juri!" Aarif and I shouted, getting up to chase after her. "That is not Juri food!

That is definitely not Juri food!"

When we stepped off of *Ricochet*, we were dressed in our signature outfits; the ones we wore on our wanted posters.

We wore long, poufy, and conservative Benkinian style dresses
and hats, each in a different color, with my own outfit a mix of
bright yellow and blue. While they hadn't initially appealed to
me, my time on Benkin, and Moli's initial reaction to seeing me
in one, had led to them growing on me. P'Ken had always loved
the style, and while they didn't like them at all, I had Layla and
Shun wear them on special occasions as well.

"Yael, you're flapping," P'Ken noted. "Seeing Madame
N'gwa in person still gets you this excited?"

I kept on flapping my hands, not ready to stop yet. "No.
But this is going to be the first time since I've joined the order
that the entire group will be together in one place."

"Speaking of, where is everyone?"

A reasonable observation by Layla. We'd landed on the
highest point of Defnuct-7, atop a rocky cliffside. The air was
thick, it was freezing, and there was no one to be seen.

"Maybe this is part of the test?" I thought out loud.
"Maybe they're all invisible? God, I hope my prize for passing
this test is a device that lets me turn invisible; that would be so
freaking cool."

Madame N'gwa's cackle echoed through the mountainside.

"No such luck, I'm afraid," she said, appearing from behind us. "I was just a bit slow getting here. I'm old. It happens."

"It's a pleasure as always to see you," I said, leading the
group over to her. "This is Shun, she's training alongside Layla,
and you remember my partner, P'Ken."

"Indeed I do," she said, grinning like a cat at my friend.
"Yael has helped you ripen like a fresh plum. Perhaps one day,
there will be a place for you among the order."

"Joining your ranks is my greatest dream," P'Ken said,

sounding like a far more mature young me.

"I'm sure it is." Madame N'gwa cackled. "Of course, I probably won't even still be alive by then." She turned her head to Layla. "Why can't you be more like her?"

Layla crossed her arms and turned away from her. "P'Ken chose to leave finishing school. You *paid* my parents to take me out of art school."

"Your mother was already a lost cause when she was your age and showed no aptitude for theft. I refused to let someone with your natural talent not achieve your full potential."

I did not need more of this drama right now, and odds were it would just go in the usual circles if I allowed it to continue as normal. That left me with two options: break it up, and ask where the rest of the order was, or do something profoundly stupid.

"Madame N'gwa, I believe Layla's learned enough that, if she so chose, she could become a great thief at any point," I said, choosing the latter option and picking up from when I'd gotten interrupted during our video call. "Once the matter of this killer android/cyborg is settled, I think you should consider letting Layla return to her original studies."

Everyone looked at me curiously, save for Shun, who appeared completely disinterested. "I'm surprised to hear you say that, Yael," Madame N'gwa hummed.

"Yeah, so am I," Layla followed.

"Do you know what you're doing?" P'Ken whispered.

The answer to her very good question was a resounding "No".

"I just think she's learned most of what she has to, and she already has a bounty that puts most others to shame," I said, coming up with this as I went along. "Yes, that's mostly because of her relation to you, but she's still been crucial to me pulling off some major heists. She's nearly an adult, and she's smart enough to choose her own path from here."

Madame N'gwa rolled her head around, cracking her neck. She then went down her body, cracking every other part of it, finishing with her toes. When she was done, her face went blank.

"I will think about this and have an answer for you once your true initiation is complete."

"Thank you," I said, smiling and nodding. Of course, my smile wasn't nearly as big or bright as Layla's. "I appreciate it."

N'gwa nodded back at me. "Now then, let's not keep the others waiting any longer."

"I don't see, smell, or hear anyone else," Shun said.

My hero laughed. "Genetic enhancements are helpful. They allow one to better survive the harsh universe we live in. But they don't change your perception of reality."

She clapped her hands, and in the blink of an eye, the entire Order of the Banshee, as well as tables filled with food and booze, appeared all around us, *Ricochet* was nowhere to be seen, and our ears were suddenly greeted to blasting classical music.

"Welcome, Yael!" many of the Banshees cheered, while others chuckled.

"How... how did you—?"

"Impressed?" Madame N'gwa cut her great granddaughter off. "Yael, Layla, please say hello to everyone. P'Ken, you and Shun may get straight to enjoying yourselves. Indulge your primal instincts and be prepared to share your greatest stories."

"Wait!" I shouted as N'gwa turned around and walked away. "Why are we partying?

We're in danger, right now."

Madame N'gwa shook her head. "No. No, we're not." She walked further away, over to our sisters, and left the four of us twiddling our thumbs.

I had to believe she knew what she was doing. That if our attacker showed up here before my test, the rest of the Banshees could handle them. But something about that didn't seem right. Yes, I'd once again been blown away by what the Banshees were capable of, and I desperately wanted to know how Madame N'gwa had pulled off that trick, but at the end of the day, none of the rest of them were fighters.

My train of thought was cut off as Layla wrapped her arms around me.

"Thank you! Thank you! Thank you! Thank you! Thank you!" She looked up at me with a twinkle in her eyes. "I knew you wouldn't let me down! Well, no, I didn't, but I'm still really grateful. Thank you!"

Standing against Madame N'gwa made me want to vomit. A little bit had even come up my throat while I'd done so. But as much as I wanted to constantly please and impress her, Layla was my responsibility, and with her only being months away from adulthood, what was best for her was whatever she wanted to do.

"Of course. Now come on, go introduce Shun to your aunties. I'll catch up in a minute."

"Got it."

Grinning and bouncing up and down, Layla took the hand of a somehow still unimpressed Shun and led her into the crowd. For an aspiring thief, she sure didn't have much of a reaction to seeing all the best thieves in the universe in person.

"I ask again: do you know what you're doing?" P'Ken

asked. "The last thing we need right now is to make an enemy of Madame N'gwa."

"And you know the last thing I *want* is to make her our enemy. But I'm not about to force Layla to stay home and run a pickle business." I sighed and made some other strange noises with my mouth. "If things do go south though, can I count on you to have my back?"

P'Ken raised her stick off the ground. "I think you're making a big mistake, and when this comes back to bite us in the arse, I won't let you hear the end of it." She flipped her stick around and raised it up. "But that doesn't change that the answer to your question is Always."

I licked my lips as I gripped her stick. She then gripped it, right above where my hand was, and we continued to grip it back and forth until both of our hands reached the top.

"Come on. Let's go get drunk."

It was absolutely wild seeing all of my sisters together. There were those I'd spent plenty of time getting to know, like Beatriz Nunez, Lioness, and Electric Ellie, those who didn't care much for me, like Shion the Librarian, Yami, and Pony Tamer, and those I hadn't spent much time with yet, like Athena York, Go-Go Granny, and the only addition to the order more recent than me, Minty.

The one thing most of them had in common, apart from being elderly and brilliant thieves? Being jealous of my bounty and notoriety.

"That Shun kid of yours looks like she'd make a good bodyguard, but how is she as a thief?" Athena asked, actually talking to me for a change since she'd been drinking with Electric Ellie, who was especially excited to see me. "Is there a brain on top of all that muscle?"

I sipped my shrimp cocktail flavored cocktail. "She isn't Banshee level, if that's what you're asking, but she's pretty bright. Graduated the Utozin Naval Academy at 14."

"What made her choose to abandon that path and follow you?" Ellie asked, sucking on her black-gloved finger. "Was it the joys of shocking people both physically and emotionally?"

"That's your thing, darling, and it will never be anyone else's," Athena said, comforting her friend with a hand on her shoulder as she flipped her curly brown hair. "But it is a good question. Layla is the Madame's project, Marcos is someone I've even been impressed by, and that other buffoon you've told us about wants to be a "gentleman thief". What does she want?"

"Honestly, I'm not too sure," I answered, finishing up my drink and going in for another. "She doesn't like talking about herself much, and I respect that."

"You trust someone you don't know the motivations of?"

"Shun's put her life on the line for me more than once. The most excited I've ever seen her was when she got her bounty. She's one of us."

Moli had tried getting Shun to open up a few times, but never to much success. We suspected she was somewhere on the Autism spectrum like us, but she denied she was, and we weren't about to force her to get tested. Still, the smile she wore when she held her wanted poster was unforgettable, and the kind of thing that couldn't be faked.

Ellie excitedly clapped her hands. "I'm eager to see what she'll be like when she's drinking three glasses of prune juice a day." She softly laughed to herself. "Fucking prunes."

Athena sneered as she popped a sweet, pungent, and crispy cherry in her mouth. "Trust is a funny thing. It's something every person needs to survive and thrive. We are social creatures after all, and a proper relationship cannot be forged without it. And yet giving it to someone who doesn't deserve it can cause our demise in an instant."

Ellie continued to clap, generating electricity between her hands. "What is trust but educated faith? When you believe what someone says at face value, it's no different than believing in an uncaring god. It doesn't matter if you've known someone for a century, a decade, or a day; if you're not questioning everything, you're setting yourself up to fail."

I opened my mouth to respond to that BS, but nothing came out. My face and legs froze up, and my hand moved on its own to tug at my hair. Athena snapped her fingers in my face, but that didn't achieve anything. She and Ellie snickered as they walked off.

"Our poor little sister is going to die," Ellie hummed.

Fuck. Fuck, shit, fuck. As I regained control of my body, I rolled my jaw around and bounced up and down. I hadn't frozen up around the other Banshees in years, and now I'd humiliated myself. Had they gotten in my head about Shun? No, that wasn't it. I trusted her as much as I did any of the other kids. Was I nervous about the initiation? Apparently, I had reason to be, since it could kill me. More likely, I wasn't as out of my slump as I'd thought.

"Yael." Losing my foot and stumbling around, I turned to see Madame N'gwa, her face blank. "It's time."

I nodded, and followed her up a nearby hill. N'gwa remained silent as we walked, but she occasionally looked back at me. Maybe she was mad at me for earlier, or maybe I was imagining it, but each glance into my eyes was filled with judgment.

Atop the hill was a campfire, and surrounding it were books it could easily burn up if they got any closer.

"What is this?" I asked.

Madame N'gwa paced around the campfire. "Journals filled with some of the greatest stories ever lived by Banshees. Some written by myself, some written by our sisters, and some written by those who lived generations ago." She widened her eyes and pointed her tongue at me. "Experiencing all the universe has to offer is why we as an organization exist. And in the name of that goal, we have found ways to survive beyond what the rest of humanity thinks we as a species are capable of." She pulled sand out of her pocket and threw it into the flames, turning them a vibrant purple. "There is a reason we only accept the oldest and the smartest. But we believed your brain was large and developed enough to overlook your youth. Now, we will see if we were right to do so. Sit down."

I did as she said, getting down on the ground and criss-crossing my legs. "What exactly am I doing?"

Madame N'gwa's expression didn't change. "I'm sending you on a journey inside your mind. Should you succeed, you will reach the peak of humanity's potential and never need to be afraid again. Should you fail, you will either die or be rendered a vegetable. Are you ready?"

She hadn't actually answered my question. And it really would have been nice if she'd mentioned this initiation could kill me before we'd come here. Still, if this was the only way I could protect my family, then I'd do it, no matter the risk.

"Let's get started."

CHAPTER 10: MOLINA

I'd barely slept the past several nights, but the investigation was progressing well.

Kaybell and I had spoken to every general Morphea had pointed us to, from General Tomaso, who was always out to make Father look bad, to General Hossington, a dirty old man, to my former captain, General Asparago, who resented my entire family.

All of them were seemingly innocent, but something I'd noticed over time was that nearly all of the generals Morphea was suspicious of were nobles, primarily dukes. With how unpopular many of Kay's policies were among the nobility, and given that Father was one of Kaybell's closest allies, it was possible he'd been killed as an attack on her.

"Where did you say Griffin went?"

"You think I listened to that dolt?"

I pulled out a chair and took a seat across from Marcos at a table in the royal library. This section of the palace held the largest collection of physical books in the universe, only rivaled by the Xyconia Library on Pilan 7, and in its computers was a near infinite supply of records dating back to the dawn of modern society.

"Don't you ever think you'd be happier if you tried being friends with him instead of constantly being at each other's throats?" I asked.

Marcos didn't look up from the tablet they were working on. "A year from now, I'll never have to speak to him again. What would be the point?"

"I know you want to be an independent contractor, but Griffin and the others are gonna be top-rate thieves, and you may end up working with them down the line."

"I'll happily assist Shun in the future, but Layla, while I do like her, doesn't have what it takes, and Griffin doesn't have half a brain."

I leaned back in my chair and raised my hands above my head, cracking them. "You know, a problem Yael and I used to have was that she thought she was so much smarter than me and better in every way, and didn't respect my mind or abilities. We were only able to be happy together when she let that way of thinking go."

Marcos chuckled. "You really think she still doesn't think that way?"

I slammed my hands down onto the table. "Excuse me?"

"Don't get me wrong, Professor, you have my full respect, and you're absolutely smarter and more skilled than most of the incompetent fools who fill the stars. But one genius speaking about another, Yael is on an entirely different level from any of us. She knows it, and, deep down, you know it. Frankly, she should be the one leading this investigation."

I wasn't about to lose my cool at a kid. I was far too well trained for that. But damn if this wasn't a sore spot they were going after. I'd been trying to help them, and yet their response was to insult me and my marriage? They couldn't be more disrespectful.

"Focus on the research and be quiet," I said, grabbing a tablet for my own use.

"Whatever," they murmured.

Turning my attention to the files, I read about several of Father's enemies outside of the Sunrisers. The first one who stood out to me was Kredix Kor, a drug kingpin whose empire spanned three galaxies. Back when he was a captain, Father had nearly single-handedly brought down his entire operation. Next, there was Ranveer Rukh, who, as the most wanted male thief in the universe, and was viewed by many as an equivalent to Madame N'gwa. It was his capture that directly resulted in Father being promoted to general. The last criminal who stood out to me in my first hour of reading was Angus Arinadate, a warlord who had nearly formed a third major empire in the universe before the Sunrisers, under Father's leadership, had stopped him.

"I return with news!" Griffin shouted, breaking rule #1 of being in a library. "And bagels!" He set multiple bags down on the table and took a seat next to Marcos. "Cykebian delis have the best variety of shmear, I swear."

I straightened my back and went into professor mode. "Griffin, I asked you to do research with Marcos. Where have you been?"

"No need to worry, I was helping in my own way."

"Oh yeah?" Marcos snorted. "How's that?"

Griffin rolled his eyes at Marcos. "Well, you were suspicious of Prince Megz, so I got in on a game of light-squash with him and his sisters and talked to him a little."

"And you were careful not to give away that he was a suspect?"

"Of course. I started talking about romance and led the conversation to his relationship with Morphea. He confirmed that everything she told you was true. He freely admits he gets off on hurting women in bed, but he doesn't see it as different from any other kink. The only thing he regrets is not stopping as soon as Morphea told him to. He assumed she was getting into the foreplay, and for that mistake, he seemed truly remorseful and didn't blame your father for striking him at all."

I'd meant to have this conversation myself so I could read Megz's face and body language. As things stood, I had to go off Griffin's word alone. Based on how he'd presented himself to me since we'd arrived, I had every reason to believe what he was saying. There was no excusing what he did to Morphea, but being a creep didn't make him a murderer.

"Thank you, Griffin. Good work taking initiative."

Griffin grinned, proud of himself, while Marcos mimed vomiting.

"I actually have one more thing to report," Griffin said, riding this high.

"Oh, this should be good. What, did you fall in love with—"

"I'm in love!"

The room went silent for a moment.

"Holy shit, I was joking."

"Griffin, what are you talking about?" I asked.

The blue-eyed blonde pulled his hands to his heart. "Princess Jolla Kraken Bythora. I swear by the gods, she may be the most perfect woman I've ever met."

My brain raised red flags, its alarm was set to red alert, and my bones were screaming "Abort!" I didn't know where this was coming from, but I needed to put the kibosh on it immediately.

Marcos took a deep breath in, grinning nearly as wide as Griffin. "Ohhhhhh, this is too good. Please say more."

"Do not insult *or* encourage him," I said. "What are you talking about?"

Griffin giggled, rolling his hands around each other. "What's not to get? She's stunningly beautiful, she's a brilliant light-squash player, far better than Megz and Wink, she's classy and cultured, and her dark sense of humor is a bit odd, but I find it adorable."

Marcos burst out laughing, while I grit my teeth and cringed, trying to figure out what the Hell I was supposed to say.

"Griffin. Kid." I paused to exhale. "You did catch the part the other night where she mentioned that she missed getting to torture people, right?"

Griffin waved me off. "It's not like she actually does it anymore. And even the most perfect of women have flaws. I'm sure I could fix her and make her see what a horrid tradition she practiced."

I wanted to slam my head against the table. Only a horny teenager could think getting into bed with someone who'd cruelly insulted him and who considered torture fun was a good idea.

"Please, please, please ask her out soon," Marcos pleaded. "I want to record your rejection."

"If *you* think I'll fail, Platyperson, then I know I'll succeed."

"Are you sure you aren't rushing things?" I asked. "You've only known her a few days."

"And yet I feel like I've known her all my life."

I wasn't so old that I couldn't understand his point of view, especially since he'd once shared with me in confidence that despite having taken many girls on dates, he was still a virgin. He wanted love, recognition, and sexual gratification, and here he was in a position to ask out one of the most powerful women in the universe who, yes, was quite attractive.

"It may feel like that, but in reality, I've known the twins a lot longer than you. They've always been bad news."

"And so was Emperor Kaybell, yet you're giving her a second chance. What's different here?"

"The difference is I can take care of and protect myself if things go bad. You can't."

Griffin's smile faded as he looked down at his hands. "Everyone deserves a shot at redemption. Everyone."

I couldn't disagree with that. Kaybell had committed countless atrocities, and yet I deeply wanted us to be best friends again. I'd done awful things myself. Kaybell had only tortured Yael because I'd allowed her to. In general, as a former Sunriser, I had to believe in the system's capacity for rehabilitation.

Wait a second.

I picked my elbows up and slammed them down as thoughts and old memories raced to the front of my mind. There were Sunriser generals who would have benefited from getting Father out of the way, criminals who would have wanted revenge on him, and nobles who would have wanted to make a move against Kaybell. But there was only one man I could think of who fit all three labels.

And I was going to pay him a visit.

CHAPTER 11: YAEL

"What the fuck?"

What the fuck? What the fuck? What the fuck? my words echoed through the air in some other woman's voice. That is, assuming there *was* air wherever I was.

All around me was nothing but an empty white void. Then, the nothingness seemed to push against itself, forming cracks. And from the cracks sprung a new setting: a setting I hadn't seen in a very long time.

"Oh, so is this what we're doing?" I asked, standing in front of the average-sized Cykebian house I'd grown up in. "A little trip down memory lane? Cause unless you're gonna make me relive the time I tried Mega Flare Gummy Worms and then washed them down with The Hottest Beer in the Universe TM, I don't see how this could kill me."

The thud of a dusty old book being shut rang through my ears. Turning around, I found Shion the Librarian, or, more likely, some type of psychic manifestation of her. Whatever was happening right now was an area of science they hadn't taught in school, so I wasn't entirely sure.

Shion was by far the tallest Banshee, standing three heads above me. She dressed in long, flowing brown and forest green robes, with ornate gold jewelry on her ears, neck, and wrists. Her flawless, if naturally wrinkly, skin, was a dark shade of brown, and her eyes were the color of olives, one green and one black.

"Like so many, your origins are humble," she began. "The nothing daughter of two picklers. However, it wasn't long before your path diverged from the norm."

Loose pages blew through a burst of wind, and from them formed replicas of Mom, Dad, and little five year-old me, all dressed up for school in my uncomfortable uniform.

"I don't wanna go to pwivate school!" tiny Yael pleaded. "I wanna go to Pre-K with my friends!"

Dad bent down on one knee and put a hand on my shoulder, giving me the same smile he used on customers. "Kreplach, you heard what all the doctors said. You aren't like other kids.

You're… gifted."

"Beyond gifted," Mom said, beaming with pride. "You're unlike anyone else they've ever seen. That's why you got this scholarship. Opportunities like this don't come for everyone.

That's why you need to take full advantage of it. If… *when* you succeed at this school, you'll be able to do anything you want."

Tiny Yael pouted and crossed her arms as I turned around, pouted, and crossed my arms at Shion. "Why are you showing me this?"

Shion's face didn't shift. "They loved and cared for you as their everything, and yet you do nothing to repay them."

"Nothing? Uh, I send them loads of gidgits every month. They've been paid back in full for everything they gave and did for me, many times over."

"But do you ever see them?"

"Of course not. I'm a thief."

Shion backhanded me across the face, and not only was I not fast enough to dodge, but it actually stung. Did my enhancements not work here? My surgeon should have mentioned something about that.

"85% of the Banshees remained in contact with their parents up until the day their parents die. We do not begrudge the 15% who did not, as they either never knew their parents or came from abusive homes. Being a thief, alone, isn't an excuse. So what have you to say?"

I moaned like a cat, stretching my mouth and arms out in different directions. Of all the stupid things for this test to be, it had to be this. I'd been hoping for some impossible to solve riddles or being forced to play a game of chess against myself, but not being talked down to about being a bad daughter.

"I have to say that I'm happy with the life and family I've put together for myself, and they're not a part of it. The people I've surrounded myself with don't judge me, but my parents would, and that's not something I need to deal with."

Shion re-opened the book in her hand. "You say you're happy, but you can't lie to yourself."

The pages of her book burst out of their binds and flew straight at me. I shielded my eyes, but instead of making contact, they swarmed around me, buzzing like bees. No matter where I looked, there was only black and white.

After a minute, the pages went flaccid and collapsed to

the ground, dissolving into nothingness, and my environment had changed. Sunset hung over medium-sized Yael as she sat over the edge of the roof of Emperor Kalaben High School, head in her tablet.

"Ah, crap," I said through clenched teeth.

Medium-sized Yael cried her heart out, snot dripping from her nose, and threw her tablet off the roof. She then roared hard enough to make my heart pound.

Gentle footsteps pitter-pattered across the rooftop, and just as in reality, I was joined on the edge by Molina. After only seeing her wear her sexy, revealing leather outfits for so long, it was a bit surreal seeing medium-sized Molina in what used to be her standard attire, looking like she was heading to a business-casual dinner party.

"Hey."

The same lump that formed in medium-sized Yael's throat at that moment formed in mine. "Hey."

Medium-sized Moli kicked her legs and took medium-sized Yael's hand, clenching it. "This isn't fair."

Medium-sized Yael snickered through her tears. "No shit. I ace every damn test, do better than any other applicant in history, and I'm rejected for being mentally unfit? It's so fucked up." She clenched her Moli's hand back. "How could you get in and not me?!"

I turned away from the sight of my greatest failure. Not getting rejected from the Sunrisers, but making Moli cry. No matter how hurt I was, it was cruel and unfair of me to have said that. No matter the Moli, real or imaginary, I couldn't stand to see her in pain. And yet, my ego had always brought her only that. I thought I'd gotten that under control, but I'd been so confident that us being together was enough for her that I'd ignored what was really going on in her head.

"Perhaps you'd be happier if things had gone differently this day," Lioness said, clad in her signature faux lion fur coat, Shion no longer anywhere to be seen. "Perhaps you were meant to be a Sunriser, not a Banshee."

"Come on, Lioness, you know me better than that." She stared at me coldly as she licked her hand and wiped it all over her face. "Right. You're not really, Lioness. You're me. Or something. Either way, no. Definitely not."

"Are you sure? You may have a higher bounty and more notoriety than most of us, but you still pale in comparison to our experience and abilities."

"Duh! You're all way older than me and apparently have superpowers. That second part is why I'm here."

A bottle of milk appeared out of nowhere in Lioness's hand and she chugged it back, leaving her with a milk mustache. That, of course, meant she had to clean herself again.

"But again, are you happy? You're the worst of the best, but you could have been the best of the worst."

"Oh my gods, yes!" I sighed. "I love my job. I love being a thief. That's not the problem."

Lioness smirked. "So you admit there's a problem?"

I popped my lips. "Yes. Fine. Some things have been bugging me lately. I haven't been the best wife, but I know I can do better. I haven't been the best mentor, but I'm trying to do better. And, well, I... I—"

"Say it."

I bowed my head and shifted around. "I don't wanna."

"Say it."

"Look, we're in my mind, you know what I'm thinking."

"Say it."

"Fucking hell, shut up!"

My screaming was met by the screaming of Yael from fifteen years ago. No longer on my high school's rooftop, I was hovering through a museum, watching myself run for my life from security during my first heist. It was a time before I had enhancements, before I had *Ricochet*, and before I really knew what I was doing. It was a miracle I'd gotten out at all, let alone with my anonymity intact.

As the choir of myselves died out, a different sound filled my ears. Once again, the Banshee guiding me had changed, and now Moonriver stood behind me, singing a beautiful tune.

Around the same height as me, but far wider, Moonriver had a light tan, a bald head, and was dressed in a dark blue dress covered in feathers. She lacked the ability to speak in any traditional language, but she was such a gifted singer, she could communicate her thoughts with near complete accuracy to anyone above a certain level of intelligence.

"No, I wasn't exactly a natural when I started out," I admitted. "My Sunriser training didn't all directly translate and, in actuality, left me with some bad habits, but that's why I got my enhancements to compensate, and convinced Jellz to show me the ropes. To make sure I never did anything as stupid as set off a basic museum alarm system again."

With the museum guards unable to fire their blasters without risking hitting any of the priceless paintings and artifacts around us, they had no choice but to bet on their speed and hope they could catch me. Nervous as I was though, crying, freaking out that I was gonna go to jail, and thinking that I should have stayed home, I was never in any danger. Even before receiving my enhancements, I'd been at the peak of physical health and conditioning. Those doofuses never had a chance at catching me.

Moonriver sang, showing off her full range and ability to sing everything from soprano to bass. I didn't see her too often, so even seeing an imaginary version of her perform was awesome. As things stood, she was my third favorite Banshee, and her music- and sound-themed capers were always fun to hear about.

"You always believed in me! Why are you suggesting I shouldn't have become a thief?" I slapped my forehead. "Right. Not you. Me. But that would mean I think I shouldn't have become a thief. That doesn't make any sense."

Moonriver tilted her head, softly whistling.

"Okay, Yael. Focus." I flipped over and stood up on my hands. "I can't just keep jumping around. That assassin could show up at any moment, and I have to be ready. So what's going on here? Why am I thinking this way?"

I clenched my eyes shut and took a deep breath in and out.

No, I hadn't been happy in a long time. By all rights, I should have been. I had everyone and everything I needed, plus infamy and riches beyond my wildest dreams. I should have been ecstatic. But even if I fixed things with Moli and Layla, darkness would still consume my world. Did I blame being a thief on that? Did I think I could have somehow made a better life for myself if I'd stayed in the pickle business?

Of course not! That was stupid! All I knew was I was miserable and, for the life of me, I couldn't figure out why. It was the one damn puzzle I couldn't solve.

Panting hard, I did a series of handstand pushups as I continued to think.

Is my subconscious seeing something that I'm not? Could it be that the problem isn't that I'm a thief, but that I think there's a problem because I'm a thief? This vision thing had started with my parents, who I didn't want to see because of my profession, but I was 99% sure they weren't the issue. I loved Mom and Dad, but it had been fifteen years since I'd seen them. The desire to see them wouldn't have just started eating away at me recently.

"You seem like you could use some help opening up."

My arms collapsed under me as I fell on my side.

"Moonriver?" I opened my eyes, hoping to the gods I'd misheard the voice.

I hadn't.

Standing over me now wasn't any of the Banshees, but instead, my worst nightmare. "It's so wonderful to be able to play with you again," Emperor Kaybell taunted.

My surroundings had changed once again, and I now found myself trapped in the *Noriker*'s interrogation chamber. I couldn't move a muscle, and I was completely at her mercy, her special torture device hooked up to my body.

"Madame N'gwa!" I shouted. "Get me out of here! Wake me up! I can't go through this again!"

Kaybell guffawed. "No one's coming to save you, peasant. You're all mine."

"No. No, no. Please don't. Please don't—AHHHHHHH!"

My brain went through a blender, ground into chunks and juices. At the same time, my toes were picked from my feet like grapes from a vine. One by one. Slowly. I wasn't sure how long I screamed, but by the time she turned the machine off, I was out of breath.

Kaybell cupped her hand around my chin. "What do you want, Yael? Why are you so unhappy?"

I choked on my own spit as I tried to answer. Even if I had gotten the words out, I would have just said, "I don't know".

The emperor threw my head back and stepped away. "Do you think maybe Molina doesn't love you as much as you love her? I mean, she could have had me, and I mean, just look at us; there's no contest." Her voice trailed off into laughter. And she wasn't wrong; she was way hotter than me. "Maybe it's because you two don't actually have much in common."

"More… than you, bitch," I grunted.

"Mmm, I don't know about that." From her waist, she drew a sword. "Do you care about her special interest at all?"

Before I could even try and answer, she ran the sword through my chest. Blood erupted from my mouth, and I started choking on it, all the while she twisted the blade around to cause me maximum agony.

"Madame N'gwa," I panted. "Please. I can't do this. There has to be another way."

My plea was met by Kaybell ripping the sword out of me and covering me in the blood waterfalling out of my chest. If this was reality, that would have killed me. But because I was here, there was only suffering.

"What do you want, Yael?" she asked in a harsher tone. "Make up your mind!"

I couldn't speak. I was in too much pain, my tears and snot were mixing with my blood, and she'd caused some major internal damage. I couldn't give an answer even if I knew what to say.

"All right, you need a greater incentive?"

Kaybell clapped her hands and, in response, the room extended. Out of nowhere, Aarif and P'Ken appeared, also strapped to their chairs, with the same device hooked up to them as me.

No, I thought. *This didn't happen. This isn't happening. None of this is real.*

Those thoughts didn't help me as my ears were filled by my family's screams. And it wasn't their current selves. It was them as they had been the day I'd been tortured in real life. P'Ken was just a kid.

"Tell me what I want to hear, vermin!" Kaybell exclaimed. "Or I'll let them fry."

The effects of the device hit me too at that moment, the hole in my chest expanding to consume my entire torso. A flaming poker skewered me, and knives were plunged just a little bit into my scalp so that they hurt like Hell, but didn't reach the brain.

"Last chance, peasant!"

P'Ken shouldn't have been going through this. In reality, Layla and Shun shouldn't have had to worry about the threat that was coming for us. I was their teacher. They were kids.

P'Ken was just a kid.

Layla and Shun were just kids. They're all just *kids*.

Oh my gods.

"Well, Yael? What's it gonna be?!"

I answered her question by flexing my muscles, breaking free of my restraints, and punching her hard enough to break her neck and send her corpse flying across the room. And then the room, and everyone else inside it, disappeared.

All the pain went away too. In its place was a sense of peace I hadn't felt in ages. I now stood under a clear blue sky, right outside my school, with Madame N'gwa at my side.

"Well?" she asked, jingling her bells. "Have you solved the equation?"

Taking another deep breath, I exhaled and grinned at what I'd built.

"When P'Ken first told me she wanted to be my apprentice, I thought I was too young to have one. Honestly, that initial thought was probably right. But I took her on anyway. And a few years later, I agreed to train Layla for you. I didn't need to take on Marcos, as there were definitely other programmers I could have hired. And by the point Griffin and Shun came around, it was like I was handing out apprenticeships."

"And you know why?"

All five of my students appeared in front of us, while Aarif and Molina appeared behind me, patting me on the back and giving me a kiss on the cheek, respectively.

"Because as annoying or frustrating as they can be, I love kids. I love sharing my passions and loves, and kids, especially ones who are eager to impress you, soak that shit up like sponges. I love spending time with them and watching them learn and grow. More than the thrill of stealing, they're why I still do this job. I mean, I peaked pretty damn early, and all I have left to do is surpass you. But think about what they'll all be able to accomplish."

"I haven't heard an answer."

I laughed as my extended family faded away. "I love them. I love them like they're my own. But I want someone who truly is my own too. And I shouldn't let my less than savory career get in the way of that."

I cried again, not in agony, but with joy. I turned around and faced not Madame N'gwa, but Moli. "I want to have a baby."

Saying that outl oud sent euphoria through my body, but it was short lived, as out of nowhere came the biggest headache I'd ever had.

What the Hell was going on? Why wasn't I waking up if I'd done what I had to? Was there actually more to this damn test?

"Yael," Madame N'gwa hummed, shutting my eyes with her ice-cold fingertips. "Relax. And listen."

———

I gasped as my eyes opened. I was back in reality, and, much as I was having a hard time breathing and my head was still ringing, I was alive.

But based on the smell of the air, possibly not for long.

I leaped up to my feet and saw that, beneath the hilltop I was on, fire and smoke had consumed the area where we'd been partying. I was too late.

"Shit, shit, shit, shit, shit!"

The Banshees could all be dead. My family could all be dead. But I had to hope for the best. I had to hope that my heroes, students, and friends were all smart enough to survive for however long the android or robot had been here.

Pushing the pain in my throat and head away, I tore my dress so I could fight in it and leaped to the bottom of the hill. I sprinted through the smoke, looking for any sign of life.

I didn't see any of the Banshees, but I didn't see any of their corpses either. I listened for footsteps, but heard nothing except the crackling flames.

My heart pounded against my chest as I tried to figure out what happened. And I was given a clue as the assassin stepped out of the smoke, in front of me, not trying to take me by surprise. And in their hands, hanging by their collars, were Shun and P'Ken, battered, broken, and bloodied.

I couldn't tell if they were dead or unconscious.

I ground my teeth, narrowed my eyes, and my face grew as hot as the fire surrounding us. "What have you done?"

The assassin threw their bodies to the ground, giggling again.

"Yael Pavnick, you must die for your sins."

I clenched my fists and took my stance. "No. You're the one dying here."

CHAPTER 12: MOLINA

Rolltaro H. Galopire, duke of Kreshent and Sunriser general, was a man I'd once held as much respect for as for any other superior officer. That was before he was discovered to be extorting those living on his land for a far greater sum of gidgits than was legally taxable in the Cykebain Empire. Kaybell's father overlooked his crimes, let him off with a warning, and pardoned him, much to the chagrin of my own. He'd at least wanted to demote Galopire or, in the best-case scenario, have him dishonorably discharged, but he'd been unable to get the votes from other generals to make either happen. Even still, Father never made any secret that he wasn't fond of him, and with the power he did have on his own, practically isolated him from the rest of the organization and stripped him of any actual responsibilities.

I had to check his file after coming to my initial suspicion to be sure, but it came as no surprise that he was a member of the political faction seeking to restore the slave trade, arguing not only that it was the will of the gods, but that it would help the economies of worlds further away from Cykeb. If Galopire had killed Father, he would have gotten revenge for how he'd been treated, he would have a chance to become supreme general, and he would have taken Kaybell's bishop.

The only thing that confused, and worried, me, was that Morphea knew all this better than anyone, and yet she hadn't put him on the list of names for us to talk to. It could have been a simple oversight, or she could have had a personal motivation, but if Galopire did turn out to be involved, that would incriminate her as well.

At dinner, I informed Kay of my theory, while she told me about her follow-up meeting with General Asparago. Asparago claimed that while she did indeed hate me, she still respected my father, and only questioned his parenting skills. While she was currently vying for the supreme general position and mildly sadistic, she said she never would have killed an innocent man unless it was for the greater good, and that only the guilty deserved to face her wrath.

Kaybell mostly believed her story, but kept her on our list of suspects. As for my newest suspicion, she agreed that if any general was responsible, it was most likely Galopire. She'd only ever spoken to him once or twice, but I'd told her all about his crimes and his relationship with my father.

The next morning, Kay and I flew to Galopire's estate on Kreshent, Father having essentially banished him from Zenith Command and forced him to work from home. Griffin elected to stay behind to go riding with Wink and Jolla, the latter of whom he was still planning on asking out. I'd tried to get Marcos to at least come up with us, but I hadn't even managed to get them out of bed.

Lives of hedonism and excess weren't anything unusual among the nobility, but even Kay snickered at how far this man took it. All across the grounds were marble fountains flowing with wine, solid gold statues of himself, which couldn't have been more proportionately inaccurate, a security force made up of Cykerdroids that had been partially built with gold, despite that making them substantially less durable, and massive screens displayed self-produced films Galopire had starred in.

"Be honest, is this how you picture my mind?" Kaybell asked as we landed next to the central mansion.

"No, your statues actually look like you."

Kay laughed as she took my hand, her soldiers leading us off the ship. She believed Galopire wouldn't have the nerve to make a move directly against the emperor, but given we were on his territory and greatly outnumbered, I'd convinced Kay to at least have a few soldiers and Cykerdroids go in with us. Additionally, while I loved my sword, it wasn't gonna cut it here, so I'd also taken the most powerful sidearm the royal armory had to offer and strapped it to the other side of my waist.

"Emperor Kaybell, it's an honor to have you in my home," the pale, overweight man with a blonde mohawk said, bowing as we entered his ornate sitting room. "May I get you anything? Anything at all?"

"No, thank you," she said as we sat down on a comfy sofa, her guards and robots remaining on their feet.

The hideously ostentatious room Galopire had decorated was, naturally, filled with gold sculptures and paintings of himself. It was also fucking freezing, the cooling system blasting harder than it ever should. If I had to guess, Galopire kept his house this way so he had an excuse to walk around in six layers of silk, velvet, leather, and fur.

"Ms. Langstone, I apologize for not making an appearance at your father's funeral," Galopire said, sitting down in his recliner. "I know it was expected of me, but I knew your father and… well, he wouldn't have wanted me there."

He was openly admitting they weren't fond of each other. If he was the killer, at this point, that would have been perfectly reasonable to admit. After all, he didn't know yet that we knew Father *had* been murdered. That is, unless one of the other generals was working with him and had informed him of our investigation before our arrival.

"I understand," I said. "I know you had a history."

"Mmm." Galopire adjusted his cravat. "I'm sure the emperor didn't drop by just to pay a visit or find out why I wasn't in attendance. How can I help you?"

Kaybell primped her hair. "Lord Galopire, have you been satisfied with my performance as emperor these past few years?"

"You'd have me beheaded if I said no, wouldn't you?" He laughed to himself, filling the otherwise silent room. "I kid, of course. The girl I knew when she was growing up may have ordered that, but everyone knows you've gone soft."

My head shifted to Kay on its own, worrying that that comment would make her explode.

Surprisingly, however, she managed to keep her cool, not appearing phased at all. Of course, Kay's ranting may have been preferable to Gaolpire's continued laughter.

"No, I won't have you executed for speaking your truth," Kay said with a straight face. "Answer honestly."

Galopire bounced his head up and down, resting his tongue on his lower lip and salivating. "No, your highness. I have not been. Nor have many of your other most important subjects. You've been neglecting our needs in favor of helping hapless commoners, no offense Ms. Langstone, and over-preparing for a war your father already ensured we could win."

Again, I readied myself for Kay to scream in my ear, but she remained composed. "You seem fairly comfortable here, and the majority of other dukes live lives of similar luxury. As for our army and weapons, yes, we could have most likely beaten the Utozins no matter what they threw at us, but if our firepower is so great that they can't even compare, we can end a war as quickly as it starts, without needless bloodshed. And even if you believe my policies here are extreme, you yourself are a proponent of the return of the slave trade, and I'd argue that's an equally extreme take, just on the other side of the spectrum."

Hmm. I pinned a note to my brain to discuss with Kay later.

"Your highness, if you'd allow me, I could explain to you in, oh, I'd say an hour, how this isn't a matter of opposing extreme views, but one of logic and fantasy. As a duke, I am among the most well-bred and well-educated people in the universe, and I am here to provide counsel on how the empire should be run, just as I did for your father."

"I'm well aware of the things many of you wanted my father to do," Kay said through gritted teeth, not losing her temper yet, but now on the verge of it.

"We actually have a few more questions for you," I said before Galopire could respond. "With my father's passing, do you have any interest in taking his place as supreme general?"

Galopire tapped his foot against the black marble floor. "I believe I could fit the role quite well, but going after that position would be a fruitless endeavor. The winds tell me the position will either be going to Han or your sister." He bowed his head. "I'm afraid being excommunicated from the command center ripped away my chances of ever fulfilling my potential."

"And do you regret the crimes you committed that led to that happening?"

Galopire picked his head up and cracked his neck multiple times, continuing to tap his foot. "I do. But we all make mistakes. Such as, I don't know, giving up a chance to capture the entire Order of the Banshee."

He snickered as Kay nearly shot up from her seat. Luckily, I got my hand over to hers and calmed her a little before she lost it.

"That was both of you, wasn't it?" he continued. "The captain who lost her nerve and the first officer who let her emotions get the best of her?"

Kay's hand trembled under mine.

"Did you know, your highness, that there were many who felt your complete and utter failure as a Sunriser should have resulted in you being disinherited? Of course, we're not too fond of your brother either. Now, your sisters? They'd make excellent emperors."

"Did you *kill* Drenian Langstone?" I breathed, getting straight to the point as I tried to stop whatever game he was playing.

Galopire burst out laughing, pounding both of his feet against the floor. "He was really murdered? I hadn't even thought of that. Meanwhile I was here thinking that you'd caught on to my latest business venture. So silly of me. I should have know you stupid girls couldn't have figured me out."

"Who do you think you are to speak to me this way?" Kay spat.

The tapping of Galopire's foot escalated in speed. "Me? I'm your humble servant. Of course, in the near future, I hope to be something much more."

"And what's that?"

Galopire smirked. "A bringer of justice."

Kay's eyes widened as she pulled away from me and launched up to her feet.

"Shoot him!" Kaybell ordered, and at the exact same moment, Galopire slammed his foot against the floor, cracking through it.

Galopire's chair flipped around, throwing him down to a lower level of the estate. His Cykerdroids filled the room and, with the element of surprise, blasted away our guards and our own Cykerdroids.

"Get down!" I shouted, tackling Kay to the floor as the shootout took place. "He must have had them programmed to follow a specific pattern of his foot tapping. What do we do?"

"Dance with me!"

"What?!"

Kaybell took my hands, stood us both up, and spun me around, guiding each of my steps so that only she was hit by the incoming blaster fire, while I was completely unscathed.

"Are you okay?" I panicked as we continued to dance together.

"I'm fine. Enhancements, remember?"

"Yeah, but these are Cykerdroids!"

"And I'm the fucking emperor! You think I'd let any-one get enhancements on par with mine?" Kay lifted me off the floor as she ran on the wall and decapitated the Cykerdroids coming at us from the right with a series of fierce kicks. "You're looking at the strongest woman in the universe."

For the split second after Kay put me down, I was able to catch my breath. And that was necessary not just because we were in the middle of combat, but because of the power Kay was displaying, and the way her sweat glistened in the light.

"Other side!" she called out.

We resumed dancing over the remaining Cykerdroids. The only thing separating this from one of the numerous Sunriser galas we'd attended together being that we were in real danger and not social danger.

With a few more kicks from Kay's flawless legs, the room was cleared. Of course, given the size of the estate, there were bound to be more.

"Let's get out of here," I said. "Fast."

Kay nodded and took the lead, moving the way we'd come in, while I trailed after her. Calling yourself the strongest woman in the universe was a bold claim, but she may have been right. I couldn't picture Yael or Shun pulling off what she'd just done, let alone any of the fatcats who'd gotten enhancements in the past few years.

"Hey, about before," I started as we made our way down a particularly long hallway. "When you told me about preparing for war with the Utozins, you didn't say anything about wanting to prevent bloodshed. Did you make that up just now to try and impress me?"

Kay smirked. "As if I'd need to lie to impress you. No, I didn't make that up."

"Then why didn't you say that before?"

"Honestly? I was already working to show you how much I've changed, and I didn't want to go overboard all at once. I didn't want you thinking I'd gone, as that pompous fool put it, "soft."

I had no words to say in response to that. I could only smile with pride… and possibly another sin. I tried to force that part down and focus on how far my best friend had come.

Turning a corner, we immediately retreated two steps back as blaster fire blew away the wall we'd momentarily stepped in front of.

"Dance again?" I asked, my heart racing from the nostalgic experience.

Kay shook her head. "Cover me."

While she dove back around the corner to attack head on, I drew my blaster and fired at our enemies while maintaining cover. Kay was doing the real work, but I was glad to be helpful at all.

The sound of crushing metal mixed with the monotonous humming of the blaster fire to grind against my ears, but I kept on shooting, imagining the awesome ways Kaybell was dismantling each of them.

"All clear!" she called out after a few moments.

I went around the corner to find Kay standing over a pile of dead machines and scrap metal. The lasers were starting to take their toll on her, her outfit destroyed and blood coming from every part of her body, especially her head, but she was still grinning like nothing was wrong.

"You know, it's a really good thing you weren't this strong when you were trying to kill Yael," I laughed.

Kay dusted herself off. "Tell her I'd like a rematch sometime."

The idea of sitting on the side, sipping a drink, watching

Yael and Kay go at it with nothing on the line had me shaking at the ankles. The sweat, the moves, the cute workout outfits…

"Kaybell!"

I was too late. I'd been distracted. While I'd been fantasizing, a single Cykerdroid appeared from around the other side of the hallway and fired at Kay. I'd been too slow to warn her, and a full-powered shot hit her in the back of the head.

She collapsed to the floor.

"No, no, no!" I fired at the Cykerdroid as I rushed to Kay's side. "Please tell me you're okay."

Kay didn't move or answer. I put my fingers to her neck, and she was breathing, but only barely. That meant I could breathe again.

If there were any more Cykerdroids beyond this one, we were probably screwed. But if this was the last one, or at least the last one that found us, maybe I could get us out of here.

I threw my blaster away and instead drew my sword. Running serpentine with as much speed as I could muster, I charged the Cykerdroid. It landed a few stray shots, the sudden pain in my legs nearly bringing me down, but I refused to fall.

My sword couldn't pierce a Cykerdroid. That would be ridiculous. But this asshole had made his regiment with gold. And in his vanity, he'd given them all massive weak spots.

I ran my sword through the piece of gold which made up its right shoulder and then twisted it around. From the outside, Cykerdroids may have been incredibly durable, but their insides were so intricate that if any part of them was severely damaged, the whole system would fail.

I ripped my sword out of the machine and sheathed it back as the Cykerdroid froze and static flew off of it in every direction.

It was a lucky thing that development of cybernetics had been halted for so long, or else that probably wouldn't have worked.

Luck wasn't actually on my side, though. And Galoprie wasn't the fool I'd assumed he was. The dead Cykerdroid's eyes glowed red. And in place of the endless blaster fire, my ears were my by a ticking sound.

"Kay!" I screamed, running back over to her and picking her up by her armpits. "We have to move! Now!"

"Wh… what?" she whispered.

"That thing is gonna blow!"

I had no idea what kind of reach or power this explosion would have. All I knew was that I probably couldn't survive it. Maybe Kay would be able to, but I was screwed. I wasn't sure what was worse: dying with Yael thinking I was mad at her, or not being able to avenge Father.

"Hey! Kay!"

Somehow still having it in her to do so, Kay tackled me back down, and covered my body entirely with her own. She was going to take the full brunt of the explosion for me.

"Kay, don't do th—"

The bomb inside the Cykerdroid went off, destroying the entire section of the house, rubble crashing down around us, and making fire and smoke the only things I could see. Kaybell had positioned herself perfectly, the explosion not touching me at all, but I couldn't make out what condition she was in, and my deafened ears couldn't make out a thing audibly.

As I stood back up once again, soot at my feet, rubble continued to fall. Everything was so blurry, my sight not much better than my hearing.

"Kay!" I called out, walking down the hallway. "Kay,

where are you?"

I'd been thinking about what a tragedy my own death would be, but Kay's would be just as great. The scum who hated her and wanted to make life miserable for the common man would win. And she would miss out on prospering from the fruits of her hard work.

"Fuuuuuuuuuuck."

I spun around on my feet. Still not able to hear right, I wasn't sure at first if Galoprie had reappeared.

He hadn't.

Out of the ashes, Kaybell rose, covered in the stuff from head to toe. Blood was gushing out of her head, but she was still standing.

"Thank the gods," I said, running over and hugging her. "You idiot. I don't care how strong you are. That could have killed you. You're the emperor, you can't go sacrificing yourself for nothing like that."

Her arm stiff and slow to move, Kay hugged me back. "You're not nothing. You're everything. And I'd sacrifice myself for you a million times."

Tears ran down my filthy face and, as they did so, I had a single thought. A horrible, awful, terrible thought.

I wanted to kiss her.

CHAPTER 13: YAEL

Sweat dripped down every inch of my body, the heat of the flames around us bearing down on me as the smoke made it a struggle to breathe. My initiation hadn't made me any stronger, faster, or more durable, and my head was still splitting, but I knew I had it in me to kick this thing's ass.

Before I could take a step forward, they threw my friends' lifeless bodies in front of me. I knew it was stupid to break from my stance, but I had to know if they were still alive. I bent down and put my fingers to each of their throats.

I coughed as I tried to breathe a sigh of relief. Neither of them were dead. Of course, that just made me wonder: why hadn't this unstoppable killing machine finished the job?

"I know you're not much of a talker, but, uh, thanks for letting them live," I said, standing back up. "This mean your beef is only with me? Gods, why did I mention beef? If you hadn't shown up, I could be eating right now."

The assassin popped out their razor-bladed katars and electrified them like they had last time. I retook my stance and looked down at my friends. My first priority had to be getting them out of here. Even if the assassin didn't want to kill them, it probably wouldn't mind them winding up as collateral damage. I had to fight them and distract them, while also getting Shun and P'Ken to safety. I had to do two things at once.

Following Madame N'gwa's advice, I did what seemed like the most counterintuitive thing I could and closed my eyes. She'd also advised taking deep breaths for my first time, but with all the smoke around, that wasn't happening.

"Yael Pavnick, you must die for your sins."

"Yeah, yeah. I get it."

The sound of their rapid, heavy steps banged against my ears as they charged toward me. I had to fight *and* run away. I had to travel down two different paths. I had to live two different stories.

Popping my eyes open, I grabbed the assassin's wrists at the moment they went in to strike, using all my strength to hold them back. At the same time, I picked up Shun and P'Ken like sacks of potatoes and ran away with all my speed.

And at the same time I pulled that off, my brain cracked like an egg, the gooey juices going all over the place as the first me collapsed to my knees.

"What the Hell?" the assassin asked, the weirdness of what was going on finally prompting them to say something outside of their usual phrase.

I would have made a snarky remark, but I was too busy feeling like my head had been chopped in half. The second me was experiencing the same agony, but the adrenaline running through my blood kept me moving. Still, I wouldn't last long. The strain on both of my bodies was too much, and no matter how long I felt like I could keep it going, if it went on too long, I was dead.

Gently putting my friends down in a crater, I clapped my hands and restored reality to normal, dissipating the Yael who'd been left to fight the assassin. The sensation of my brain coming back together was better than an orgasm, but it also left me equally exhausted.

My knees buckled under me, my body wanting to collapse, but I couldn't let that happen. I could sleep this off like a bad hangover once I'd made sure the assassin would never bother us again.

Spinning around on my heels, I ran back the way I'd come, not stopping until I was back where I started. The assassin hadn't moved one step away from where I'd left them.

"You know, I was expecting you to chase after me once I put myself back together," I said. "Feeling tired?"

They took a single step toward me. "Explain what you just did."

"Sorry, buddy," I said, taking my stance once again and readying myself for the real fight to start. "Trade secret."

———

"Yael," Madame N'gwa hummed, shutting my eyes with her ice-cold fingertips. "Relax. And listen."

I did as my sister asked to the best of my ability, going completely numb.

"The Order of the Banshee was formed 978 years ago for two purposes. Firstly, it was to allow the best of the best thieves in the universe to find companionship and to learn from each other's successes and failures. The second reason, however, was its primary purpose. The universe is endless, and the amount of experiences to have in it are infinite. There are more adventures to be had than any single person can go on in a single lifetime, even one that lasts as long as mine. As a collective, we are able to share not only information and tips with each other, but stories. We can live vicariously through each other and, as a result, we can live fuller, more complete lives than anyone else. We can be more complete people. For what are humans but the stories that make up our existences?"

I'd known all of this for ages, and parts of it were repeated at every Banshee meeting. By this point, I'd told all of my top thirty stories, and also heard over a dozen from the others that put each and every one of them to shame. But I had no idea what any of this had to do with the weird trip down memory lane I'd gone on.

"Of course, the universe is a dangerous place," Madame N'gwa continued. "And as a group of women far past our physical prime, we've needed to develop a way to allow ourselves to overcome any obstacle. Approximately 600 years ago, the Banshees of their day found just that. They weren't the strongest or fastest or most athletic, but they were the smartest. And they could exploit that."

Madame N'gwa opened my eyes with her fingertips. Her appearance remained unchanged, but she now held a yellow apple.

"At every point in life, we are faced with making decisions. You can drop the apple, you can toss it into the air, or you can take a bite out of it. Each action will have a different impact on your story, however minor. But what if you wish to do all three?"

Two other Madame N'gwa's appeared next to the original, all identical in appearance.

One tossed their apple into the air, another dropped it down into the endless void we were standing in, and the third took a bite from it.

"This is the power of The True Adventurer." I squinted my eyes. "Cloning?"

The three Madame N'gwa's snickered as they merged back into one. The remaining apple both did and didn't have a bite taken out of it, and that wrinkled my brain.

"Not quite. To put it crudely, it's a mild form of reality warping. Through someone else's eyes, we change their perception of our actions. We can allow ourselves to be captured, while also making a quick getaway. We can go on a vacation while also going on the most exciting heist of our lives. We can take two exciting jobs at once. Do you get it?"

I shook my head. "Not really, no. What's the science behind this?"

Madame N'gwa grinned at me like I was a dumb kid. Which to her, I supposed I was.

"We're not all scientists, Yael. We're thieves. You know more about those fields of knowledge than the vast majority of us. If you're interested in exploring the how of this ability, then we'll gladly support your research. But for now, focus on the why."

"The only why I care about right now is protecting my family," I said.

"And that's understandable. But much like we aren't scientists, we aren't fighters. We're adventurers who balk at the restrictive nature of society, not warriors who live for bloodshed. Use this ability as you see fit, but never forget its true purpose. Never stop seeking out new stories."

I didn't even have to think about my list of the weirdest things that had ever happened to me, because this? This right here? This broke the fucking scale.

"Okay, let me see if I've got this right," I sighed. "I can make other people see I'm doing things other than what I'm really doing, but I'm actually doing all of the things at once, and I'll carry memories of all the events even once I've turned the power off?"

"Something like that."

Madame N'gwa put a hand on my shoulder. "A word of advice: don't try splitting yourself into any more than two selves to start. Your brain will likely barely be able to handle that much, and any more will kill you instantly. Understand?"

I nodded.

"Good. Then make us proud. And bring us back some grand tales."

I smiled back at her. I definitely didn't understand any of this, but right now, if I really had a superpower I could use to beat the assassin, I wasn't gonna look a gift horse in the mouth. I was gonna ride that horse to victory.

"Wait, hold on, what if one of my multiple selves dies?"

———————

"Custard cream on a cracker!" I screamed at the top of my lungs as a laser from the assassin's wrist both did and didn't cut me in half.

The trials I'd been through had made my pain tolerance higher than most, but there was now a memory in my mind of my torso being severed from my legs, and that burnt my eyes with the heat of the sun.

The assassin charged at me and swung their katars around, but I ducked and dodged out of the way of each of their attacks. I took the brief chances I had to strike back, kicking their face and stomach, but they weren't phased at all.

I altered the assassin's perception of reality over and over again, allowing them to think they were killing me repeatedly, all while I ran circles around them, attacking from every angle in the hopes of finding a weak point. To my horror, there weren't any.

All I succeeded in doing was bloodying my fists and breaking my own bones. On top of that, even though I'd only used my new power a few times and I was still in the middle of energizing combat, I was getting sleepy and exhausted. I couldn't keep being The True Adventurer without any thought. It may have been my only real weapon against the assassin, but I had to better pick and choose when I used it.

I did a triple back tuck to put distance between us and cracked my neck.

"You know, if you told me why you hated me, maybe we could talk things through and I wouldn't have to kill you."

They raised their katars above their head and, a moment later, lightning blasted out of them in every direction. I was pretty damn fast, but especially with how drowsy I was getting, I wasn't nearly quick enough to dodge lightning.

"Shit! Crap! Sprock!"

With me down on my knees, paralyzed, the assassin went straight for my neck with their katar. I didn't have any other choice but to shut my eyes and warp reality.

I was barely able to move, but I crawled away while my other self was decapitated. I ended up falling on my face as I experienced the feeling of getting beheaded.

I could see why this ability was mostly used to run away and explore. Using it to fight put too much strain on the mind and body. But Madame N'gwa wouldn't have given it to me now if it couldn't get the job done.

The assassin appeared in front of me and picked me up by my throat. Just like last time, they pummeled my face. Over and over and over again, splitting my skull.

"Tell me how you're playing these tricks, and I'll let your friends live."

I stuttered as I struggled to speak. "See? Communication? That's good. And you know, you may have had some ground to stand on if you hadn't already let them live once."

They threw me down on my back, cracking my spine.

"You think I care about their miserable lives? I only thought it might be nice to keep them as pets. But your power is far more valuable."

Blood and saliva dripped down my chin. "Go chase a meteor, ya dumb yellow belly." That comment got holes put through each of my kneecaps, courtesy of her hand lasers. "Fuck!"

"Last chance, Yael Pavnick."

I had to end this now. And there was only one way I could think to do that. I had to put every last bit of strength and energy I had into one final move and pray that it did the trick.

"Okay," I said. "You want to know how I keep faking my death?"

They didn't answer but continued to stare down at me.

"I'll tell you in Hell."

Breaking some more bones, I used my core strength to launch myself up and grabbed the assassin's shoulders, pulling myself onto and doing a handstand on them.

The assassin threw me off, but with the power of The True Adventurer, they also didn't, and I was still hanging on to them. They raised their arm to shoot me again and finish me off, while I adjusted my grip to stay on top of them. And the moment before they fired, I grabbed their arm and pointed their hand up at their face.

The resulting explosion sent me flying off of them and back onto my ass. I was completely wiped out and had nothing else in me. Even before the smoke had finished clearing, I had a funny feeling they were still alive. I could only hope they were injured enough that Juri would be able to finish the job.

My eyes widened and a chill went down my spine. The smoke cleared, and, of course, they were indeed still standing. But that wasn't why I was in shock.

I'd blown their mask off. And in the process, I'd revealed their face. *Her* face, I presumed. She had soft, porcelain skin, cerulean eyes, and amber hair. She wore a full face of makeup, a bright red shade of lipstick, and had half a dozen earrings in each ear.

Most notable of all? She couldn't have been older than twelve. "Who... who are you?" I asked.

She spat blood out of her mouth as she sneered at me.

"I am Princess Kaya Langstone Bythora, heir to the Cykebian throne. And you stole my Mommy!"

CHAPTER 14: MOLINA

We'd only done it by the skin of our teeth, but we'd gotten off Kreshent alive. After Kaybell took the explosion for me, we didn't run into anymore Cykerdroids in the mansion itself, and her remaining men who'd stayed on board the ship came to our rescue and protected us from the remaining robots on the estate.

I was shaken up, but unhurt, save for a few minor injuries, while Kay required immediate treatment. With the crack medical team and technology aboard her ship, there was a good chance she'd be mostly back on her feet by the time we reached Cykeb, but that didn't make me any less worried about her. Something could always go wrong.

True enough to form, I could hear Kay whisper in her sleep as she recovered that she was going to have General Galopire skinned alive for his crimes. And while that was a grotesque image and he may not have been Father's killer, I couldn't argue that if anyone deserved such a fate, it was him.

Or at least, that's what I'd thought in the moment. I wasn't sure if I believed that, or if I was letting my new feelings get the best of me. For gods' sake, I shouldn't have ever even thought about what I had. I was a married woman and I loved Yael. I loved her so, so much.

But it had been so long since I'd been happy with her. And as much as I'd missed her during our time apart, I'd always been happy when Kaybell and I were friends, fighting the good fight together.

Maybe Marcos was right. Maybe Yael really *was* better than me. Maybe she was too much better than me for our relationship to last. If I'd ended up with Kaybell, there would have been so much I could have accomplished and done for the people of the universe as empress, as opposed to the practically nothing I'd ended up with with Yael.

I shook my head, tears flying off my face. I wanted to stop thinking about this and think about anything else instead. I tried so hard thinking about all the reasons Yael was amazing and all the brilliant times we'd had together before things went south.

But I kept returning to one thing: Kaybell had tried sacrificing herself because she loved me. Yael would have tried sacrificing herself because she loved me *and* because she looked down on the rest of us to the point she felt it was her responsibility alone to protect us all.

Thank the gods for slumber, or else these thoughts would have tormented me the entire voyage.

"You all should have seen the way Molina handled that Cykerdroid with only her sword," a bandaged up Kaybell said at the head of the dinner table, several hours later. "She was brilliant."

I sniffed as I sipped my wine. "You were barely conscious enough to notice."

"I'm sure you were simply fabulous," Griffin commented, sitting next to me while Marcos continued to not come out of their room. "Jolla, did you know I'm almost as talented a swordsman as she is?"

Jolla and Wink snickered together.

"I miss swords."

"It was such fun sticking them into peasants' eyes."

Megz rolled his eyes. "You're both terrible."

"I'm only continuing the conversation," Jolla said. She turned her head to Griffin. "They're old and a bit crude, but I adore weapons of all sorts. Perhaps you could show me how to best wield one sometime?"

Griffin practically skyrocketed out of his seat and through the ceiling as dumbfounded joy overtook his face. "Yes! I mean, yes, that would be grand."

"Splendid."

I turned to Kaybell as Griffin quietly congratulated himself. She shrugged at me, just as surprised by this turn of events as I'd been. Griffin and Jolla getting together may not have been as bad an outcome as Kay and I making a mistake, but I still didn't trust the blue-haired demon.

"I appreciate the kind words, but you're the one who did all the work back there," I said. "I could have done all the same things if I had your enhancements, sure, but, well, I don't." I bit my lip. "But I mean, your doctors are the best and know how to do the procedure safely, so maybe I could get some before I go home?"

Kaybell hesitated, freezing for a moment before she sipped her wine. "Yes. Yes, absolutely, if that's what you'd like, it would be no problem for me to arrange that." Cringing, Kaybell set her jewel-encrusted goblet down, her hand shaking. "Moli-na, I haven't been entirely honest with you. There's a secret I've been keeping. I was afraid if I told you too soon it would scare you away again, but I need to get this off my chest."

Oh fuck. Was this where things unraveled? Was this where I realized I'd been duped by Kay again, and she was still a complete monster? Would I have to lead my students in an escape? And did a part of me hope that was all about to happen so there wouldn't be any chance of me being unfaithful? Fuck!

"You can tell me anything, Kay," I said nervously, Griffin's eyes on me, while Kaybell's siblings directed their gaze toward her.

Kaybell nodded, clenching her eyes shut for a moment. "Do you remember when Galopire said that my father had already sufficiently prepared the empire for war with The Utozin Authority?"

"I do."

"Yes, well, he wasn't only referring to measures he'd already taken. Father had a course of action in mind that would have further sharpened our already existing edge."

"And what was that?" I asked, my legs trembling underneath the table.

Kay took a deep breath in and out. Around the table, Megz, Jolla, and Wink's faces had gone sullen, while Griffin was hanging on the same edge as me.

"He planned on drafting tens of billions of civilians across the empire into our army. That alone wasn't something I took issue with. It's an honor to live in the Cykebian Empire, and everyone's duty to serve it in its time of need. But there was a second step to his plan. He was going to force all of the drafted citizens to receive genetic enhancements, despite knowing that, in all likelihood, 85% of them would die in the process. "That still leaves billions," he'd said. Combined with his belief that restoring the slave trade would be essential to rebuilding the economy *after* the war? I had to do something. And I did the only thing I could."

I clenched my hands around my legs, holding them in place. The sight of her tears made my eyes just as wet.

"Kay…"

"I killed him, Molina. I killed my own father." While Griffin appeared confused as to how he should feel and what he should say, Megz shared tears with Kay and I, and the twins' bangs hung over their eyes. "I've gotten this amazing second chance with you because of how much your father meant to you, while you're having dinner with a woman who killed hers."

This wasn't where I'd expected she was going at all. And I wasn't sure if it was better or worse.

"He was the greatest man I've ever known," Megz said. "But he had to be stopped."

"We felt his actions were completely appropriate," Jolla said.

"But that didn't mean he wasn't an abusive bastard," Wink followed.

"We're glad he's burning in Hell," they finished in unison.

Tensing up my entire body, I unhooked my hands from around my legs, and then breathed out. The room had gone cold, but I was weirdly warm.

Kaybell had told me all about the harsh and unforgiving way she'd been raised. Emperor Stephen had beaten her for as long as she could walk. Any time she did something to displease him, whether it was apologizing to someone or missing out on a perfect score on a test, his fist went across her face.

"Did you… did you think I'd judge you for this?" I asked.

"Of course I did," Kaybell whimpered. "Don't you?"

I shook my head. "Megz, Jolla, and Wink are right. You may not have been a Sunriser any more when this happened, but you did what any Sunriser would have. You didn't let your personal feelings get in the way of what was best for the universe. You did the right thing."

Kaybell dabbed at the tears and snot of her face with her handkerchief. "You… you really think so? You don't think patricide is unforgivable, even with what you're going through?"

"No. Not at all."

A smile cracked through Kaybell's tears. "Thank you. Thank you so much."

The room went silent. The only thing I could hear was the pounding of my heart against my chest. What she thought of as her deep, dark secret only made me respect her more. She'd done the hardest thing a daughter could ever do for the greater good. Had our positions been switched, I wasn't sure I'd be able to go through with it.

Kaybell had successfully molded herself into what I always knew she could be: a hero. And I was so damn proud. I was proud of her, and I was proud of myself for inspiring such a massive transformation. In a way, my impact on her had been what saved the universe.

I wasn't going to cheat on Yael. No matter what thoughts or feelings I experienced, I couldn't let that happen. But there was no longer any doubt in my mind that I wanted my best friend back, and I wasn't going to let my fear of making a mistake stop me from getting as close to her as I'd once been.

It was risky. I knew that. But it was what I needed.

Griffin coughed. "So then. How about dessert?

After dinner, Kaybell needed more rest, so she went to bed early. I was exhausted, so going to sleep early was my plan as well, but first I wanted to check in on the student I hadn't seen all day.

"Marcos?" I called out, knocking on their door. "You in there?"

There was no response.

"Okay, well, Kaybell gave me a key card that opens every door in the palace, so I'm coming in anyway."

"You can't do that!" Marcos shouted, finally responding. "These are *my* private quarters!"

I hovered my card over the entrance and buzzed it open. "They're guest quarters, and I'm your guardian. Get over it."

Inside the room, Marcos was curled up in a ball on their bed in their platypus hoodie, with their hover chair close by. They still hadn't unpacked at all, all of the clothes they'd been wearing the past few days just crammed back into their bag.

"What do you want?" they asked.

"To see how you're doing. Staying in bed all day usually isn't a good sign."

Marcos snorted. "I'm fine. You can leave now."

I rolled my eyes as I sat down next to them on the bed. "You know I was a teenager once too, right? I know what hormone-fueled angst is like."

They flipped over onto their other side, turning away from me. "Make your own bed before you come into mine."

I rested my hands on my hips. "What's that supposed to mean?"

Marcos clicked their tongue. "It means you think you're past being a teenager, but you're the married woman nursing a schoolyard crush."

"Excuse me?"

"What? You think you're slick? It's been obvious since you met back up with the emperor."

I swallowed nervously. Where could they have gotten this idea from? I hadn't started feeling that way till today, and this was the first time they'd seen me since.

"Try not to be so confused," Marcos continued, as if they knew what I was thinking. "One of Yael's key lessons to me has been that even if you think other people are dumb and you can't understand them, you should still be able to figure out more about them then they know about themselves."

Marcos flipped back over, facing me again, and gave me the stink eye. "I have a moderate amount of respect for you, Professor, but Yael is my true mentor. If you break her heart, I will destroy you. And I'm fairly certain Ms. Amatyn would actually kill you."

"P'Ken *is* very scary," I quietly muttered. "Listen, you have nothing to worry about. Yes, Kaybell is incredible and gorgeous, and I'm beyond happy with how she's bettered herself, but Yael is the only love of my life. I will always be faithful to her. I promise."

Saying this all out loud to someone else was reassuring. More so than just thinking it in my head. It really felt like I believed every word I was saying. I loved Yael. I loved my beautiful wife. And no amount of temptation would taint that love.

"So we'll be returning home as soon as your father's killer is caught?" Marcos asked. "No further delay?"

I nodded. "That's the plan."

Ideally, we'd be able to stay a little longer than that. Some time to just relax with Kay like we used to during shore leaves sounded wonderful. But depending on how long the investigation took, I really would need to get back to Yael as soon as possible.

"But come on, are you really gonna tell me that's the only reason you've been keeping yourself cooped up?" I asked. "Talk to me."

Marcos groaned, pushing down on the mattress and sitting up. "You're not going away until I tell you, are you?"

"That's correct."

"Right. Well… you see—"

"Ah!" Griffin called out from behind me, cutting them off. "Professor, I was looking all over for you."

I shifted around to face Griffin, who held in his hands a neatly tied bouquet of vibrant flowers which seemed to have been picked from the royal gardens.

"Please tell me those aren't for Jolla."

"They are indeed!" Griffin proclaimed proudly, pulling them close to his chest. "I know things got rather dour and serious at dinner, but I think now is the time to ask her out. You may not approve in general, but I was hoping you could tell me if this arrangement was good enough for her."

Marcos cackled. "What? Did you spend hours putting that together for her yourself?"

"As a matter of fact, I did. Any true noble should know how to put together an elegant flower arrangement."

I wanted to believe there was more to the twins than met the eye, but it was difficult to get past them taking pleasure in gouging out people's eyes and other such horrors. Ultimately though, they were victims of their father's abuse, just like Kaybell. That wasn't an excuse, but maybe if I spent more time with them, I could help inspire change like I had in their big sister.

"It's beautiful," I said truthfully. "But try to not be too let down if she rejects you."

"No, no, no," Griffin said, waving a finger at me. "Negativity is the enemy. I won't be letting it in my head at all." He nodded. "Thank you, Professor."

With his head held high, Griffin marched off to his potential doom.

"I suppose we'll see how that goes," I said, turning back to Marcos. "What were you saying a minute ago?"

Marcos had been talking about knowing things about people before they knew them about themselves. I couldn't do that. But I could still pick up on the signs in front of me. And there was a big, flashing red one in the form of the tears in Marcos' eyes.

"Holy shit."

"Don't say a word," Marcos growled, flopped down onto their back. "Not one."

"Holy shit," I repeated. "You're jealous." Marcos made a series of weird, loud noises with their mouth. "Listen, Griffin probably isn't gonna succeed. I can't believe you're *both* into this girl, but you'll have your chance with Jolla."

"*Fucking* Hell you're daft," Marcos breathed. "Try again."

Moving past his rude comment, I gave further thought to what they meant. And it only took me a moment to reach the, to my credit, far less obvious conclusion.

"You mean...?"

"Yup. It's as humiliating as it sounds."

I stammered for words as I tried to picture what Marcos wanted. "You treat him like shit."

"Because he's an incompetent buffoon who deserves nothing but scorn and ridicule."

They paused as they wiped their eyes. "But also he's hot and adorable and I love him."

Yup. Definitely a teenager.

"Look, I know it's not easy, it may even seem like the hardest thing in the world, but the best thing you can do is be honest with him about how you feel. It'll make you a lot happier in the long run. If I'd figured my shit out back in high school and told Yael how I felt, we may not have missed out on spending an extra decade together."

"That's easy for you to say. She's loved you back since day one." Marcos gripped the comforter, digging their nails into it. "What's so special about you anyway? What makes these amazing, brilliant, powerful women fall for you? I truly mean no offense, Professor, but you got where you did through nepotism, and you are thoroughly average in every way."

They said "no offense" and yet I felt pretty damned offended. Partially because I'd long ago realized that what they were saying was true.

"We're not talking about me right now. We're talking about you. And I don't think anyone but Yael and Kaybell would question you're the most special out of the three of us here."

Marcos ripped the comforter apart, the sound of the tearing fabric resembling the laser fire I'd been caught up in earlier. The material the comforter was made from was pretty thick, but while Marcos may have been born without the ability to use their legs, they still worked their arms plenty.

"Where has being special gotten me? Used by my parents since I was three to commit cyber crimes for them? Not even getting to enjoy the fruits of my labor as they spent every last gidgit I made for them on themselves and their hedonistic, drug-obsessed friends? Running away from home before I was literally worked to death? Becoming an egotistical asshole who's basically ensured the man I love will never love me back? Sounds like a great fucking life."

There was nothing I could say about Marcos' awful upbringing. Even if I knew what to say, it would be hollow. I couldn't relate to them at all. I'd always been eager to impress Father and gleefully did the work I was given.

No, I couldn't say anything there. But I did know a few things about romance.

I lay next to Marcos. "Griffin thinks you're a dick, yeah. Because you are a dick. If you like that about yourself, keep being you and try redirecting that energy away from him. If you don't like that about yourself, it's never too late to change."

I patted them on the shoulder. "Remember why you first came to Yael? You wanted to learn how to be your own boss so you wouldn't have to work for anyone else ever again. Take that attitude and apply it here. Take charge of your life, apologize to Griffin, and tell him how you feel before he makes a big mistake."

Marcos breathed heavily, in and out, over and over again, as they wiped their hands all over their face, clearing away their tears and probably making their already present acne even worse.

They pushed themselves up, out of bed, and into their chair.

"Sorry, Professor. I can't do that." They hovered over to the door frame before stopping. "For the record, I meant it when I said no offense." They turned their head around. "You were lucky to be born average."

CHAPTER 15: YAEL

"I'm sorry… what?"

Kaya panted as she wiped blood off her face and brushed her hair out of her eyes with her gloved hands. If she was an android, some freak had chosen to make the most dangerous thing in the universe look like a little girl. But if she was a cyborg, then someone had *turned* a little girl into the most dangerous thing in the universe. And I didn't know how she got the idea that Molina was her mom or how she had her hair, but her last name gave me a damn good place to start looking for answers.

"You heard me, you degenerate," she snarled. "You tore my mothers apart. Don't deny it."

I still couldn't move at all. I didn't know where anyone else was right now, which meant my only option was to keep this conversation going as long as possible. Fortunately, that was my specialty.

"Your mothers being… Molina and Kaybell?"

"That's *Emperor* Kaybell to you, peasant! And yes, I was born through an artificial combination of their genetics."

Not an unusual way to have a kid these days. It certainly

made more sense than Moli giving birth twelve years ago and never telling me.

"Okay… listen. I don't know what you've been told, but I'm not the bad guy here. Molina *chose* me over Kaybell when she discovered what a sadistic monster she is. And if Kaybell's filled your mind with that same poisonous bullshit, then I am so sorry. But you don't have to be her weapon."

Kaya laughed hysterically with all the joy and innocence of a normal girl her age.

"You're as dumb as Kenneth Roz, lead singer of The Duroc Boys. But nowhere near as cute." She pressed her thumb against her chest. "Emperor Kaybell is an angel. She has never treated me with anything but love and compassion."

"She turned you into a cyborg!"

"Because she was worried about me! You've been living in the middle of nowhere, so you probably don't know, but the greatest war the universe has ever seen is on its way. She only wanted to ensure that I'd be safe."

"*And* she sent you to kill me."

Kaya laughed again, this time so hard she pounded her chest. "You're supposed to be a genius, but you're so blinded by your hate that you can't see the facts. Mother didn't send me to kill you. She's always talking about wanting to make things right with you and becoming friends. I'm here because I want to be here. And because I want nothing more than you dead."

I shook my head as my heart pounded against my chest, each pump of blood feeling like a laser was going straight through it.

"I don't understand."

"Shocker."

"No, stop. Listen. Say I believe Kaybell's turned over a new leaf and has nothing to do with this. What do you think's gonna happen here? You kill me and Molina will go running back to her? Unless I'm missing a really big piece of this story, she doesn't even know you exist. You were made without her permission."

"But I'm still her daughter. And with you out of the way, the veil blinding her and making her think she's fine with settling for mediocrity will be lifted. She'll happily embrace her true family."

This was too weird. This was too much. My brain couldn't handle this much new information right now. But if I stopped talking, she'd just finish what she came here to do.

"Shun and P'Ken!" I shouted.

"You could have easily disabled them without hurting them, but you made them suffer. If Kaybell didn't teach you to do that, then why? And what makes you think you're prepared to take another life?"

This time, she giggled. It sounded just like Moli's giggle at her age.

"Some things are genetic," she said. "My family's enjoyed torturing lesser forms of life for thousands of years. Just because Mother decided to turn her back on that tradition doesn't mean I shouldn't get to enjoy myself. I play the role of *her* perfect angel, of course, but fortunately, I've had my aunts to help nurture my proclivities. They've given me *many* tasty subjects to experiment on."

I couldn't believe this. Kaybell had to be involved somehow. Kaya had to be an android who'd been programmed to believe everything she was telling me. Because if she was telling the truth? Then she wasn't a monster. She was just some poor kid who had the bad luck of coming from an evil genetic pool, and who wanted her moms to be together.

I wouldn't just not be able to kill her then. I wouldn't *want* to kill her. But the feeling wasn't mutual.

Kaya raised her hand up and, with a grin spread across her face that more than resembled the look Kaybell had given me while she'd tortured me, charged up a blast.

"Kaya… you don't have to do this."

"You're right. But I really want to. And I'm kinda used to getting what I want. Sorry. Comes with being a princess."

I tried to move any muscle I could, but nothing happened. I tried tapping into the power of The True Adventurer again, but that only made my splitting headache worse. I was helpless.

"Any last words?"

I swallowed. I'd never thought about my final words. I'd always thought I'd get out of every bad situation and live forever. I really had no idea what to say that could be remotely meaningful.

"I…"

Before I could say anything else, a canister was thrown down onto the ground, between Kaya and me. And from it dispensed a neon yellow and blue gas. It was my special "Yael's Sleepy Time Fuck You Cocktail Gas."

The charge of Kaya's beam dissipated as we both choked on the stuff. And I could only hope that she'd be joining me in slumber.

Waking up once again in my bed on *Ricochet*, my physical injuries had mostly been healed, though less efficiently than last time. My brain, meanwhile, still felt like it had been flattened by a truck. I wasn't gonna be fighting *or* using the power of The

True Adventurer again anytime soon. Even if I could, there was no way I'd survive a third ass kicking from Kaya.

"Good morning, Professor."

I blinked repeatedly until I was able to make out Layla sitting next to me. It made sense she'd been the one to treat me. P'Ken was probably still down and in need of treatment herself, and Layla didn't have nearly as much medical training as her, which explained why I still felt like garbage.

"Hey, Layla," I groaned, sitting up and rubbing my eyes. "Was… was that you who saved my ass back there with the knockout gas?"

She nodded. "We weren't sure before if she was a cyborg or an android, so we didn't think about using it. But when I heard her explaining to you who she was, I knew the gas would work. So I waited till you were done getting information out of her and then threw it."

I grinned as I licked my lips. "Smart. And very stealthy on your part. I didn't even notice you. How long were you there?"

Layla lowered her head. "The whole time. Long before you showed up. I wanted to help Shun and P'Ken fight, but… I was too scared. I'm sorry."

"Don't be. Seriously. You wouldn't have managed to actually do anything to Kaya, and you ended up saving the day. We're all alive because of you."

Layla smiled back at me. "Thank you, Professor."

"Mmm." I stretched my arms out, cracking them real good. "Where is everyone right now? I'm guessing the other Banshees all left."

Layla rolled her eyes. "I wish. They all stuck around to make sure you woke up. And because they're interested in seeing how this whole situation plays out. Shun and P'Ken are still asleep in their own rooms, and Aarif is watching our diminutive prisoner. I stuck her behind one of the ship's force fields. I thought about killing her while she was unconscious so she was no longer a threat but… you know…"

"She's a kid. I get it."

My legs were like twigs that were about to snap, but I pushed myself up anyway. I had the patience of a child, so I knew firsthand it wouldn't do me any favors to keep Kaya waiting.

"What's the plan?" Layla asked.

"You go look after Shun and P'Ken and let me know if and when they wake up. I'm gonna go pay our guest a visit." I patted her on the back as I walked away. "Seriously. Great job."

I walked out of my room, Layla following behind me with a hop in her step. While she went into P'Ken's room, I went downstairs and over to Aarif.

"There she is!" Aarif called out with excitement. "The unkillable Yael Pavnick!"

We high-fived and clasped our hands, and with how drained I was, I didn't even need to hold back most of my strength.

"Dude, you have missed so much," I said. "I think I'm magic now."

"Of course you are. You get all the cool stuff."

"You have a cyborg dog."

"*We* have a cyborg dog."

Turning around, I looked through the transparent force-field at Kaya, who was boxed into a small corner of the ship. Her eyes were closed and she sat with her legs crossed.

"You talk to her at all?" I asked.

"Yeah. Asked her if she was meditating. Turned out she's

got a music player built into her. She's been listening to some teen boy band called EZ Street. I asked if I could listen in an attempt to bond with her, and she said she was going to eat my heart."

"Right. Okay." I clapped my hands together.

"Music time's over Kaya. We need to chat."

Kaya peeked one of her eyes open and smirked. Opening her other eye, she stood up as if without a care in the world.

"What do you want, Evil Incarnate? I'm trying to listen to my future concubines."

I crossed my arms and looked her dead in the eyes. "You certainly seem relaxed."

"Why wouldn't I be?"

"Um, maybe because you're our prisoner."

Kaya shook her head as her smirk grew. "Gods, how does Mother think you're so smart? Let me spell out your situation for you since you haven't figured it out. You're not gonna let me die, or else you already would have killed me. That means you're gonna have to feed me sooner or later. And the second you take down this forcefield to give me food and water, I'm gonna rip your head off. We can talk in the meantime if you want, but keeping me from listening to my music is only gonna make me want to do especially horrible things to your friends. So if I were you, I'd enjoy my last three days of life instead. Tick Tock."

I *had* thought of all of that, but I'd really hoped she hadn't. Shit. Neither of her moms was stupid, and one of them was Moli, so I should have expected she'd have a good head on her shoulders.

"No, no I don't think I want to enjoy myself. Which is unusual for me, but yeah, I'd rather talk."

Kaya hung her arms at her side, pushed her lower lip out, and wiggled her head.

"So, how old are you exactly?"

"Twelve. Biologically and mentally. Practically a teenager. I was only actually born two years ago after Mother ascended to the throne. She understandably didn't have time to deal with a messy, needy baby, so she had me artificially aged up past the bulk of my childhood."

"Shit," Aarif said. "That's horrible."

"She robbed you of one of the best parts of life," I said. "How could you forgive her for that?"

"Forgive her? I'm grateful. Why would I ever want to be a helpless baby, debasing myself by spitting up everywhere and crying all day? Your childhood may have been a highlight because you had the honor of being friends with my mother, but my glory lies in the future."

I bobbed my head up and down while Aarif silently mouthed "Wow."

"And I bet you're also gonna say it was super responsible of Kaybell to let you travel through space on your own. If she doesn't know you came to kill me, where does she think you are?"

Kaya's grin spread across her face. "I told her I wanted to explore the stars I was born to rule over. She knows there's no one and no thing that can hurt me, so she only told me to call often, take plenty of pictures, and to be back in three months. With that much time, I of course didn't come straight for you. I had some fun, first. I went to some of the most renowned restaurants and spas in the universe, slaughtered a few armies to test my strength, and caught some killer concerts."

She giggled and blushed. "Kissed my first hunky boy *at* a killer concert. Obviously didn't send Mother pictures of that. Even if I hadn't been successful in tracking you down, I wouldn't have considered the trip a waste." She narrowed her eyes. "Are you sure you wouldn't rather go roll around in the mud, or whatever it is you peasants do for fun? It's half of what makes life worth living and I can't seem to wrap my head around what your endgame is here."

I wasn't even sure what my endgame was here. The facts were I couldn't kill her, no prison could hold her, and Kaybell clearly couldn't control her. If she was Moli's daughter, then it was her job to be a good influence on her. But since she wasn't around, by transitive property as her wife, that duty fell to me.

I had three days to convince her that murder and torture were wrong. I couldn't waste any time.

"Well, I was thinking that maybe we could—"

"Silence, vermin," she cut me off, casting her eyes down. "You mentioned your cyborg dog before. I'd like to meet her."

Aarif and I exchanged a quick glance before he spoke. "You wanna meet Juri? I mean, I know she's the best, but aren't girls like you all about pure breeds and stuff like that?"

"Uh, no. A cute doggie to snuggle is a cute doggie to snuggle. Add in the fact that she's a deadly killing machine who was probably the most advanced cyborg before I came around, and she sounds like the perfect pet. I'll admit, in this one, singular way: I'm jealous."

Aarif chuckled to himself as he rolled his shoulders and popped his collar. "Well, you know, I'm the one who put Juri together. So that's pretty cool, right?"

"Phhh, no," Kaya bristled, dismissing him. "Engineers

are just glorified servants. Always doing someone else's manual labor. It's their creations and employers that matter, not them."

She clapped her hands together and smiled innocently, bouncing on the balls of her feet. "May I please meet Juri? I promise I won't bite. And if she likes me, after I massacre the rest of you worthless peons, I can give her a good home."

She wasn't getting past the forcefield, and if this was what she really wanted, then I could give it to her as a show of good faith. Only thing I wasn't sure about was Juri's reaction. She tended to be a pretty good judge of people, and if Kaya didn't like how Juri treated her, well… I remembered what being a hormonal twelve-year-old girl was like.

"Okay, sure," I said. "Aarif, go get Juri."

"Aye aye, Captain." He pointed at Kaya and gave her the stank eye. "Don't try anything funny with my girl."

Kaya waved her hand in front of her wrinkled nose as Aarif went down to the engine room. "Thank the gods he's gone. His smell is somehow even fouler than yours."

I couldn't for the life of me figure out how much of what she was saying came from her, and how much of it came from imitating her aunts. Or Kaybell. Kaybell had to be involved somehow. There was no way she could have changed as much as Kaya had described.

"Hey, a minute ago you said that fun was half of what made life worth living. I agree with that, but… what do you think the other half is?"

Kaya sat back down and crossed her legs. "Power. What else?"

I shrugged. "What's so appealing about power?"

"Simple-minded fool," Kaya groaned, rolling her eyes.

"Power is everything. It's the ability to live your life however you wish. To do whatever you want. To make anything you want happen. And to make others obey your whims."

I wagged my finger at her. "To me, most of that doesn't sound like power. It's freedom."

"You say that as if there's a difference. Those in power have the most freedom and get to decide who else has it."

"And why does it matter to you what other people do?"

"I am the crown princess of the Holy Cykebian Empire and they are my subjects. It's my right to shape the universe and those in it as I see fit."

"Yes, but *why* do you want to do that?"

For the first time since we'd started, I got her to hesitate. "I don't understand the question."

"All right, here comes the best dog in every possible dimension in every possible reality in the multiverse: Juri!" Aarif walked her in before I could continue that conversation.

"OMG!" Kaya squealed as she crawled over to the forcefield, the biggest grin on her face. "She's adorable!"

Juri scampered over to the forcefield and met her eyes. Fortunately, she was a pretty smart dog, so she knew better than to try licking someone through the forcefield. Not again.

BARK! BARK!

"You have such a beautiful coat," Kaya cooed. "It's a shame your owners couldn't have stuck to dog grooming and stayed out of the business of their betters. They may have had a future."

BARK! BARK!

"What's that? You secretly hate your owners and you want to come live with me?" Kaya glared up at us. "We can communicate because we're both cyborgs."

"Bullshit," Aarif replied instantly. "You're messing with us."

Kaya pouted and made puppy dog eyes. "I'm sorry, Aarif. I just feel bad for Juri because she's stuck with owners who are stinky losers that don't pet her right. Her words, not mine."

Steam practically came out of Aarif's head. No one joked about his bond with Juri. But he had to keep it together.

BARK! BARK!

"Aarif fantasizes about doing *what* to you?! You dirty, man!"

"Oh, you little bitch!"

While Aarif continued to rant at Kaya about how he'd never do anything inappropriate to Juri and how strong their bond was, I restrained him to make sure he didn't disable the forcefield to go after her, and Kaya laughed so hard she fell over onto her back.

This was gonna be a long three days.

CHAPTER 16: MOLINA

Miracles were as rare as Yael cleaning our bedroom without me making her, but they did happen. A pen could drop and land on its point. One of the twelve legendary swords forged by Master Kibao could be found in a cavern at the bottom of an ocean, after being thought destroyed millennia ago. I'd even heard of someone surviving after having their head severed from the rest of their body.

Apparently, miracles could get even more shocking than that. Griffin Cirico could land a date with Princess Jolla Kraken Bythora.

"This is so wrong," I said.

While Kaybell's men were rounding up General Galopire and bringing him to Cykeb for investigation, the emperor and I were spying on Griffin and Jolla's lunch date at the latter's favorite restaurant, *Portmanteau*, where its exclusive guests could eat the endangered marine life swimming around them in tanks. Kaybell had had secret cameras installed all throughout the restaurant the previous night, and from our cloaked shuttle craft, we could see everything that was going on inside.

"Perhaps, but I wasn't about to miss this," Kaybell said, popping an oyster in her mouth. "Jolla's never been on a date, and I need to make sure she doesn't embarrass the family."

"Wait, she's never been on a date? I'd have thought she'd have flocks of suitors."

"Oh they come. And then she scares them off."

We both laughed. While Griffin certainly wouldn't appreciate my actions, a part of me was happy we were doing this. Jolla seemed to be going along with Kaybell's decrees, and even if she ever decided to go against them, Griffin was nobility, but when it came to looking after my students, I couldn't be too safe.

"So, what with torture off the table, what do you do for leisure?" Griffin asked as a waiter brought them crystal water bottles.

"Hunting has made an adequate substitute," Jolla answered. "The larger the beast, the more satisfying it is to bring down. Alas, I'm starting to get bored. It's *all* Wink ever wants to do. My true passion is marine biology."

"Is that so? And here I thought you just liked how fish tasted."

Jolla smiled down at her menu. "Do you know where my middle name comes from?" Griffin shook his head. "It's an ancient myth from Earth. A gargantuan, squid-like beast with three heads and ten arms, each equipped with razor-sharp claws. It brought down countless ships and piled up even more bodies on the ocean floor."

"And your parents, when looking at their newborn baby, decided to name you after that monster?"

Not looking away from the menu, Jolla reached her hand over to her bottle and twirled the straw in it around with her fingertip.

"I'm the youngest member of the royal family. I even came out after Wink. In all likelihood, I'll never hold any real power." Jolla lifted her head back up. "But what lies below the surface is what's truly dangerous. Kings and queens couldn't do anything about the kraken. They couldn't even do anything about sharks or stingrays. Kaybell can have the universe. But just like the horrors of the depths, I'll be what people really have to worry about."

She had Griffin's undivided attention, the poor dolt not taking his wide eyes off her once as she sipped her drink.

"Also, I find some of the anatomy fascinating. Did you know that seahorse enzymes are how we first developed the ability for cis males to give birth?"

"I do now!" The two laughed together, and I tried not to cringe. "I'm afraid there isn't much time to learn things like that in my, uh, Sunriser training."

Jolla rolled her head around. "You can drop the act and relax around me."

What?

"I'm sorry?"

Jolla took another sip from her drink. "You don't have to pretend you want to be one of those goody-goods. We know what you're about. You, Marcos... Molina."

Without waiting to see how Griffin responded, I turned off the monitors and faced Kaybell. She looked back at me, nonchalant.

"Is there a problem?"

"I don't know. You tell me."

What was her game here? She'd known all along that we'd lied, and she'd gone along with it? Why? What was her game here? I'd let my guard down, and now there was a spear running through my heart.

Kaybell sighed. "Yes, we knew all along that the three of you worked directly alongside Yael. The Sunrisers may not know about Griffin and Marcos yet, but I have full dossiers on them. More than that, I know that you and Yael are… married. And I'm fine with that, though you'll excuse me if I slap my face for sabotaging myself. I even know where your school is located."

My eyes flickered, over and over again, on their own.

"Why'd you let me lie, then?" I asked. "And if you were serious about wanting to make things right and you knew where we live, why didn't you ever come to see us? To see me?"

"In order, I went along with your lie, and instructed my siblings to do the same, because it was what you felt comfortable telling me. I figured you'd tell me the truth about your career and all about the exciting heists you'd gone on once I earned back your trust. As for why I never went to see you…" Kaybell trailed off and snickered. "Why did Yael never track you down during the decade we were together? Hmm?"

I tugged at my hair. "Because as much as she missed me, she wanted to leave her old life in the past."

Kay nodded. "The entire time we were friends, I was a terrible person. I was afraid that seeing you again… seeing Yael… would bring out the worst in me. The Bythora in me." She raised her hand and rested her delicate palm on the side of my face. "I see now that I was a fool. You don't bring out the worst in me. Only the best."

I lowered my head and shook it. I was so stupid. She'd done everything possible to re-earn my trust and I was still doubting her. She'd always have her secrets, it came with her position, but I had to let go of the past and accept that things were different now. She was different now. Any secrets, any seemingly devious motivations she had… they weren't ones I needed to worry about.

"Thank you," I said, leaning forward in my seat. "Should we, um, get back to spying on the kids?"

Kay leaned forward a little in her own seat. "We shall."

Our lips were only a pointer finger away from each other's. My heart told me to close the gap, Kaybell's power and warmth calling out to me, but my brain shut that down. I may not have been as smart as most of the people around me, but I at least knew better than to sabotage my life over a nostalgic whim.

I hit the button I'd pressed before, turned the monitors back on, and returned my focus to those.

A waiter was walking away from Griffin and Jolla's, looking like he'd taken their orders, and the two teens were laughing together, seemingly having moved past the same bumps we had.

"So why train to be a thief at all?" Jolla asked. "Your family name may not garner much respect, but you still stand above the unwashed masses."

"Not the words I'd use to describe commoners, but I know what you mean," Griffin said with a smile. "In reality, nobles don't typically turn to lives of crime. But they do in works of fiction. There are all sorts of tales of gentlemen thieves, high-class nobles robbing their fellow elites for the greater good, all the while charming women around their worlds fawn over them." Griffin bounced in his seat. "The truth is, I'm the baby of my family too. I have six older brothers. There isn't even a chance of me ever being a baron like my father. That's something Burton's always been happy to remind me; he's the oldest.

While they all plotted and schemed against each other for power, I didn't even bother. Being at the bottom meant I was safe. And reading stories of these fabulous, devilishly handsome noblemen pulling off the most intricate and creative of heists was how I spent my time. And eventually I thought: why can't that be me?"

A smile crept up my face listening to Griffin. He wasn't a prodigy like Yael, Layla, or Marcos. He didn't have decades of brutal training like Kaybell and Shun. He didn't even have the parental support I'd had going for me. But he was tough. Damn tough. He was laser-focused on achieving his dream, no matter how many setbacks he faced. And even if his occasional incompetence could be frustrating, as his teacher, I was gonna make sure he got everything he wanted.

"Well, if you ask me, you already have the devilishly handsome part down," Jolla said, inching her hand across the table and putting it over Griffin's.

Griffin shivered. He looked down at their hands and then back up at Jolla's face. "You were making fun of me pretty harshly. Did you only agree to go out with me because you think I'm hot?"

Jolla shrugged. "Didn't you only ask me out because you think *I'm* hot?" Griffin went silent for a moment.

"I'm okay with this."

———

General Galopire had seen better days. Kay evidently hadn't taken almost being killed lightly, and had him beaten to a bloody pulp. His face was black and blue, his lip was torn, and his awful-looking mohawk had been shaved off. And because some habits died hard, he'd been stripped down before being marched through the palace on his way to the dungeon, exposing the black and blue marks and scars Kay's men had left all over him.

I would have felt bad for him if he wasn't everything wrong with Cykebian nobility.

Kaybell promised me that she didn't usually do things like this, that she only did it because he nearly killed us. I believed her, and only made her agree to not take things any further.

"I'll be the first to admit," he said, trapped against the wall by a forcefield, "mistakes have been made."

Kaybell scoffed. "You've done more than make mistakes. The only punishment appropriate for your crimes is death."

The dank, dark, foul-smelling dungeon we stood in was one of several underneath the palace. Emperor Stephen had enjoyed filling them up and allowing criminals to lose their minds and wither away into dust. Kay, however, primarily used the dungeons as a place to store criminals as they awaited her judgment, and when she gave the thumbs down, it meant anything from a swift death to community service, with no room for lifetime incarceration.

"That may be true," Galopire said, smirking. "But you wouldn't be down here if you didn't want something from me. Is it details on my trafficking network? I'll give up every man I was working with in exchange for my life."

Of course he would. Men like him had no honor.

"You *will* give us that information, but there's something else first," Kaybell said. "You may not have killed my father, but now that you know he *was* murdered, we thought you might have an idea who did," I said.

Galopire stretched his neck out. "Oh really? And why's that?"

"You were bold enough to try and make a move against me," Kaybell answered. "A foolish decision, I could never be killed by the likes of you, but a bold one. The fact that you took that initiative without checking in with anyone else tells me you must hold quite a great deal of influence among the nobles who wish to see me ousted as emperor."

Galopire flashed his overly white, obviously fake teeth. "Losing touch with most of my former co-workers has led to me making... *other* arrangements, yes."

I stepped right in front of the forcefield. "Tell us what you know, and you might see a sun again."

"You know, you wouldn't have to offer me anything if you weren't so radically against torture," Galopire laughed. "It's not like I'm made of particularly tough stuff."

Kaybell turned her harsh eyes to me, before looking back at Galopire. "I'd think given your current placement in the pecking order, you'd be able to understand that this is a better way of doing things."

Galopire shook his head. "I have no loyalty to those I work with. Or to anyone for that matter. But my principles? Those I hold dear. And I know in my heart, blessed by the gods, what criminal scum and common filth deserve."

During my time in the Sunrisers, I'd been in the dark regarding the practices of the modern nobility, but I'd been fully aware how many of them saw me. Saw my entire family. In their eyes, we had no right holding as much power and authority as we did. I made friends and allies among them, but I knew they were always judging me.

"I'll talk," he continued, cracking his knuckles. "But I'm not sure you'll like what I have to say."

"Spit it out," Kaybell ordered authoritatively.

Galopire licked his lips, cringing in pain as he reached where it was torn. It was nice seeing that smug look wiped off his face.

"The truth is, I don't believe any of my peers were responsible. Nor do I believe Drenian's murder was meant as an attack on you. He had plenty of enemies on his own, and in none of *our* discussions regarding what to do about you was his death a popular idea among anyone but myself. They may have hated that pretender as much as I did, but they deemed killing him more trouble than he was worth."

"So you have nothing then?" I spat. "Is that what you're saying?"

"I'm getting there," he replied, shutting his eyes. "Among his enemies, there's one who stands out with both the most motivation and the best opportunity."

"And that is?"

Galopire's eyes bulged open. "Morphea Langstone."

If I could have slapped him through the forcefield, I would have. Morphea was a lot of things, and she'd never treated me right, but I knew she loved Father more than anyone.

"Morphea was not our Father's enemy," I stated.

"No? Because from the few friends I still have at Zenith Command, I've heard several stories of them furiously arguing in Drenian's office. Swearing at each other, throwing and breaking things, the whole shebang. And now, she stands as one of the top two candidates to become supreme general. Seems rather suspicious to me."

I clenched my fists and lost control of my breath. I finally had a chance to have a good relationship with my sister, and I wasn't about to throw that away based on the nonsensical suspicions of a bastard like Galopire. He knew nothing about her. He knew nothing about anything. We could walk away and leave him here to rot and no wrongdoing would have been–

"Hey," Kay said, taking my head. "It's okay."

She carefully caressed my knuckles, making soft but firm movements. She slowed down my heart and cooled down my brain. After all the times I'd had to do this for her, I was relieved she could pay me back. My mind had just been going to some dark places.

Kaybell stepped up to the forcefield. "And say it definitely *was* an attack on me. Who would you assume was guilty then?"

Galopire grinned.

"The only person it could be. Our glorious leader." He didn't say anything after that.

He winked.

CHAPTER 17: YAEL

Why did people hurt others? Rather, why did they take pleasure in doing so? That was the question I needed to answer if I was going to save Kaya from herself, and the rest of us from her.

With nobles and royals, at least it was obvious. They held unchecked power and authority and got a kick out of throwing those around. They saw most other people as lesser forms of life and themselves as one step below the gods. They were self-righteous bastards who'd convinced themselves that not only was there nothing wrong with tormenting others for fun, but that the people they did it to deserved it. It was tradition to them, no different from lighting candles or releasing spider monkeys on holidays.

That may have been the type of sadism Kaya held, but the issue went deeper. And since this toxic shit was baked into her DNA, I needed to understand as much as possible if I gonna find an answer.

While I worked on getting to the bottom of this, I decided to keep approaching Kaya from different angles. She saw me as her worst enemy and Aarif had been a bust, but maybe she'd get along better with someone closer to her own age.

"Hi, Kaya," Layla said, approaching the forcefield, tablet in hand. "I'm Layla N'gwa."

"The Prodigal Daughter," Kaya hummed, not bothering to stand up or open her eyes. "As far as rapscallion rats go, your pedigree is top rate."

I may have been busy thinking, but like Hell was I not gonna make sure Layla was safe while doing this. She and Kaya were alone, but with one-way camera lenses in both of our eyes, I could see and hear everything she saw and heard from my room.

"I'm not proud of my heritage," she said. "I was forced down the path of the thief. If it were up to me, I wouldn't have that nickname, I wouldn't have a bounty, and I wouldn't be here right now. But I do and I am."

"Not a fan of Madame N'gwa?" Kaya purred. "Are you a fan of Yael? Let me out of here, and I'll take care of them both for you."

Layla, to her credit, didn't seem to let her face or body show any response to that offer.

Kaya couldn't be allowed to hold any more cards than she already did. "I hear *you're* a fan of EZ Street."

Kaya still didn't open her eyes, but she did giggle. "Is this the part where you pretend to be interested in the same things as me?"

"Who's pretending?" Layla laughed with her. "I want, no, I *need* Gianni to dance all over me."

"An understandable wish. He is the hottest."

"But Jamal is a close second." Layla turned on her tablet. "You know they released a new music video while you and Yael were asleep?"

"What?!" Kaya's eyes shot open. "Without any prior announcement?!"

"Yeah! A surprise drop. Sexy as all Hell."

Kaya jumped up to her feet, the resulting thud echoing through the ship. "Show me now." Layla obliged, pulling up the new single "Always Like a Bridge" for Kaya on her tablet, the widest grin I'd seen yet plastered on the pre-teen's face. I'd been surprised when Layla offered to use her knowledge of boy bands to bond with Kaya, as I'd thought she was more into high art. She responded by saying that there was nothing wrong with having some guilty pleasures… especially when they came with abs.

Listening to the song, I didn't think there was any pleasure to be garnered from it, guilty or otherwise. If Kaya hadn't beaten most of my blood out of me, some probably would have been coming out of my ears. I was no music expert, so I couldn't finely critique what was wrong with it like I could a cup of soup, but it was trashy garbage. I'd made sure Layla had been listening to plenty of badass rock and, when this was all over, I'd have to do the same for Kaya.

"That. Was. Amazing!" Kaya squealed as the video finished. "Let's watch it again!"

"Totally!"

Oh god, why?

Kaya and Layla watched the video for a second time. This time around, the two of them sang along with the chorus. The first go around was painful enough, but while Layla could carry a tune, Kaya had possibly the worst singing voice I'd ever heard. And I'd listened to *Moli's* attempts at singing.

Five minutes later, the video ended once more, Kaya moaning as she dropped down and rolled over onto her back, placing her hands over her heart.

"Four years, Layla. Then they'll be mine. All mine."

"I've never thought about being a princess, but I won't lie, this makes me jealous." Layla bit her thumbnail. "Come to think of it, why didn't Emperor Kaybell ever announce to the universe that there was a new princess?"

Kaya sat back up, still in a good mood. "She was overprotective for the longest time. I was confined to the palace and my existence was known to only a select few. It's why I was able to guilt her into letting me go on this trip. She plans to make a formal announcement about me upon my return to Cykeb."

"I see. Hey, how about we watch the video five more times, and focus on a different boy each time?"

Fucking Hell. I'd have rather taken another beating at this point.

"You do that too?"

"Every true EZ stan should."

I put my hands over my ears in a vain attempt to block out the music, but because of how the lenses worked, that did nothing to help me. They did indeed watch the video five more times, and important brain cells I could have used to save us in the future died. If I ever heard Layla or Kaya shout, "Lie down!" again, I was gonna crack.

"Oh my gods, you are too much fun!" Kaya cheered, bouncing up and down. "Are you sure you don't wanna kill Yael with me? Torture her a little for making you into a criminal?"

Layla shook her head. "There is a part of me that hates Yael for doing my g-gma's bidding these past few years. For helping her rip me away from my school and all my friends, and ruining my last few years as a kid. But while there's a lot of things about the past two years I regret, getting to know Yael isn't one of them. She's a great woman."

Kaya scoffed.

"I'm serious, Princess. She's brilliant and kind and kind of an asshole, but also kinda funny. Come on, aren't you the least bit curious to find out how she was able to win your mother over?"

Kaya slammed her fists against the forcefield, sending her flying back against the wall. "Kaya!" Layla shouted as she shot up. "Are you okay?"

"Of course I am, you insipid fool," Kaya groaned, dusting herself off. "I'm indestructible." She walked back up to Layla, her eyes, filled with joy and excitement moments ago, now cold and dead. "I know how smart Yael Pavnick is. I know how impressive she is. I'm even willing to concede the slightest possibility that there was no deception involved in seducing Mother. But the fact remains my mothers were going to wind up together, were *destined* to be together, before she showed up. She defied the will of the gods. And for that, I can never forgive her."

Layla bobbed her head and continued biting her nails, at a loss for words. I was pretty sure Kaya was wrong. Moli had never been romantically interested in Kaybell, and us not meeting back up wouldn't have changed that. Even if she did end up tempted by the idea of becoming empress, she would have run away the second the torture devices came out.

Now, if I'd been competing against the apparently "new and improved" Kaybell? Maybe I would have had something to worry about.

Many sadists were fueled by rage, with no healthy method of getting their aggression out. They were hurt or traumatized, and the only way they could make themselves feel better was to make others hurt as well. It would make a lot of sense if Kaya was this way, given how one of her moms had been completely absent in her life, the mom she'd been left with sounded like she'd been treating her more like a pet, and there was no telling what her aunts may have done.

The only thing was that the joy this type of sadist felt from inflicting pain tended to be short-lived, with depression quickly following. I wasn't getting that vibe from Kaya.

This required further thought.

With the first of our days having passed by, Shun and P'Ken had woken up and been brought up to speed. The former had suggested abandoning *Ricochet* and leaving Kaya here to die, a plan I hated for two distinct reasons. She was even less of a people person than me, so I wasn't about to send her to talk to Kaya anyway. P'Ken, however, volunteered for duty, saying she knew exactly what to do.

While I lay in bed eating my second-favorite gummies—I'd run out of my favorites—and sipping a beer, I repeatedly tried calling Moli a dozen more times. This was something she kinda, super needed to know about, and I missed her so, so much. But she still didn't pick up. She must have really hated me right now.

P'Ken got Kaya's attention by slamming her stick down in front of the forcefield.

"Oh goodie," Kaya moaned, having just been humming "Always Like a Bridge."

"You."

Standing tall with perfect posture, P'Ken glared down at Kaya, not saying a word. Her body was rigid, and her eyes were filled with disappointment. She was in full headmistress mode.

"What? Not gonna say anything?" Kaya snickered. "You wanna let me out and take me on again? You were already stupid enough to try it once."

P'Ken didn't flinch or respond. That pissed Kaya off.

"Come on, Whip Cracker. Talk to me. What made you think someone without even enhancements stood a chance against me after seeing what I did to your friends?"

P'Ken remained stalwart and silent.

"Answer me, dammit!" Kaya growled. "I asked you a question, peasant. Answer me now or I'll—"

"Or you'll what?" P'Ken cut her off, finally choosing to speak and raising an eyebrow. "You can't do anything right now. And if I had to guess, this is the first time in your life you've been in such a position. You may have put on a brave face at first, but I'd say by now, the little baby is getting cranky."

Eyes bulging, Kaya popped her katars out of her arms. "Keep talking. See what happens."

"I'm guessing this is also normal behavior for you. You don't like something or someone, and you immediately resort to violence. Do you think behavior like that is appropriate for high society?"

"What the Hell would you know about high society?"

Kaya managed to get to P'Ken a little with that one. Her eyes blinked uncontrollably for a couple seconds.

"You don't know anything about me, do you?" P'Ken asked, regaining her composure.

"Why would I? Mother, Yael, Layla, Marcos Domingo,

and Shun Segisteel are the only members of your operation who matter. The rest of you are human refuse. Well, except for Juri. May I talk to her instead of you?"

They knew about Marcos? Shit! A problem for later.

P'Ken clicked her tongue. "I am P'Ken Amatyn, daughter of Lulu Amatyn, headmistress of the St. Shiala School for Girls."

"And why is it important for me to know that your mother is a glorified babysitter?"

P'Ken slammed her cane down on the floor. "The St. Shiala School for Girls is the most respected finishing school in the Cykebian Empire. It's where your mother went and, in a few years, it's where you'll go." She picked her cane up, twirled it around, and rested it on her shoulder. "It's also a school attended by almost nothing but spoiled brats. I should know. I spent the better part of my life being bullied by them. And that's all *you* are. A spoiled brat."

Kaya, getting more and more pissed off, laughed with heavy breath as she clanged her katars together, electrifying them. "Keep talking, bitch. You're asking for it."

"Keep making threats. See where that gets you. A teacher does not fear her students."

"You *should* be afraid of me. Everyone should. And I'm not your damn student."

P'Ken tapped her cane against her shoulder, halting the conversation for a moment. "Why did Emperor Kaybell create you?"

"Ex… excuse me?!"

"It's a simple question. Why did she make you? It isn't as if you were a consensual decision between your mothers who wanted to have a child together. And if the emperor just wanted *a* child, she wouldn't have needed to use Molina's DNA."

"Shut up."

"I think I have an answer. Or at least, an educated guess. Kaybell was so heartbroken over losing Molina that she wanted to still have a piece of her in her life. And someone who was 50% her would fit that bill. That's why she's been so protective of you. She doesn't want to lose her for a second time. When she looks at you, she doesn't really see you. Only her."

The invincible cyborg cried. It was a clean cry, but the tears were plentiful.

"Why are you doing this to me? Why?! You're only making me want to kill you even more!"

"Quiet!" P'Ken shouted back, slamming her cane down once more. "And quit your sniveling. It isn't ladylike in the slightest."

Kaya panted as she wiped her tears from her red cheeks. "Why?"

P'Ken smirked. "You're not used to being treated this way. You're used to getting every little thing you want. Your mother gives you nearly everything imaginable, and you have your aunts to indulge your darker side. And of course there's no one to stop you from bullying all your servants, and no one capable of standing up to you. There's not one person in your life who tells you "No". Well, that's changing now. You want out of that prison, you want me to be silent, and I say no."

Kaya fell to her knees, continuing to cry. "Who do you think you are? Some kind of evil psychologist?"

"No. I am the greatest apprentice of Yael Pavnick. And the most important thing she ever taught me was how to spot someone's weakness and use it against them."

What was happening here was actually kinda gross considering P'Ken was a grown woman essentially bullying a child into submission, but also I couldn't help but beam with pride at how far she'd come, even if she was pants-crappingly terrifying.

"I'll... I'll kill you last," Kaya sniffled. "I'll make you watch as everyone else dies."

"Still making threats, even now." P'Ken bent down to meet Kaya at eye level. "Still crying. Hell, this whole crusade you've gone on to murder Yael is one big temper tantrum. You can't stand the idea that Molina would ever choose a commoner over a princess, because, as a princess yourself, that means *you* may not always get what you want."

"No!" Kaya shouted, hysterical, slamming her fists against the floor and shaking the whole ship. "That's not it at all! I just want my Mommies and I to be happy together. I just want us to be a family."

P'Ken set her stick down and raised her gloved hand. She slowly and softly put it against the forcefield. She was burning herself pretty badly, but she took the pain and didn't show it at all.

"Molina loves Yael and only Yael. She is one of the most compassionate women I have ever met. She could never love a daughter with as twisted an idea of fun as yours." P'Ken pressed her hand harder against the forcefield. "Your family will never be together. But if you want Molina in your life at all, you can't be this person. Become more like your mothers, stop thinking it's okay for you to treat people however you wish, and quit being such a brat!"

Escalating her volume on the final word, P'Ken pulled her burnt hand off the forcefield.

Kaya, meanwhile, curled up into a ball as she continued to sob.

P'Ken picked herself back up and walked away, not smiling, but with her posture still perfect, she was clearly satisfied with the results of her work. Ideally, some of what she said to the kid would get through to her… but she may have gone a bit too far.

The final major cause of sadism was insecurity. It was the feeling that one wasn't good enough, and the need to bring other people down to compensate. These sadists were weak-minded and typically cowardly, and they exclusively targeted those with no chance of being able to stand up to them.

Kaya may have had bad blood, she may have been tyrannical, she may have been hurt, and she may have felt it was her right to do as she pleased, but after hearing everything Layla and P'Ken had gotten out of her, I was convinced that this was where most of her issues stemmed from.

It was day three. Kaya was lying flat on her back in her prison, starving and exhausted.

No matter what, today she was being let out. But not before we had one more conversation. "G'mornin, Kaya," I said, approaching the makeshift cell, glass of water in hand. "I've got water for you. No food, because your stomach probably couldn't handle what I eat, but we'll go see the Banshees about that a little later. Sound good?"

Kaya cracked her neck as she sat up. Her eyes were red and there were enormous bags underneath them.

"You're in a cheerful mood for a corpse," she groaned.

"Have you accepted the inevitable?"

"Mmmmm, no. Can't say I have." I set the glass of water down on the floor, right in front of the forcefield. "In fact, I'm planning on having a damn good day, starting by showing *you* the coolest thing in the world."

"I think you'll find I already have plenty of experience with genocide."

I held myself back from rolling my eyes. It was not her fault she thought that way.

From the inside of my dress, I pulled out my tablet, and cued up one of the videos I'd pulled up the previous night. I plopped down on the floor and held the tablet out so both of us could see it.

"Wrestling?" Kaya scoffed as the video played. "Of course you'd enjoy such foolishness."

"Don't be so quick to judge. Have you ever given it a chance?" Kaya shook her head, turning away. "Come on, Kaya. Watch one clip and listen to what I have to say. After that, you can decide if you wanna watch more, or if you'd like to come out."

I pushed the glass of water against the forcefield with my foot. A few seconds later, I had Kaya's attention again.

"One clip."

I nodded as I closed out the video I'd been playing. That had just been a random, if still cool as Hell, match. I knew exactly which one she really needed to see.

"What we have here is a classic bout," I said, pressing play. "Lazuli vs Dragonius. This was the climax of a saga that lasted over two years. Dragonius had worked his way through Lazuli's team, The Knights of Stone, and defeated them, nay, shattered them, one by one. Lazuli, the youngest member of his team, was the only one left who could stop him from claiming the championship title."

While I was speaking, Dragonius whaled on Lazuli. He had the immediate advantage and was practically toying with his physically inferior opponent. The piledriver, the power slam, and, of course, his signature firebreath all made appearances. There was nothing Lazuli could do.

"What dribble," Kaya mocked. "What enjoyment is there to bad when the violence is all fake?"

I shook my head and clicked my tongue as Lazuli struggled to get up before the referee ended the match.

"That's the thing. It isn't fake. Well, not mostly. The storylines and personas are fake, and competitors don't get nearly as hurt as they seem to, but there's still a level of reality to it all. These talented athletes and actors are still putting their bodies on the line for our enjoyment. Serious injuries do happen. And while Dragonius may not actually want to murder Lazuli in real life, off-camera, they still seem to hate each other's guts."

Lazuli got back up just in time and hit Dragonius with everything he had, successfully landing three consecutive Canadian destroyers and a jackhammer. And none of it even seemed to phase Dragonius.

"If there's something you're trying to tell me, spit it out instead of wasting my time with this nonsense."

"This nonsense *is* what I'm trying to tell you. Although I'd prefer you not call it that."

Dragonius got Lazuli down on the mat again, but refused to let the ref count, throwing him aside. He pounded in Lazuli's face with his clawed fists, drawing blood and knocking out teeth.

"Dragonius may be one of the baddest bad guys of all, but he didn't have to be," I continued. "The son of a human woman and a dragon, he never knew either of his parents. Throughout his childhood, he was bullied for his heritage and beaten up countless times. He set out to become the strongest not just so no one could ever mess with him again, but so he could hurt everyone else the way he'd been hurt."

Lazuli tried tapping out, but Dragonius wouldn't even let him do that. He picked up him, threw him against the ropes, and resumed comboing him with his after his. He wasn't just planning on winning this match. He was going for the kill.

"I couldn't care less about this Neanderthal's backstory," Kaya said.

"You sure? Cause it sounds pretty familiar to me."

Kaya sneered. "Are you implying I'm anything like this mindless buffoon? I *have* my mother, and I've only ever tormented others, not the other way around. I don't need to work to be the strongest because I already am."

"Yeah, yeah, I hear ya. But let me ask you this: What did you feel the *first* time you hurt someone?"

Against all odds, Lazuli managed to stand back up after Dragonius' onslaught was finished.

"Excuse me?"

"I'm curious. How did it happen? What prompted it to happen? And what did you feel when you were finished with them?"

Dragonius couldn't believe what was happening. He'd exhausted himself while he'd been having his fun, and yet Lazuli still seemed to have as much energy as when they'd begun.

"I... why does it matter?"

"Answer the question."

Kaya took a deep breath. "It was a servant girl. One slightly younger than myself. She was cleaning my chambers, and when I entered them, I startled her. She knocked over a vase of flowers filled with water all over my bed. For that, I slapped her. And the tingles that went through me were like nothing I'd felt before. So I hit her again. And again. Eventually I had her down on the floor, begging for mercy. And so I kept her from feeling any more pain by breaking her neck. I was a bit shocked by what I'd done, but I loved it. And fortunately, Aunt Wink found me before Mother. She had her guards clean things up, and told me if I ever wanted to continue experimenting, I'd need only ask her. From that day on, I felt freedom beyond comparison."

Even running on empty, Dragonius was still too much for Lazuli to handle. Lazuli was able to avoid taking too many more hits, but they still weren't able to hurt Dragonius. He needed a plan.

"I've never intentionally killed *anyone*," I said. "Juri killed some people back on the *Mangalarga*, but aside from that, nah. I do love fighting, though. Not just wrestling but combat in and of itself. It's thrilling, it's fun, and it gets the blood pumping. And I think some good old-fashioned, non-murderous violence is what you need."

Kaya didn't respond, her eyes now glued to the screen as Dragonius continued to try and finish off Lazuli.

"You target those who are weaker than you. Those who you see as beneath you. And you get pleasure from tormenting them because you know what you really are. A scared little girl who couldn't hope to beat someone in a fair, equal fight. A pathetic child who isn't worthy of inheriting the throne."

Kaya punched the forcefield, this time bracing herself

so she wasn't sent flying back. As she continued to punch the forcefield, she screamed. "Who the Hell do you think you are to speak to me like this?! You're nothing! Less than nothing! And in a matter of minutes, you and everyone you love will be dead!"

I set the tablet down, paused the video, and turned to face Kaya.

"Who do I think I am? Well, considering one of your moms is my wife... that makes you my kid too."

"Silence!" she demanded, continuing to bang against the forcefield.

"And unlike the mother you're used to, I'm gonna be straight with you. You don't hate me. And you don't blame me for your bio moms not being together. You blame yourself."

Kaya continued to scream profanity and strike the forcefield as the tears that hadn't escaped her eyes yesterday made their way down her face now.

"Why would I blame myself for that? That doesn't even make sense!"

"Kids blaming themselves for things their parents do never makes sense. Just like parents blaming their kids for their own mistakes never makes sense. It's all bullshit our stupid brains trick us into believing. You hurt others because it makes you feel better about yourself, but if you want to really prove your worth, you'll find scenarios where you can compete evenly. If that means fighting, well, I think after I master my new power, I'll be able to give you a run for your money, and it'd be a good way to get out your aggression. And if not, the universe is your oyster. You can explore everything it has to offer. Moli and I will be happy to show you around and get to know the real you. You can learn swordplay from her, listen to boybands with

Layla, learn how to be a proper lady from P'Ken, and play with Juri to your heart's content. But first you need to accept what you've done."

"I have done nothing wrong! I am the crown princess! The universe isn't my oyster, it's my plaything!"

"Keep telling yourself that! See where it gets you!"

Kaya whimpered as her strikes grew weaker and slower and her tears and snot became more prominent.

"I don't… I won't…" A high-pitched scream shattered my eardrums. "Mother thinks I'm perfect. She's the only one who does. I try my hardest to impress my aunts when we torture together, but they still make fun of me. And my own uncle is frightened of me." Kaya shook her head, completely messing up her hair. "She'd never forgive me."

I snorted. "You think so? Let me tell you, she's a lot older than you, and has probably done way more horrible things. But from the sound of it, despite how hard it is to believe, she's turned over a new leaf. And you can do the same. You need only forgive yourself first. Or are you gonna tell me that as good as murder and torture make you feel, you don't end up feeling even worse about yourself when you're done."

The screaming and banging stopped. Kaya's crying and sniffling stopped. She fell over and buried her face in her hands, before looking back at me.

"Yael Pavnick… you must help me."

I breathed the heaviest sigh of relief as I smiled and grabbed my tablet. And from it, I disabled the forcefield.

Immediately, Kaya charged at me. But not to attack. She retracted her katars, and wrapped her arms around me. For a change, I got to experience what it was like when I trapped my family in my bear hugs. I fucking loved it.

"I'm sorry. I'm so sorry. I'm so, so sorry."

"Shh," I said, brushing her hair. "It's okay. It's okay. I forgive you."

The baby-faced little girl looked up at me, sniffling. "So… how did Lazuli win?"

I cast my smile down at her. "I'll show you."

When I'd gone on my quest inside my head, I thought what I wanted was a baby. But that wasn't the only thing that could give me renewed purpose. It could also be an artificially aged-up two-year-old with homicidal tendencies, crippling self-deprecation issues, and a desperate need of discipline.

Kaya could be my future.

CHAPTER 18: MOLINA

The idea that Wink might have killed Father didn't surprise me as much as I wished it did, but for Kaybell, it was unthinkable. Despite how off-putting I found them, her siblings were the people she held most dear, which was why I'd deliberately kept her in the dark when I'd suspected Megz.

Still, that only made her want to talk to Wink more. She needed to confirm that she wasn't plotting against her sister to take the throne. I wasn't sure what to think. Galopire would definitely lie to save his own skin, but he'd also sell out his boss.

After talking it over, we decided that discussing things with Wink casually would be best, rather than performing a straight interrogation and asking her directly. Kaybell knew how important it was that we got the truth out of her, but she also didn't want to damage their relationship if this was all a mistake. So, the next morning, the three of us set out to Hoca-Hikaru for a hunting trip.

Hoca-Hikaru was listed every year among the top ten hunting destinations for Cykebian nobles and other wealthy elites. The planet had been modified so that the leaves of the trees, the flowers, and the grass were all constantly shifting color, making camouflage impossible, and forcing hunters to think of their feet. In the past, that and its multitude of different biospheres were its main draw, but ever since Kay legalized genetic engineering, the people who owned the planet had been engineering animals to make them stronger, faster, smarter, and more aggressive.

I'd never liked hunting, but I'd begrudgingly gone on a few trips with Kaybell and her father before. I could stand the general idea at this point, provided we ate what we shot, but what they were doing to the animals here was grotesque. Of course, Wink disagreed, and thought the modifications only made for a more satisfying kill.

"So Wink, I hear Jolla is studying marine biology," I said, the three of us bundled up in coats and furs, blaster rifles draped over our arms as we searched for red-eyed polar bears in the arctic biosphere. "Do you plan on studying anything?"

"Why would I do that?"

"Because there's something you're interested in?"

Wink shook her head. "I already know everything I need to. Even if there was more for me to learn, I only finished basic lessons with my dull, old tutors last year. Why would I go straight back to that?"

"She always had lower marks than the rest of us," Kaybell whispered in my ear.

"You say that as if it matters. Why does a princess need to understand math or agriculture?"

The answer seemed obvious to me: they were important things to know about for anyone in line to become emperor. I'd studied them plenty as a Sunriser, but if I'd become Kaybell's empress, I certainly could have continued my studies. Either Wink didn't want to be emperor after all, or she only cared about the power and title, and nothing else.

"I would ideally like to see you do more than hunt though your 20s," Kaybell said. "You're capable of so much more."

Wink scoffed. "Is this why you came with me? To lecture me about my life?" She turned her head around and glared at us both with death in her eyes. "You aren't Mother."

Kay froze for a moment, before shaking it off. "Yes, but unlike Mother, I'm the one that's still here for you."

"She only left *because* of you," Wink said, spinning around on the balls of her feet, allowing the ice to do the work. "Though I suppose I should blame you as well, Molina. You are the one responsible for all of this."

A needle went through the back of my brain. I'd only been trying my best to make casual conversation, but I'd ended up stepping into something I really shouldn't have.

"Mother was the one who couldn't accept that things needed to change," Kay said. "You're lucky that I—"

"That you what?" Wink cut her off. "That you didn't kill her, too?"

A red-eyed polar bear's howl echoed in the distance, loose snow and icicles dropping down the mountainsides around us. I could feel the ice underneath our boots growing thinner.

"I would never hurt Mother. Just like I'd never hurt you. But she chose her principles over her responsibilities as empress regent, and her responsibilities as a mother. That's not my fault." Kay's breath was visible as she turned to me. "Nor is it Molina's."

Wink sniffed, glaring at me specifically like I was a tundra ant to be squashed. Caressing her rifle with her purple gorilla-skin gloved hands, she loaded and raised it, and turned back around.

"Why don't we continue the hunt in silence? We can talk more at dinner."

Wink walked forward slowly and carefully so that she neither cracked the ice, nor alerted any nearby animals. She may have had a specific target in mind, but her lust for blood would likely settle for anything.

"Did you kill my father?"

Kaybell's eyes widened at me getting straight to the point. That wasn't the plan. But Wink wasn't exactly giving me reasons to put my faith in her right now.

Wink didn't turn around or stop walking. "Oh. So that's what this is about. I can't say that's much better. Where did you get this preposterous idea?"

I followed behind Wink, and Kaybell followed behind me. "General Galopire."

"The man who tried to kill you both? Why would you ever believe a word from his vulgar tongue?"

"We don't," Kay was sure to say before I could respond. "He was trying to save his head by telling us what he knew, and he pointed us to you. We're just following up on the lead like we would any other."

Wink shook her head. "You insult me, sister. I'm hurt. I never liked the supreme general, but I've followed your rules to a tee. I wouldn't break them for him. What motivation would I have even had?"

"Well, there's something else Galopire told us."

"Molina, don't."

I clenched my fists. This was our last lead, and if we didn't find the killer soon, the trail would go colder than our surroundings. Kaybell didn't want to play hardball with her sister, but I had to. I had no choice.

"He said that you're the leader of a coalition of nobles who seek to overthrow Kaybell for both her social policies and her use of government funds. Naturally, that would result in you getting to skip ahead of Megz in the line of succession and put you on the throne. My father was one of Kaybell's most powerful allies, and any opposition against her would seek to take him off the board."

I stomped down on the ice, cracking it.

"Look me in the eyes, and tell me the truth."

My voice was hard and my breath clouded the air around me. Kaybell's harsh glare weighed heavy on my shoulders, but I'd forgiven her for so much that she should be able to forgive me for this.

Wink cackled as she did as I asked and looked straight at me. "Really, sister? You're going to allow her to disrespect a princess of the Cykebian Empire like this?"

Kay lowered her head. "Answer the question."

Wink bit down on her cracked bottom lip. She bit down so hard she drew blood, seemingly for the sole purpose of licking it up.

"I haven't killed anyone in over a year. I swear it on Father's grave."

"So you deny everything Galopire said?" I pushed.

"She already answered, Molina," Kaybell said. "It's done. Leave her alone."

I got close enough to Wink that it was impossible to distinguish our breath from each other's. "I want to hear her say it."

More blood trickled down Wink's chin. Rather than slurp

it all up at once again, Wink dipped her tongue in the pool multiple times, savoring the taste.

"Yes. He spoke nothing but lies."

A gust of wind brushed past us, blowing snow in our faces. My knees shook, both from the freezing cold and the rage in my heart. I didn't believe her. Galopire had no reason to single her out specifically. If he was trying to mess with me, he would have accused Kay herself, and Wink had every reason to wish to see her sister removed from the throne. She was lying.

But there was nothing I could do. "Wink, I—"

Before I could finish my fake apology, a red-eyed polar bear got the drop on us, flanking us from behind. My heart pounded as it got within mauling distance, but it didn't get the chance to strike. With one shot to the head, Wink brought down the graceful creature, its brains splattering all over us.

Wink spat on its corpse. "You two can carry that."

Wink walked off on her own, not waiting for us to pick up the dead bear. "Kaybell…"

"Don't, Molina. I think Wink had the right idea about continuing this trip in silence."

I cringed for more than one reason as we raised the bear up in our arms. This couldn't be how the investigation ended. There had to be a conclusive clue I'd missed.

There had to be.

I'd had a long day, I was tired, and I was ready to sleep it off like Yael did her bi-daily hangovers. I'd changed into my pajamas, I'd brushed my teeth, and I'd taken care of my skin. All that was left for me to do before I tucked myself into the luxurious bed Kaybell had provided for my stay was to brush my hair.

Standing in front of the bathroom mirror, I went over everything I'd been told in the past week for the umpteenth time, just as I'd done for the majority of the hunting trip. No matter how many times I repeated every conversation I'd had in my head or thought about every file I'd read, I couldn't figure it would. As much as I believed Wink was hiding something, for all I knew, we'd never even been on the right track.

I had no idea what to do. I was going to fail Father one last time.

As I finished brushing, I gave one final, hard tug on my now-straightened hair. Shutting off the light, I walked into the bedroom and was met by a knock on the door. I wasn't in the mood to talk to anyone, but if Kay had come to pay me a late-night visit, I couldn't waste the chance to apologize for earlier.

Opening the door, I wasn't met by my best friend, but by my favorite student. From the sneer on his face and the fact that he was still fully dressed though, he was no less pissed off at me.

"Griffin, hey. What's wrong?"

"What's wrong?" he echoed, incensed. "You insulted Wink's honor. You *and* the emperor. She cried her heart out to Jolla over how hurt she was, and that in turn made Jolla cry. As her boyfriend, I cannot stand for that."

I had a hard time imagining Wink genuinely crying over what we'd said. I had an equally hard time imagining that Jolla thought of Griffin as her boyfriend. Of course, if I said any of that, Griffin would say that I was judging them too harshly. I would counter that it was impossible to judge someone who waxed nostalgic about recreational torture, and he'd go off again about fixing them.

"I'm sorry," I said. "I need to get to the bottom of things, and I was only doing due diligence by confronting Wink."

"You were wasting everyone's time. The Bythora sisters have issues, believe you me, Jolla could talk about them for days straight, but their loyalty to and love for each other is unquestionable. You were played, and you hurt innocent girls as a result."

I looked down at the floor and nodded. "I already apologized to you, and I plan on making a formal apology to the others at brunch. What else do you want?"

Griffin gripped the hilt of the sword at his waist. "I've learned so much from you, Professor. And the one-on-one time we've spent together training in the fine art of the blade has been my favorite part of the past couple years, without question." He shook his head. "But you aren't Yael."

He didn't need to even raise his sword to lunge it through my heart. "Griffin, please don't—"

"You should have called her from the start," he cut me off. "You should have answered any of her countless calls. Do you have any idea what you're doing? Don't you miss her?"

I clenched my eyes in the palm of my hand. "Of course I miss her. But I'm doing my best. This is my fight."

"She's your wife. Your fight *is* her fight."

Tearing my hand away from my face, I laughed as my eyes dampened. "Dammit. You don't even realize how hard it is being her wife. Standing at her side, always being compared. I love her more than anything, but it's not fucking easy. It's been five goddamn years since I did anything for myself, and I thought I had it in me to prove I still had *some* value. But I guess not. I'm not average. I'm pathetic."

Griffin gently grabbed my chin and picked up my head.

Looking at him now, his face had softened.

"I get it. Perhaps better than anyone else could. It's not easy standing next to Layla, Shun, and Platyperson either. They're all prodigies, and I'm a wannabe. It's no wonder Yael doesn't take me into the field. I'm kept around as a courtesy."

"That's not true. You have talent. Real talent."

"And so do you. But we're comets surrounded by stars."

I dried my eyes with my sleeve. Catching Father's killer mattered more than my pride, and the longer I waited, the colder the trail would get. Much as the thought killed me, I had to entertain the idea that, after I made things right with Kaybell, my next move would be to call Yael.

"Don't lump yourself in with me," I said, forcing a smile. "You're going to be the best damn gentleman thief the universe has ever seen."

Griffin smirked back at me. "Maybe not."

"What are you talking about?"

Griffin's lips curled further up his face. "Jolla just invited me to stay. Here with her, as her personal companion."

My mouth hung open. "And… you accepted?"

Griffin continued to grin. "When I initially declared my love for her, it was primarily for her beauty. But I've gotten to know the real her over the course of our dates. And when I was comforting her as she cried, her pain was my pain. I hurt, because she hurt. If that's not true love, I don't know what is."

"But what about your dream?"

"It's a good dream. And one I'll never stop thinking about. But I could be a prince. You passed up the chance to become royalty but… that's not me."

I ran my fingers through my hair as I took a deep breath.

"Kid, you don't want to do this. I know the offer is tempting, and I know it's a hard road, but don't give up on what you really want. No matter how much you're treasured, you don't want to be someone's trophy."

Griffin's smile didn't fade. "I've already made up my mind, Professor. When you and Marcos depart Cykeb, I *won't* be going with you."

I sighed. He wasn't listening. But I'd meant it when I said we weren't the same. Maybe living in the lap of luxury as Jolla's boy-toy was all he needed to be happy. For his sake, I hoped it was.

"You were always my favorite student," I said, wrapping my arms around him.

"And you, my favorite teacher," he replied, hugging me back.

"You better come visit often."

"Of course! And if all goes well, I'll get to introduce Yael and the others to my wife."

Pulling away, I could practically see Griffin's warm, eager heart bursting out of his chest.

At the same time, once they heard about this, I could only picture Marcos's breaking.

CHAPTER 19: KAYA

This was my chance. I could do what I'd come here to do. I could kill them all, and none of them would be able to stop me. I could enjoy their screams and moans of agony, or I could blast my music and tune them all out as I cut their limbs off one by one.

But I didn't want to.

I'd always thought Mother was brilliant. I'd thought that even though she'd foolishly rejected our family's traditions, she was still the smartest woman in the universe, and I was a close second.

I'd been so wrong. P'Ken and especially Yael were operating on an entirely different level from us. In only a matter of days, they'd figured out exactly what they needed to say to hit me at my core and save themselves. Meanwhile I'd been ignorant to the truths they spoke about me all my life. They were like Penelopi and Gustra from the Kaiju Mysteries series. Only old. And without the sexy giant monsters.

"So… what happens now?"

"Now, we go find Shion the Librarian's ship. She doesn't like me much, but her ship's got the best food. And I think she'd respect me using my new powers to steal from her. Hopefully."

Yael and I walked across the rocky surface of Defnuct-7. I'd never done much walking outside before I'd left Cykeb, my palanquin bearers usually carrying me around the palace's grounds. I'd found too much walking was insufferable, and a burden a princess should never have to withstand, but in small doses it was relaxing.

Of course, I couldn't relax at all right now. The screams of the thousands I'd slaughtered echoed in the back of my brain, and for once, I didn't take pleasure in them. There was also a gaping hole in my stomach brought about by the starvation I'd been forced to endure. Only once that hole was filled would I be able to focus on my mind. And only once my mind was cleared would I be able to sleep again.

"I hope she has alligator steaks," I said, hugging myself. "They're my favorite. But that's not what I meant. What happens *after* I'm fed?"

Yael stuck her hands behind her head and looked up at the morning sky. "We'll say goodbye to the Banshees and let them know everything's cool. Then you'll call your mom and let her know that we're taking you home. We'll head to Cykeb, find Molina, since she still isn't answering my calls, and let you two get acquainted. After that, we'll take you back to the palace, and Moli, Kaybell, and I will figure out where to go from there. Ideally, we can work out some type of shared custody deal. If that's what you want, of course."

I nodded. "Even if my mothers can't be together, I still want to be with them both. And there's a great deal I can learn from you as well. Though I don't think I'd ever want to live anywhere but the royal palace. Living among the likes of you and your crew... isn't for me." I raised one of my arms so I could cough into my elbow. "You really think Molina will forgive me as easily as you have?"

"You kidding?" Yael slapped my back. "She won't just forgive you. She'll love you."

I tightened my arms around my torso. Mother had shared so many stories about all of the adventures they'd gone together and how she was the light that shined through the universe. If Yael and Mother both thought she'd love me, then they couldn't be wrong.

Except they didn't know what I knew.

"Yael… thank you. Anyone else would have killed me or left me to rot. But you only sought to help me. If I'm going to be emperor one day, I'm going to need powerful allies I can trust." I tugged on her sleeve. "Promise your princess that no matter whatever else I do or say, you'll always forgive me. Promise me that my mothers always will. And promise me you'll never, ever hurt me, or any of my family."

Yael stretched her arms out, making cat-like groans, before tugging on her hair and scratching her head. Given how fashionably she dressed, I hadn't expected her to act so common. Or so weird. But I didn't mind.

Yael took my hand with a firm grip. "I promise."

"About all of it?"

"About all of it." She rolled her eyes and smirked. "Assuming Kaybell doesn't try to kill me again. You know she stabbed me with a gamma knife, right?"

I shrugged, smiling back at her. "You had it coming."

"*Did* I though?"

———————

My combat suit was designed for peak efficiency. It was nearly as durable as I was, it couldn't be frozen, burnt, or cut, it absorbed kinetic energy, the voice synthesizer built into my now-destroyed helmet allowed me to strike fear into my enemies just by speaking, and along with all of that, it was comfortable, flexible, and allowed me my full range of motion.

Unfortunately, I also hadn't been able to have it washed in over a week, and it smelled most foul.

The crew of *Ricochet* didn't have any clothes in my size immediately ready for me, but as it turned out, P'Ken was a gifted seamstress. She asked me for my favorite color, to which I responded bright, golden-yellow, and she promised she'd have a top-quality dress for me made in a day. I told her I'd need a different dress for each day I was with them, but that made her laugh.

In the meantime, I was given a plain white t-shirt and black athletic shorts to wear. The cheap fabric irritated my skin within seconds of contact and made my body itch like it never had before. P'Ken had laughed at that too. When I nearly lost my temper and screamed at her for disrespecting me, she shut me down with a single harsh glare.

Yael may have been the genius of this operation as well as their strongest fighter, but P'Ken was the *badass*.

"Take as long as you need to speak with your Mother," P'Ken said. "Let us know when you're off."

"Yes, ma'am," I said, addressing her as I did my tutors.

She turned around and walked out of Yael's room. It was only natural that Yael would allow me to stay here. She didn't have proper accommodations for me, but hers were the nicest quarters they had, messy as they were. Her only rule was that I not touch any of her wrestling posters or the "fidgets" on her desk. I had no idea why she was so paranoid. While I had gained an appreciation for wrestling, I had no reason to touch her posters, and I'd grown far beyond the need to play with childish toys. A teenager had no need for such dalliances, and I practically was one already.

I couldn't wait for my 13th birthday so it could be official. By then, knowledge of me would be public, and the entire universe would cheer my name. The party held in my honor would be of the most epic scale, and with a show of force against the Utozin Authority, I'd show my people their futures were in good hands.

The only thing that concerned me, and cramped my stomach, was the fact that if I didn't want to embarrass myself, I'd need a date. And while any boy would be lucky to have the honor of escorting me… I'd never actually spoken to one. Or at least none my own age. Gods, why couldn't I have been telling Yael the truth when I said I'd kissed a hunky boy? Lying about it only made me crave my first kiss even more.

I took a deep breath. I'd come clean about that when I came clean about everything else.

For now, I needed to smile and act like nothing was wrong. Mother couldn't suspect I was feeling anything but flawless.

The watch P'Ken had loaned me rang and, a few moments later, a hologram of Mother's face was smiling back at me.

"Kaya!" she cheered. "You haven't called in days. I've been so worried."

"Everything is fine, Mother. More than fine in fact."

"Why aren't you calling me from your ship?" She squinted her eyes and looked around. "What filthy hole have you found yourself in?"

I held my head high. "*Ricochet.*"

Mother's eyes widened and I believed her heart skipped a beat. "You… went to see Yael Pavnick?"

"You've talked about her a great deal. And if Molina is going to be a part of my life, and of yours again, then we need to get along, right?"

Mother recomposed herself, her face turning stern. "And how is that working out?"

"Very well, actually. We got off to a rough start, but she's amazing. She's brilliant, if something of a weirdo, and she already cares about me a great deal."

"I'd say I'm surprised, but I'd be lying. No one can resist the charm of my perfect angel." She primped her hair. "To be clear, she knows who you are?"

"She does. And she doesn't care. I believe it helped that I explained how much you've changed. She's fully ready to be your friend and an ally of the royal family."

Mother laughed. "You did something I've been afraid to do for so long. Reaching out into one's past is never easy, and with the darkness consuming mine, I never could. Thank you so much for doing this."

My heart pounded against my chest. I didn't deserve her thanks. I wasn't being honest at all. Not one bit.

"Anything for you," I said. "How are things proceeding with your investigation? Are you and Molina still having a good time together? Have you told her about me?"

Mother rolled her chin and sighed. "Alas, our trail has gone cold. Molina and I are having a small fight right now on top of that, and, no, I haven't told her." She fixed her collar and smiled warmly. "But you've inspired me. I'm going to make sure our fight ends today, and I'm going to tell her all about you, and how perfect you are."

I held back tears. "Thank you, Mother. Yael will be escorting me back to Cykeb, so we'll all be together soon."

"I'm looking forward to it. And please, tell Yael how sorry I am once more. Also that if she lets you go near any boys, I'll have her flayed." She laughed. "I'm only kidding. Love you, sweetie."

"Love you, too."

We blew kisses at each other and the call ended.

I threw myself down onto Yael's bed and ignored its appallingly low thread count as I cried into her pillow. I'd fucked up. I'd majorly fucked up. I couldn't hold the truth in any longer, but I couldn't tell anyone either. Why did having a conscience have to hurt so much?

Something pounded against the door. It didn't sound like someone knocking, and they'd agreed to give me privacy while I spoke to Mother. That only left one possibility in my mind.

And it was a possibility I desperately needed to snuggle right now.

I got out of bed as the pounding against the door continued, and upon opening it, I was tackled to the floor by the most precious and deadly dog I'd ever met, and my face was assaulted by her loving tongue.

"Hey, girl!"

I giggled as Juri enjoyed the taste of my face. I hadn't realized from looking at her how heavy she was, but with how much machinery was inside her, it made sense. Running my fingers through her curly brown fur, she barked. I couldn't actually understand her, but I wished I could.

Even though I couldn't, I could tell she was happy.

More than I wished I could understand her, I wished she could understand me. We were the two most advanced cyborgs in the universe, after all. Both soft and cute on the outside, but unimaginably deadly on the inside.

"How did it feel tearing up the *Mangalarga*?" I asked, rolling around the floor with her. "Did you enjoy yourself? Did the pain and death of your enemies bring you satisfaction?"

Juri got off of me and licked my hand.

"Or did you regret what your masters made you do?"

I stood up and grabbed one of the dog treats Yael kept in a bag next to her bed. The second it was free from its plastic prison, Juri jumped up and grabbed it from me with her teeth. She was too adorable.

"No master made me do what I did," I said. "My aunts may have encouraged me and given me subjects to practice on, but killing that first servant girl was all me. Every last innocent person I killed instantly or tortured to a slow death, I did it for no reason but my own personal pleasure. And I really did love every second of it. But I never realized until now how I was killing myself, too." I bent down and pet Juri's head as she continued to chew with her stronger-than-steel jaws. "Do you wish you'd stayed a normal dog?"

BARK! BARK!

"Probably not. Your masters would be rotting in prison. But if Mother had only allowed me to be a normal kid… I wouldn't have been able to hurt anyone. I still could have had my guards do my dirty work for me, but I wouldn't have been able to come close to bringing the scale of pain and death I've wrought." I looked down at my clenched fists, my knuckles recently caked in blood, but my fingers still perfectly manicured. "My safety comes first. It may not be my place to kill whoever I wish, but my life does matter more."

I put my hands down and looked down at Juri, who didn't even look like she was paying attention, relaxed and wrapped around my leg. I bent down, gave her a big hug, and stuck my face right into her fur.

"Well, you seem to have made yourself at home."

Aarif stood in the doorway. I didn't even need to smell him to know he'd been working on the engine; he was covered in grease. Juri abandoned me at the sight of him, running over and cuddling his leg.

"You couldn't be bothered to shower before addressing me, *engineer?*"

He opened his mouth to speak, but quickly closed it, breathing out through his nose. "I was just looking for Juri." I rolled my eyes as he walked further into the room. "I thought you were trying to not be awful now. Why are you still looking at me like I'm the scum of the Earth? You seem fine with the others."

Foolish peasants always needed things explained to them. Slowly. Did they not understand how annoying that was for their betters?

"The others are all accomplished, independent women who've successfully made their names known throughout the universe. I may not respect their chosen field, but I respect that. There's a reason your bounty is lower than even Shun's. You do nothing but whatever they tell you. You fill a role a thousand others could. You're nothing but the help."

He pursed his lips and mockingly placed his hand over his heart. "Was Shion's food that bad? It upset your little tummy and make you a cranky baby? No? Okay, well either way, I'm not letting a preteen girl talk to me that way."

"I hope you don't expect me to speak to you as an equal."

"Actually, yeah, I do. And so does Yael. So if you don't want to piss in her cereal at dinner tonight, you'll drop the attitude."

He was such an annoying idiot.

I blew strands of hair out of my face and I got up and lay back on the bed. "Whatever."

"Nah, not whatever," he said, standing over me. "This isn't gonna fly."

I didn't bother responding. He could keep talking, but I wasn't gonna bother listening. I turned on some Duroc Boys and tuned out. Kenneth Roz was probably even dumber than this loser, but by the gods you could grate cheese on his abs and cut slices with his cheekbones.

I was going to be the most desired teen in the universe once I was unveiled, but that was entirely based on my status and upbringing. Were I left to find boys on my own without any of that, would they still think I was cute? I liked to think so, but probably not. I had a baby face, I had no hips or ass, and no matter what creams or lotions I used, my pores wouldn't stop getting bigger. I was so fucking ug…

"Kaya!" Aarif screamed, loud enough to be heard. "You're listening to your music, aren't you?"

I laughed in his face as I shut it off.

"You think you're real funny," he said. "All right, since your attention span is no better than Yael's, I'll skip to the cliff-notes. I could be way richer and way more famous if I struck out on my own and went legit. You know from Juri I've got the brains to back that up. I stay because Yael is my girl, my ride or *die,* and I love the adventures following her takes me on, and while a higher bounty would be nice, I don't care all that much. I live my life the way *I* want to. And for the record, even if I was, "the help", I'd still be owed respect."

He may as well have been talking to a wall. Not because I'd turned my music back on, but because I'd been entranced by the art on his arms. A Cerberus eating broccoli and carrots, a realistic mouth with rotted teeth, and an ancient typewriter made entirely from bone were just some of the tattoos adorning his body.

I hopped off the bed and pinched his forearm, where the typewriter was situated. "Hey, hey, personal space, come on!"

I examined it closely. It was highly detailed and well done. "Whenever one of my victims in the torture chamber had an interesting tattoo or marking, I would cut it off and keep it as a trophy."

"Not getting any ideas are you?"

"No, no, I'm done with that." My attention shifted to his tattoo of a dragon and a chicken eating a giant meatball together. "I'd like a tattoo for myself though. Nothing ostentatious. Just a small little one. Mother would have a heart attack, but it isn't really anything compared to what else I have to tell her, now is it?"

Aarif grinned. Why was this foolish guttersnipe *grinning?* "You know, this is exactly how Yael and I met."

I raised an eyebrow. "Really?"

"Yup. I was talking to a full bar about the serious problem I was having, but she walked up to me to poke and look at my tattoos."

"You can hardly blame us. For someone satisfied to stand behind all of his friends, your choice in aesthetic certainly demands attention. A bit of a contradiction, don't you think?"

"Not at all. It's the same deal, actually. My tattoos are for me. I get them because they make me happy, not to impress anyone. I don't care what anyone thinks about them, although touching them without permission is a different story. Point is, I've heard how much you need the forgiveness of your moms. And I get that. But what they think of you isn't nearly as import-ant as what you think of yourself. We already found one major part of you you hate. Maybe do some more soul searching and see what else you find."

Aarif walked away, leaving the room, shutting the door behind the following Juri.

Once he was gone, I allowed my tears to resume flowing. I didn't think an engineer would have any words worth listening to, but I could feel what he'd said in my heart. There was some truth and logic to them that had hit home.

Perhaps he was slightly smarter than the average com-moner after all.

CHAPTER 20: MOLINA

"So that's it? He's quitting?"

Griffin leaving the school early sucked. Partially because he was a good kid with a ton of potential, and partially because now I'd have to find a way to convince Layla to learn swordplay. But as bad as I felt, my feelings couldn't compare to the gut punch Marcos took. Not that they were going to show it.

I'd waited till the morning to tell them so they could at least get to sleep, but there was nothing I could do to stop them from having a shitty day. I could take them to see some real platypuses later, but the smile that would put on their face would only be surface level.

While I couldn't do anything significant to help them, I at least knew what I needed to do to help myself. Griffin's words had stuck with me and kept me up all night. I needed to swallow my pride and be honest with myself.

Marcos attacked me with a flurry of flying fists. Not in real life, but in the video game we were playing on our watches. I barely had any experience with virtual entertainment or the like, but I'd figured it was best to talk to them while they were having fun, and it was either this or replacing bankers' statements with images of penises.

"I always knew Posh Boy didn't have it in him. You really suck at this, by the way."

Denial. It was a feeling I understood all too well. Picking up a chair, I moved it in front of the door and sat down in it so Marcos couldn't hover away from the conversation we needed to have. From the irritated way they rolled their eyes, they knew what I was doing.

"You know, Yael and I weren't always a happy couple," I said, trying to remember what the controls to this game were.

"Really?" they mocked, holding out the first syllable. "I never would have guessed."

"As soon as we're done here, I'm calling her. You don't need to tell me how bad a wife I've been again." I ran out of health, an animation of Marcos's character burning mine to death playing. "Despite knowing each other all our lives, there were a long ten years when we weren't together at all. Where we didn't even speak once. And you know why?"

"Because the Sunrisers suck?"

"Because she *left* me. She decided on a whim that she was going to be a thief, and she didn't have it in her to tell me or even her parents that she was running away. While she doesn't regret leaving Cykeb at all, she realized years ago how badly she screwed up not saying goodbye or staying in touch. She lunged a blade through my heart. But I didn't ignore that pain. I took it, I let it pass, and I moved on, even if I couldn't block out thoughts about her entirely. I met other people and found other things that brought me joy. And eventually, destiny brought us back together, and allowed my heart to fully mend."

While I was mostly getting destroyed once more, I did manage to land a single hit on Marcos by mashing buttons. "If you and Griffin are meant to be, he'll realize staying with Jolla is a mistake. And he'll find his way back to you."

I wasn't sure if I believed in destiny, but it sounded better than a series of extreme coincidences leading to us meeting back up. More religious and spiritual than either of us, Kaybell believed in destiny. She thought us ending up at the academy together was destiny. But if there was one thing I'd ever learned from Yael, it was the importance of freedom. Destiny spat in the face of freedom.

Not unsurprisingly at all, Marcos's reaction to my heartfelt speech was to pause the game and sarcastically clap.

"That was good. Higher than your usual level of oratory skill. I'm guessing you practiced in the mirror?" They snickered. "Yes, I'm disappointed. The man you love falling for someone else sucks, but I'll be fine. I got all my sobbing and sulking out of my system when Griffin first declared his love; two people at hot and horny as them, of course they were going to wind up fucking. Once I'm working on my own and filthy rich, I'll find a man far superior to that dolt. And I'll never think about him again."

I leaned back in my chair and smirked back at them. "Or you could tell him how you feel, save me the trouble of telling Yael how I lost one of her students, and yourself the trouble of having to find someone else."

"I do believe we've already had this conversation."

"Yeah, well, sometimes kids need things told to them more than once before they get it." I leaned over to Marcos's watch and restarted the game. "You have all the power here. Your future is yours to forge."

Marcos shut their eyes and took out the rest of my health while keeping them closed.

Only after an animation played of their character kicking mine into the sun did they reopen their eyes.

"Let me know how things go with Yael. When you have your own love life sorted out, I may consider taking your advice." They cracked their neck. "See you at brunch when you're done."

They hovered out of the room and left me all alone, the game shutting off on its own. Despite the tough face they were putting on, I'd seen the state they were in days ago. They'd fallen for Griffin *hard*. And no matter how hard they resisted, when push came to shove, with me doing some of the pushing, they'd make the right call.

Making the right call was something I needed to do too.

I tapped my watch and dialed Yael. After a minute, she still hadn't responded, which made me worry she was mad about all the calls I'd ignored, but eventually, her face appeared, and she didn't look angry at all. Rather, she was relieved.

"Fucking goddamn holy shit, finally!" she shouted at the top of her lungs, her teeth, rotted to the core by a decade of endless consumption of beer and candy, shining as if they were pearly whites. "I was so worried! Well, not really, I know you're badass enough to handle yourself, but still, big time glad you're okay."

I smiled back at her. I was so stupid. She exuded nothing but love for me and was the most beautiful, most perfectly weird woman in the universe. How could I have ever even thought about cheating on her?

She was the perfect partner. And that was only going to make what I had to say harder. "I've missed you too. And I'm sorry I haven't been answering my watch. There's been a lot going on."

Yael nervously laughed. "Yeah, same story over here. But you go first. What happened? Weren't Griffin and Marcos supposed to be helping you to relax?"

I folded my hands in front of my face, focusing myself on what I needed to say. "They were. But then we discovered that my father didn't die of natural causes after all. He was murdered."

"What?!" Yael shouted in horror. "By the gods. I'm so sorry, Moli. Do you know who did it?"

"That's what we've been busy with. We're investigating his case, but so far haven't had any luck."

"You can't blame yourself for that. I mean, apart from any information Marcos can steal, you basically have no resources to work with."

"Not entirely true. I still have a few connections and know some people around here who owe me favors, so I've gotten a few leads."

She didn't need to know about Kaybell's involvement right now. As far as she knew, she was still the demonic monster that haunted her nightmares. When we were together again, I'd tell her the full story, and explain to her in person how Kay had changed.

"Are you all right?" Yael asked. "Are the kids?"

"We're all fine. Well, except Marcos. Griffin found a girlfriend and it turns out Marcos is into him."

"Whaaaaaaat?" Yael's mouth stretched across her face. "That's crazy."

I laughed with her. "Yeah. Yeah, it is. Listen, I know we weren't exactly in the best place when I left, and, if it's all right with you, I'd love to clear the air."

Yael furiously nodded. "Yes. Yes. 100%. I am fully prepared and ready for this, like you have no idea. You are talking to a brand new Yael. Perfect wife 2.0!"

That got another laugh out of me. "Great. So, um, I've been struggling with a sense of emptiness. I've been missing the purpose, drive, and sense of accomplishment which all drove me for so long. And that's why I've been ignoring your calls. Everyone told me from the start of the investigation the smart thing to do would be to call you and let you piece the mystery together, but I wanted so badly to prove I could do it myself, and to be the one to get justice for Father. I'm sorry I worried you."

Yael's smile faded as she wrinkled her face. She rolled her shoulders back as she fidgeted around in her seat and pounded her fists together.

"I wish you could have picked up the first time I called and told me all of this, but… I get it. I get you want to be more than a teacher, and you saw this as your opportunity to do just that. And you thought if you talked to me, you'd be tempted to ask for help."

"So you're not mad?"

"How could I be mad? Frustrated, sure, but mad? I'm the reason you're in this position in the first place. It'd be really shitty of me to judge you for trying to get out of it in your own way."

I breathed a sigh of relief. "I'm happy to hear you say that. But the investigation has gone cold. I couldn't do it on my own after all. And so, I'd appreciate it if you could come to Cykeb and help."

"Say no more. Drenian was an amazing man, and his killer can't get away with it. I swear I'll catch them."

"Thanks, baby. So much."

"Of course. And please don't beat yourself up over this. You still have so much to offer the universe."

Swallowing my pride and asking for help was the easy part of this conversation. Now came the hard part.

"You're right. I do. I may not be as special as you or Aarif or most of the kids, but I know I'm still capable of a great deal." I swallowed a lump that weighed more than Juri. "And I know I'm never going to achieve anything while I'm tethered to the school."

Yael's eyes flickered. "Well, that's not a problem. Layla may not even be continuing her training, and Marcos only needs another year. Then there's just another year for Griffin and Shun, and we'll be done."

I shook my head. "I can't wait that long. Working on this investigation, I've felt more alive than I have in a long time. I've felt… things I probably shouldn't have. And I can't go back."

"Moli… what are you saying?"

I slammed my fists against my legs. Why couldn't this have been one of her awe-inspiring super-genius moments? Why couldn't she figure out what I was thinking and say it all for me?

Maybe she had figured it out. She could have read my mind and been too heartbroken to say it. I wasn't sure which option was worse.

"After we catch the killer, I need to leave," I said, my throat burning. "Following Father's path didn't work for me, and following yours hasn't worked either. I need to find one that works for *me*. I need to not be someone else's trophy."

"I… I… I," Yael stuttered, her eyes watering. "You know I don't see you like that."

"I know you don't. Because you're amazing. But it's what I am."

Yael shook her head so fast it would have made me nauseous if I wasn't already violently so.

"You don't have to do this alone. I'll always support you."

"I know you will. But you have obligations. Your jobs and the kids. I can't let you abandon all that for me." Tears streamed down her face. And I couldn't hold back mine any longer either. "I'm so sorry, baby, but I think we need to go long distance for a while."

Yael buried her face in her hands. Vomit worked its way up my throat as my heart called me a dumbass and punished me for my behavior by electrocuting itself. No matter what my body told me though, I knew this was the right decision for myself.

"Moli… you were right."

"Huh?"

"You were right that there's been something bothering me, too. Besides the nightmares. For a long time, I've been miserable. Which makes no sense because in my case, I thought I had everything I could possibly want. But, I realized in the last few days what's been missing." She smiled up at me, continuing to cry. "I love kids. And I want to have one of my own. With you."

Now I was the one at a loss for words. This was definitely something I'd thought about before, but with all the kids we already had running around, not something I'd considered a present option. Maybe Yael had outsmarted me once again. Maybe a baby was just what we both needed.

As nice as that would have been, I doubted it. I wanted to raise a kid with Yael, absolutely, but it wouldn't make me feel any differently than being a teacher did. It had to wait.

"I don't know if I'm ready for that."

Yael sniffed as she wiped her tears on her sleeve. "Well, that might be a problem."

"What are you talking about?"

She tugged on her hair. "Let me tell you what I've been doing. And brace yourself."

———

My blood boiled as I stomped down the halls of the royal palace. Every painting I passed, I wanted to tear apart. Every suit of armor, I wanted to dismantle. Every fucking sculpture, I wanted to smash.

I'd been violated. Kaybell had violated me *again*. How could I have ever believed she'd really changed? She was the same selfish bitch she always was. And now everyone else was suffering the consequences.

Passing by a deeply confused maid, I drew my sword. I didn't care how much stronger she was than me; I was going to take Kay's head, damn the consequences.

I was going to be putting the kids in danger, but I knew between the three of us, we'd be able to make it off the planet in one piece. I'd never have a chance like this again, and I couldn't waste the opportunity. I couldn't continue living my life knowing she was out there.

This would be my first truly great contribution to the universe. I was going to assassinate the evil emperor who was mere years away from ruling over everything.

Slamming the grand doors open rather than letting them open on their own, I stomped into the dining hall, where the royal family, Griffin, and Marcos were seated.

"What the Hell is your problem?" Wink spat as all eyes turned to me. What the Hell was my problem? As if she didn't know.

"Molina, are you all right?" a deceitfully concerned Kaybell said, rising from her seat at the head of the table.

I stomped a few steps forward, raised my sword, and pointed it at her. I tried opening my mouth, but I was too livid to even speak.

"Griffie, what's going on with her?" Jolla whimpered, clinging to her new boyfriend.

"I'm not sure," Griffin said, with no idea the depths of evil inside his new girlfriend.

"Platyperson, you were speaking to her earlier, weren't you?"

"Yeah," they answered. "She was gonna call Yael. Professor, what the Hell did she say?"

I needed to say it. I needed her to know that I was onto her and all of her lies. And then I needed to strike.

"You're scaring everyone," Kaybell said. "Tell us what's wrong so we can help."

That was it. I grabbed the chair I'd been comfortably sitting in all week, and I chucked it at a staine- glass portrait, colorful shards flying everywhere.

"I know who killed my father."

"What?" Kay questioned, cowering at what I'd just done. "Who?"

Swinging my sword, I took my stance and readied myself for battle. "Our daughter."

CHAPTER 21: KAYA

I'd always known what it was like to be the center of attention.

As far back as my birth, as the smoke cleared and I stepped out of the cloning tank, over a dozen doctors, nurses, and geneticists watched me in awe. While Mother brought me a towel and a robe and introduced herself, everyone else dropped to their knees and bowed. I thought people abasing themselves before me was so cool, not realizing it was the natural order of things.

Now, I was the center of attention again. Only this time, no one was in awe of me, and no one was going to be bowing. Yael had called her entire crew and myself together in the central room of *Ricochet*, and sat us all down. She'd said there was something we all needed to discuss. And from the look in their eyes, I didn't need to be Koji of Lostl1fe with his big brain and dorky but cute glasses to figure out it was about me.

"Kaya, we know there's something you've neglected to tell us," Yael said, confirming my suspicions. "I promised I'd always forgive you, and I meant it, but I need you to explain to me what's going on, because for all I know, there's more to the story than what I do know."

I crossed my arms. I didn't want to talk about this. I shouldn't have had to talk about this.

If they were done interrogating me and forgave me no matter what, then it shouldn't have mattered what I did. I *knew* they'd be angry about this.

"It's okay," Layla said. "No one's gonna hurt you. We just need to know what we're walking into when we get to Cykeb."

More than most of the others, I trusted my EZ Sister. Her eyes were as soft as a servant girl's, but as strong as Mother's. Yael wore a small smile and incessantly tapped her foot, which could have been a sign of deception, but was more likely her ADHD. The engineer and P'Ken were both stiff and serious, and Shun was glaring at me in a way I didn't care for at all. I hadn't even spoken to that Utozin filth, so I had no idea what her problem was. Maybe it was the fact that I'd beaten her ass *twice*.

I shifted around in my seat and raised my head high. While I may not have known how they'd react to the full reality of what I'd done, I'd put my faith in them this far. I didn't want to kill any of them. I couldn't. And they weren't going to let this go.

"How much do you already know?"

Yael slapped her hand down on her leg to halt her tapping foot. "You murdered your grandpa."

Her saying it out loud felt like what I imagined other people felt when I cut their limbs off. I'd fucked up so badly.

"What we don't know is why," P'Ken followed.

There was no way to excuse what I'd done. No way to soften my story. My only option was to play it cool and be straight and to the point.

I primped my hair. "I had three problems. And killing

him solved all of them. First, when I came to kill you, I didn't want Molina around. I thought she'd be more likely to have a problem with me doing it if she had to watch. Second, I needed to get Molina to Cykeb so my mothers could spend time together and rekindle their bond. Finally, I needed Grandpa removed from his seat of power. He long ago declared his intention to keep the Sunrisers neutral during the upcoming war, and I couldn't stand for that. By killing him, his spot as supreme general was opened up and Molina had to go to Cykeb without you for the funeral, and by killing him in a way that made it look like he died naturally, I was able to trick Mother into thinking there was some type of conspiracy going on and to handle the investigation herself. Naturally, she'd bring Molina in on it, giving her the chance to apologize and explain how she'd changed, and that would give them a chance to bond."

Yael and Layla's mouths hung open, while the engineer scratched his head, Shun's glare sharpened, and P'Ken… smirked for some reason.

"Ms. Amatyn, why are you smiling?" Layla nervously broke the silence, echoing my own thoughts.

P'Ken was unphased. "However much we may disagree with the morality of her actions, and rest assured Kaya, we do, you can't deny that it was a well thought-out, clever plan. Are we sure she's Molina's and not yours, Yael?"

That wasn't the reaction I'd been expecting at all. Was it because she hadn't met Grandpa herself? Yael was the only one here who had. But maybe that wouldn't even matter. Maybe I'd overestimated how much she'd care about me killing a single person compared to everything else I'd done, regardless of who it was.

Yael shook her hair, resulting in even more fly aways than she already had. "Okay. Won't lie, kinda sad and kinda pissed. Your grandpa was a great man, and he was always good to me." She sighed. "But if that's really all there is to the story, then everything's fine. You promise you're not leaving anything out?"

I smiled, relieved. "I promise."

"Great!" Yael exclaimed, backflipping out of her seat. "Thank you for being so open."

Layla grinned and shot me two thumbs up, while P'Ken nodded at me in approval. For all the time I'd disregarded these people as criminal vermin, they'd been so kind to me that I'd somehow forgotten that they were notorious thieves who regularly worked for and with people responsible for even more deaths than me. Of course this wouldn't mean much to them. Likewise, Mother may have cared for Grandpa, but she was in no position to judge me.

But there was one person who was. One person I'd always meant to keep this all a secret from.

As everyone else got up to leave, I gasped. "How did you find out about this?!"

Their eyes all returned to me. Yael cringed, banging her fists against her legs. She'd been hoping I wouldn't think of this.

"I was talking to Moli." Fuck. "I told her about you." Fuck, fuck. "And combined with everything she's learned from her investigation, it didn't take long for her to piece together what happened."

"Fuck!" I screamed. "She wasn't supposed to know! This isn't how she was supposed to find out about me!" I bent over, panting. "She hates me, doesn't she?"

"No, no, no," Yael responded immediately, rushing over

to me. "She was surprised, definitely. She was furious, absolutely. And she was disturbed that you were made without her consent." Yael firmly grasped my hands. "But she doesn't know *you*. None of those feelings are towards you. They're aimed at the universe and Kaybell. When we get to Cykeb and introduce you, she's going to love you. In spite of everything, she will."

I easily broke away from Yael's grip and squeezed her hands instead. I needed to get some of this pain out, and she was the only one who could take it.

"My plan was working perfectly. They were the best of friends again. And now Molina's going to hate her again."

Yael grunted in pain as I cracked her bones. "She does hate her right now. And I can't blame her, either. I'd feel violated too if I were in her position." She grunted again, swearing in a language I wasn't familiar with. "But you don't need to worry. We're going to get to Cykeb in a couple days, and we're gonna straighten everything out. Okay?"

I couldn't stop panting. I couldn't stop squeezing. The louder cracks brought a sick satisfaction to my ears.

"Kaya," she moaned. "It's all gonna be okay."

"If Molina was able to forgive Kaybell for what she pulled last time," she'll be able to forgive her for this," Aarif assured me.

"She's ruled by her emotions, but her training built discipline into her," P'Ken said. "She won't do anything rash."

Layla smiled and nodded along with them, while Shun rolled her eyes. I released Yael from my grip and took control of my breath. "Okay."

"Great!" Yael cheered, bouncing. "P'Ken, please come fix my hands in my room. We'll think about what exactly to say to Molina. Shun, go help Aarif do a final check on the engines before we take off. Layla, Kaya, sit tight."

This time, I allowed them all to leave, save for Layla. Had I not experienced the power of their words firsthand, I might have continued to fear that all hope was lost and I'd ruined any chance of my family being together. But while Yael may not have had the ability to function as a polite member of society, her words could reach anyone's heart. I believed in her.

"I think someone could use a distraction," Layla said, wrapping an arm around my shoulders. "Wanna see my room?"

I sniffed. "Is it as slovenly and childish as Yael's?"

"Girl, we are children," she laughed. "But I do keep my room a bit neater." She slapped my back and moved toward the door adjacent to the ship's pitiful excuse for a kitchen. "Come on, I wanna show you my art."

"You're an artist?" I asked, following behind her, ignoring the way she'd insulted us both. "Do you also make boy band collages for your walls?"

Layla laughed even harder as we entered her quarters. "Haven't done that since I was your age."

The walls of Layla's quarters were pure white, as were the carpet, her bedding, and her desk. On its own, it would have made for a drab, lifeless environment, but all around us, on shelves, on the floor, and hanging on the wall were bright and colorful glass sculptures with a beautiful sheen. The all-white chambers only served to make them pop out even more.

Layla was as creative with her art as Aarif was with his tattoos. There was a banana tree with a family of monkeys climbing it, a Cykebian Rutal flute with musical notes coming out of it, a functioning fountain, a realistic looking T-rex fossil, and a variety of more abstract pieces I couldn't decipher at all.

I wouldn't say it out loud, but this was yet another way I was jealous. Mother was at least a musician; I didn't have a creative bone in my body.

"You made all of these? They're so pretty."

"Thanks. They're my babies."

I continued to admire the works of art around me, each of them as well-crafted as anything found in the royal palace. "This is what you want to do instead of being a thief. How anyone could look at these and think you were meant to do anything else is bewildering."

"My g-gma doesn't see any merit in *things*, only in stories. She doesn't get that this is how I *tell* my stories." Layla's eyes turned to one of the more abstract pieces on the shelf above her bed, a collection of intertwined pink, white, and sky blue shapes. "While Yael's been helping you, she's also been in negotiations with her to get me out of this life. Evidently, g-gma still hasn't made up her mind, so who knows how long I'll be waiting."

Mother had told me that Yael had studied with Molina to join the Sunrisers all through their childhoods. I'd always figured her corrupt nature was what led her astray, but the more I learned about her, the less possible that seemed. She seemed more occupied with helping others more than anything else, just like a proper Sunriser.

I'd never helped anyone in my life. And apart from attempting to bring my mothers together, which I'd partially done for myself, I'd never even tried. It was the rest of the universe's duty to cater to my whims, not the other way around. But Yael seemed to get an immense sense of joy and satisfaction out of doing things for others. It made me want to give it a try.

I ejected the katar from my right arm, startling Layla.

"Why do you have that out?" she asked, catching her breath.

"Well, I don't want to hurt innocent people anymore, but Madame N'gwa is hardly innocent. If she ends up saying "no" to Yael…" I curled my lower lip and pointed at my katar. "Eh?"

Layla grinned at me with wry amusement. Had a commoner looked at me like she did now before, I would have taken their head.

"Thanks, but I think I'll pass. I don't want her dead, just out of my way." She raised a finger and widened her eyes. "And that doesn't mean break her legs."

We giggled together. After Mother unveiled me to the rest of the universe, I'd finally get to have a few noble girls brought to the palace to serve as my companions. I could only hope some of them were as fun as Layla. I'd seriously been missing out on not getting to spend time with other teenagers.

I retracted my katar, and I turned my eyes to the abstract sculpture Layla had been admiring. "What story is that one telling?"

Layla looked at me before turning back to the sculpture. "I'm a trans girl. And a long time ago, thousands of years ago, there was a majority of people who would have had a problem with that, as opposed to the minority living on backwater planets I have to deal with now. People were imprisoned, murdered, and generally persecuted against, solely because they didn't identify with the sex they'd been assigned at birth and wanted to live their truth. This is my tribute to all of them, and a symbol of how we're allowed to live in peace today."

I'd never known any of that. Most of my studies only went back to the beginning of the Cykebian Empire, and the only groups who'd ever faced persecution within it were peasants and, in the early days, those who refused to worship Emperor Leon. The inferiority of peasants was easy to understand, but any other kind of general discrimination was completely nonsensical.

Then again, Molina was a commoner. And all the commoners I now found myself surrounded by were impressive as well, to say nothing of the entire order and the shared superpower they seemed to have. No longer torturing and killing for fun was one thing, but was I also wrong about this? Was *everything* I'd learned from my aunts wrong?

"I love it," I said.

"Thanks. I made it years ago, so there's a part of me that hates it and wants to melt it down because of how much I'd do differently now, but it'll always have a special place in my heart."

"Hmm," I smirked. "Now that you mention it, it is pretty shoddy. All of these sculptures are, actually. You really do need to get back to art school."

"Shut up," she said, mussing my hair. Weirdly, I didn't mind it. "You know, even once I'm out of here, I'll still come around to see you and Yael from time to time."

"Really? I thought you wanted to get as far away as possible."

"Well yeah… but no." She shook her head. "I hate my g-gma, my grandparents are dead, and my parents sold me out for gidgits, so they're dead to *me*. That kinda leaves this bunch of weirdos as my de facto family. Rather, this bunch, plus Molina, Griffin, and Marcos, who are also all great. When Marcos isn't being a bitchdick at least. Point is, angry and annoyed as I can get at my life, the people I've gotten to know through this torture are the best."

I looked down at my hands. They were as clean as anything could be on this ship, but I could still see the blood.

"Is that how you all see each other? As a family?"

"Kinda. Most of us don't have anyone else." Layla picked my head up by the chin and grinned. "I know you have your moms, but even if you don't want them to have shared custody, I'd say Yael is already intent on making sure you always have a home with us." She lightly punched my shoulder, not that I would have felt it if she'd gone all out. "Plus, I need someone to talk boy bands with. All my friends back home think they're trashy."

"Blasphemy!"

My aunts *were* wrong. Completely wrong. About everything. These were the first commoners I'd ever spent an extended time with, and already they'd proven to be as sweet, intelligent, and capable as Mother, if not moreso, and far beyond my aunts. I still didn't want to live anywhere except the palace from which I'd one day rule over all, but regular visits to the school could suffice.

"You don't think anyone would have a problem with me being one of you?" I asked. "Shun certainly doesn't seem to care for me."

Layla bristled. "Don't worry about Shun. No one can read her." Layla's eyes popped out of her head. "That's it!"

"That's what?" Layla grabbed my wrist and sprinted out of her room, pulling me behind her. "What are you doing?!"

"We're not done on this rock just yet!" she shouted. "I know how to break free from the Banshees!"

CHAPTER 22: MOLINA

As soon as Yael told me about Kaya, everything clicked. I'd suspected that Father's killer was either someone with something to gain from his death, someone with a grudge against him, or someone seeking to attack Kaybell by taking him out. But there was one more option I hadn't considered: this was all a set-up.

Kaybell had merged our DNA to create a daughter, but that wasn't good enough for her; she still wanted me. My ex-best friend sent her killing machine to assassinate Father, and then Yael, so that I'd be drawn to Cykeb, where she could manipulate me with her lies, and her competition would be taken out. And she specifically had Father killed because she was such a narcissist that she didn't want me to have any loved ones except her.

With the appearance of an innocent little girl, she would have easily been able to show up at Father's doorstep, pretending to sell cookies or wrapping paper, and deliver the poison into his system without arousing suspicion.

Yael agreed with my assessment that Kaya had killed Father after I shared all the suspects I'd ruled out. She was especially on board after I mentioned that Wink was my only remaining suspect, as she was evidently among those responsible for making Kaya a monster.

However, she disagreed that Kaybell was involved. Kaya had convinced her that this was all her, and that Kaybell had nothing to do with it. She told me to not do anything and to wait for them.

I couldn't do that. My wife was the most brilliant woman in the universe, but she was wrong. My "daughter" had taken advantage of her soft spot for kids and filled her head with lies, just like Kay had done to me. There was no way Yael would ever be willing to forgive Kaybell on her own.

This had the emperor written all over it. For Father, I had to take her out. "Molina, put the sword down," Kaybell said, the fear in eyes confirming all of my suspicions. "I can explain."

"Save it!" I leaped onto the table and charged across it. "Griffin, get Marcos out of here!"

Kay didn't move as I raced toward her. She was paralyzed by the knowledge that her plan was ruined. I'd spent my teenage years cutting through melons for practice, and this was going to be just as easy.

I swung my blade, the legendary Fortuna, at her neck with all my strength. It shattered on impact, while Kaybell was unscathed.

I'd forgotten about her enhancements.

I dropped the hilt of my broken blade as I fell to my knees. I was worse than average. I was worse than pathetic. I was a complete idiot. And now we were all going to die.

"G…Griffin," I stuttered, tears in my eyes and phlegm in my throat. "Why aren't you and Marcos running?"

Everyone seated at the table looked at me like I was crazy, my students included. They all thought I'd lost it. The royal family I could understand, but did Griffin and Marcos not hear what I'd said? Did they not understand I was trying to save the universe?

Kaybell, still standing, covered her mouth. This was the part where she got a haughty laugh at my expense. She'd laugh at me for my foolishness in thinking I could kill her, and about how easily she'd played me, and how I was never going to be allowed to leave Cykeb.

"Do what you want with me. But let them li—"

Kaybell interrupted me in a way I couldn't imagine was intentional as she vomited all over the floor.

"Ahhhhhh!" Jolla and Wink shrieked, leaping out of their seats and away from the table.

"What is happening right now?!" Megz questioned, equally freaked out, but still seated.

Kaybell coughed and panted as she looked into my eyes. "I'm sorry. I know that was your favorite blade."

I slammed my fists down on the table. "That's all you have to say?"

Kaybell shook her head. "I was planning on using this morning to give you a chance to apologize for yesterday. But it seems now I'm the one who has to say sorry. I understand why you'd be angry that I made her without your consent, but I assure you, she had nothing to do with Drenian's death. She's an angel."

"Yael said that's what you believe." I crawled off the table, away from where Kaybell had vomited, and glared at the twins. "But even if you're going to deny it, she told me who does know the truth."

Wink scoffed. "You're making accusations toward me *again*?"

"Griffie, are you going to let her speak to us this way?" Jolla asked.

Griffin opened his mouth, but didn't say anything. I couldn't blame him and Marcos for being so confused. They had no idea what was going on.

"What am I missing here?" Jolla and Wink squirmed as their big sister growled and glared at them as well. "Is there something about Kaya I should know?"

Between the way she spoke and the pain and fury and confusion in her eyes, I almost believed she really didn't know what was going on, and she wasn't continuing to play me.

"This peasant attempted to assassinate you mere moments ago, and you're going to listen to a thing she has to say?" Jolla questioned.

"She should be taken to the dungeon at once!" Wink exclaimed.

I laughed and sniffled simultaneously. "You're all gonna keep playing dumb, huh?"

I turned to Griffin. "Your girlfriend is still torturing and killing people for fun. Her *and* Wink. They taught Kaya, who is mine and Kaybell's daughter, and a genetically engineered cyborg, who was created without my consent or knowledge, to enjoy the same things. And she's not here right now, because she went to try and kill Yael."

Marcos snickered. "This would be a juicy story if I weren't stuck in the middle of it. Is Yael still alive?"

I nodded. "She managed to convince Kaya that what she was taught was wrong, and she's bringing her here as we speak."

I turned to Kaybell. "There's no point in denying the—"

"Our baby's a sadistic killer?" she cut me off, crying hysterically. "Like I was?" Oh no. *Oh no.*

"You really didn't know."

Kaybell collapsed face first onto the table. "She was supposed to be better than me. Better than all of us." She shook her head. "As emperor, I needed an heir. And I couldn't think of anyone better to have a child with than you. I know it was wrong. And I should have told you about her from the start. But I thought it would be best if you met her face to face. That way, you could look into her eyes and instantly love her the way I did. I didn't want any of your rage and hate toward me being projected onto her."

Yael was right. Because of course she was. I could never hope to know better about anything, not even when it came to the person I'd spent every day with for a decade, and she'd met twice.

"You say Yael saved her?" Kaybell asked. "She no longer lusts for blood?"

I nodded. "My wife's awesome like that." I bit my lip. "So she really killed my father of her own free will."

"No," Kaybell seethed. "This is not her fault." She picked herself up, motherly rage in her eyes. "Guards!" Armored soldiers burst through the doors to the dining room. Realizing the game was up, Jolla and Wink tried to flee, but they were immediately subdued by the enhanced veterans. "Take them to the dungeon to rot. I'll be with them shortly to discuss how deep their crimes go."

"No! Sister!"

"We're sorry! Please don't do this!"

"This is all wrong!" Griffin declared as they were dragged

away. "Jolla, tell them you didn't do anything!"

Jolla didn't get a chance to reply as the doors shut behind the guards.

Father's killer would never be brought to justice. She was a little girl, and, even if I wished she didn't exist, my daughter. But I'd still done what I'd set out to do. The people who turned Kaya into what she is, or maybe was, had been taken down. I may have walked in here half-cocked and braindead, but I'd still gotten the job done.

"Holy fuck," Megz muttered.

Kaybell put her hands on my shoulders, continuing to cry. "I understand if you can't forgive me for creating Kaya without your permission. And I'm so sorry I was ignorant to what Jolla and Wink were teaching her. I hope you can take some solace in my sisters being put to a stop. But even if you can't forgive me again, please, stay here and wait for Kaya to arrive. She deserves to meet you. And I truly think you'll love her." A smile peeked through her pain. "From what she tells me, she and Yael have already formed something of a bond."

Yael had told me the same thing. She'd gotten it in her head that the three of us could all raise Kaya together, and that she was exactly what the two of us needed to be happier. I didn't want that, and she wasn't what *I* needed.

But Kaybell was right about one thing. She did deserve to meet me.

"We'll continue our stay until Yael and Kaya arrive. After that? I never see you again. Am I clear?"

Kaybell nodded. "Crystal."

————

Compared to everything else, it wasn't a big deal, but losing Fortuna still pissed me off. It didn't help that I'd broken it out of sheer stupidity.

Forged by Master Ceturio Dekcon, it had seen more battle than most Sunrisers, and been wielded by at least five of the greatest swordsmen in history. When I saw it up for auction, my heart raced like it had few times before, and I spent a small fortune to acquire it. The bastard betting against me only wanted it so he could melt down the rare metal it was made from, and I couldn't let that happen. It saved my life against Galopire's Cykerdroid.

And now it was gone because I'd let my emotions get the best of me. Again.

Kaybell had acquired a vast collection of swords for herself as she'd developed an interest in the art form, and she said I could take whichever one I wanted to make up for the one I lost. It really was the *least* she could do.

There were some nice, well-crafted blades in her collection, a few of them having perfect balance and remarkably elegant hilts, but none of them possessed the same legacy as Fortuna.

Although compared to the modern weaponry they were hung up next to in the armory, they may as well have. People could call them useless antiques all they wanted; I'd seen first-hand how deadly they could still be. Of all the other people who could see that they were still valuable tools in combat, why did it have to be Kaybell?

"Professor, are you free to talk?"

I turned my attention away from an especially flimsy blade with an ostentatious hilt as Griffin came down the stairs, hunched over and with puffy cheeks.

"Of course," I said, walking over to him. "How are you holding up?"

Griffin took a breath and held it in as he clenched his eyes shut and scrunched his nose. "I thought we were in love," he said as he breathed out.

"You were. But you didn't know the depths of the darkness inside her. That's not your fault."

Tightening up again, he shook his head. "No. You don't understand. I went to see her in the dungeon. I wanted her to tell me that this was all a mistake or that Wink was the only one who was guilty." Harsh, scratchy noises came from his throat. "She told me to get lost. That she was only dating me as a joke, and I was no longer funny." His eyes dampened. "That a man being skilled at flower arranging was *lame*. That "new money" weren't real nobles." Tears escaped his eyes. "That someone like her could never love someone like me."

Jolla was responsible for my Father's murder. It was impossible for me to hate her any more than I already did. If I could, I would. I'd known she was creepy, and I'd known she was evil, but she was also a straight-up bitch.

"I'm sorry," I said. "You deserve better."

"Who could be better than a princess?" Griffin wiped his face with a handkerchief before his tears could make it far. "I'm sorry, Professor. It isn't appropriate for a nobleman to cry in public."

I wanted to tell him that being royalty wasn't everything, and that a person's heart was what mattered most. I wanted to tell him that there was a genius computer whiz who acted like the world's biggest asshole, but ultimately had a good heart who was in love with him.

But *my* heart had screwed up enough. Even if he was open to the idea of going out with Marcos, me being the one to tell him wouldn't do their relationship any favors. More than that, he'd probably be dismissive of the idea of "downgrading" from Jolla to Marcos.

"Maybe. But it's perfectly acceptable for a student to be emotionally honest with his teacher." I wrapped an arm around his shoulders. "Any of these swords look good to you?"

Griffin continued to dab at his eyes. "No. They're all pretty shoddy. Especially compared to yours."

"That's my boy," I said, slapping his back. "You know I only ever went on a single date before I got together with Yael."

"Really? Was there no one else who met your standards?"

"No, that would have been easier. The date I went on during my time at the academy with another cadet proved to me that while I may be able to feign social skills in professional situations, that ability does not extend to romantic ones."

Griffin snorted. "I can see why that wouldn't be an issue with Yael."

"Yeah," I laughed. "You're so young. Younger than I was when I gave Zanthum a shot. That heartless princess thought you didn't deserve her, but she's the one who didn't deserve you. And you have all the time in the world to find someone who does."

Griffin bent over. "I'd never been in love before. I thought she was the one."

"There's no such thing. Love is real, of course, but people are all flawed, and you never know how someone will start acting in a year or ten after you get together. I know how much pain you're in, but it's better this happened now, rather than down the line." I tightened my grip on him. "You're going to find someone who loves you and all your unique quirks. And you're going to love them just as much."

More scratchy noises from Griffin's throat, a deafening wail following after them.

Griffin wrapped his arms around me as he cried into my shoulder. "I am a real noble. And flower arranging is cool. Right?"

"Of course," I said, stroking his back. "Of course."

I didn't want to be a mom. I wasn't ready to be a mom, and it wasn't what I needed at this point in my life. But while my time as a teacher hadn't been fulfilling for me, it had at least given me practice with kids. When I did want to be a mom, and when I was ready, I was going to be the best mom possible.

"Professor?" "Yeah?"

"Are you and Yael all right?"

I wrapped my arms around him and pulled him in closer. "I'll always love her. But I don't know."

CHAPTER 23: KAYA

"Have you ever had a boyfriend?"

"Boyfriends, girlfriends, *and* non-binary partners," Layla answered. "Everyone at my school wanted a cheerleader."

I turned my head to Yael. The three of us were walking briskly to Madame N'gwa's ship before she left the worthless rock we'd spent the past several days on. Layla was so excited about her idea that she wanted to run, but I'd vetoed that idea, and told her to instead call ahead. Running led to sweat, and sweating was gross and common.

Was it wrong to still refer to certain things as common? No. Just because commoners and nobles were more alike than I thought didn't mean there weren't certain traits and behaviors associated with each group.

"What about you? Were you ever with any boys?"

Yael laughed without turning to face me. "In first grade, I gave Moli a candy ring with our initials carved into it, while wearing one of my own, and said that by eating them, we'd be best friends forever." She looked up at the planet's interminable night sky. "No, I was never with anyone else."

I stuck my hands in my shorts' pockets and scratched my legs, the shoddy material they were made from still itching intensely. P'Ken couldn't finish my new dress fast enough, and I could only hope it met my standards.

"What about P'Ken? I'd be shocked if Shun ever had a boyfriend. She's way too intense. And has way too muscular thighs."

"Why are you so curious?" Layla asked.

I kept on scratching myself. "A wise princess knows when she must seek counsel and I… I really don't know how to talk to boys."

"But didn't you say—?"

"Lying! Duh! And my moms can't help. Mother only ever had eyes for Molina, and Molina only ever went on a single bad date with a guy. I definitely don't wanna talk to my aunts right now. So, in exchange for me helping you with this, perhaps you could teach me to control boys?"

Layla stuck her tongue out and bit down on it. I'd said something wrong again. Dammit. "I can teach you how to *talk* to boys, get them to like you, and be a good girlfriend."

I pulled one of my hands out of my pocket and scratched my neck. "I suppose that will suffice. "Controlling" them does sound a little amoral, doesn't it?"

"What?" Layla laughed. "No. Controlling boys is half the fun of going out with them. That's just an advanced lesson is all."

I giggled. "Cool."

Yael abruptly stopped walking as we reached the Banshees' campsite. Madame N'gwa was waiting for us by her single-passenger ship, which looked to be an older model of my own.

"I can't do this," Yael said. "This is a mistake."

Layla and I ceased moving as well. "Come on, Professor, this is going to work."

"With everything I've seen and heard about you, I can't fathom why you're afraid of a bunch of old ladies," I said.

Yael yanked on her hair. "These old ladies are my sisters and my heroes. And I'm about to make them hate me."

"What's this about *hate?*"

Madame N'gwa had noticed us and was slowly walking toward us. Even if she was a genius with superpowers, she was still wrinkly and her bones were still weak. Old people were so gross.

"Ah, Princess Kaya, I was hoping Yael would change her mind about introducing us," she continued, standing across from us. "I am Madame N'gwa, chairwoman of the Order of the Banshee."

At least she had the decency to use my title.

"I apologize for nearly killing you all. Yael is helping me work on that."

She cackled. "Oh, sweet child. We were never in any danger."

"Phh, yeah right. I was just playing around. When I got serious, you wouldn't have stood a chance."

Madame N'gwa's eyes freakishly bulged out of her head. "Yael is an amateur with the power of The True Adventurer, and she still managed to injure you. Imagine what thirty *masters* could have done."

Her words and the confidence behind them sent a chill down my spine. I could maybe understand why Yael was afraid of her. I needed to acquire this power they had for myself. With it, no one would be able to stand against me.

"We can think about that later," Layla said. "Introducing you two isn't actually why we're here."

Madame N'gwa groaned. "If this is regarding the status of your training, Yael and I are still discussing the matter. Speaking on your own behalf right now will only harm your cause." She sharpened her eyes and pointed them at Yael. "Your teacher should know this."

Yael bounced on her feet and shook her hands as her stomach rumbled, and strange noises escaped her mouth. She'd mentioned wanting to bring one of her toys to keep her focused, but I'd told her she needed to appear strong. Perhaps I'd underestimated the depths of Yael's social ineptitude.

"Well… you see… the thing is… Madame N'gwa…"

"We're done playing your game," Layla spoke up before Yael could embarrass herself any further. "We make the rules now."

The greatest thief in the universe raised an eyebrow and smirked. "Is that so? Yael?"

"Ummmmmmmm."

I sighed. The second-hand humiliation was palpable.

"What she means to say is that she will no longer be tutoring Layla, and Layla will be returning to art school, with my mother granting her a full pardon for her crimes."

Madame N'gwa burst out laughing again. "And what, sweet little princess, makes you think I'm going to allow that? I do not fear you, nor your empire."

I imagined taking out my katars and vivisecting her, but I managed to keep the thought in my head. It still put a smile on my face, though. She had no right to speak this way.

"Of course you don't," Layla said. "You fear nothing."

Layla, to her credit, was doing a far superior job of handling herself than her mentor. Her posture was flawless, her head was held high, and she spoke clearly. P'Ken evidently lived up to her family's legacy as an instructor.

"Or at least, that's what you want people to believe," she continued. "But you wouldn't have done all this to me if you weren't afraid of one thing. You're terrified that you won't have a legacy."

Madame N'gwa shook her head. "False. I'm not afraid of that, because I have you. And you've yet to present to me any reason why I should be concerned with you not fulfilling your destiny."

Layla and I smirked at each other, before looking back at our overly arrogant adversary. "Your strength is your weakness," Yael blurted out, choking on the words.

"What she means to say is that you've trusted her with your secret weapon," I said. "And as the most recent victim of its power, I can safely say it's as dangerous as it is because I didn't see it coming."

"But if you don't let me walk away, I'll make sure *every-one* finds out about the power of The True Adventurer. You can either face your fear and give up on me, or you can take on something you never even thought to fear: defeat."

Madame N'gwa's smile disappeared in a flash, replaced by a harsh sneer.

Layla had conceived this plan after mentioning that Shun was difficult to read. She'd realized that was part of what made her seem intimidating to me, and that led her to the epiphany that if the universe was aware of the Banshees' secrets, no one would ever fear them again.

I wasn't actually intimidated by Shun, not when I'd already trounced her twice. I was merely skeptical of her acceptance. Still, while Layla may not have wanted to be the next

Madame N'gwa, she definitely had the brains to be.

"You're playing a dangerous game, children," she spat. "Yael, are you actually prepared to betray your family like this? To betray *me* like this?"

Yael pulled her head down to her chest, before launching it back up, like a turtle unsure whether it should hide in its shell. She repeated the movement again. And again. And again. While she was doing this, she actually tore some hair out of her scalp. Disgusting.

"You're the one who betrayed the order," she said, sounding sick to her stomach. "The path of the thief is meant to be a path of freedom. It's not one anyone should be forced down."

Madame N'gwa seethed, breathing in through her nose. "I've never been more disappointed in a sister." She turned to her great-granddaughter. "Layla, you are making an enemy of me and the entire order. Rest assured, if you go ahead with this, I *will* see to it that you, all of you, wind up dead. I am Madame N'gwa, and I always win."

Layla got right in her face. "I am Layla N'gwa. And I'm smarter than you."

I giggled as the old bag of bones became aghast, her mouth hanging open as she repeatedly grunted.

"Very well," she said, barely able to compose herself. "If this is the game you'd like to play, then so be it. Yael, I hope you know what this means for you."

Yael shook her head. "You don't have the authority to unilaterally kick me out of the order. You'd need to hold a vote, and you may have been able to convince everyone that Layla needed to be a thief, but I'm their sister. They won't kick me out."

Madame N'gwa clicked her tongue. "This is what I get for opening my arms to a youth. You're so naive. We are sisters, but there is still a hierarchy to these things. You have always been at the bottom, and I have always been at the top. In this order, my word is law."

"Just like cheer squad," Layla, pissed off, whispered.

Yael clenched her hand around her eyes. "This isn't what the order is supposed to be. This isn't what I dreamed of."

"Childish fantasies rarely match reality." Madame N'gwa turned around and walked away. "All of you best watch yourselves."

As her mentor paced further away, Yael's hysteria intensified. She wailed and cried at the top of her lungs as snot flew out of her nose and her knees buckled under her. Was this how degradingly I'd presented myself this morning? There had to be a more dignified way to let one's emotions out.

"By the gods. What have I done?"

Layla wrapped her arms around Yael. "The right thing. Thank you so much, Yael."

The smile I'd helped put on Layla's face made my heart more full than any kill ever had.

There was no comparison.

"Oh gods, oh gods, oh gods," Yael repeated. "My dream is dead."

"Come on," I said, hooking my arm around hers and helping her stand. "Let's get out of here."

Yael groaned for a solid minute straight as we walked back to *Ricochet*.

———

At last in the sky, it would only be four days before we arrived on Cykeb. After three months, I'd get to hug Mother again, sleep in my own bed, and ride Reaper on my private trail.

Maybe I'd change her name. I was going to be revealed to the universe and be worshiped the way I deserved to be, and, most importantly, I was going to finally meet Molina.

That was the plan at least. But I couldn't wait that long. I had to apologize at once.

"I love it!" I exclaimed, twirling around in my new golden-yellow dress. The fabric was divine, the color was exactly what I'd hoped for, and it had just the right amount of frills. "You should have your own fashion line."

"I make enough gidgits doing what I love," P'Ken said. "But thank you."

I spun around and smiled down at Yael. She was lying on the floor of the main area of *Ricochet*, still out of it, while Juri licked her face.

"Do you like it, Yael?"

She moaned like she'd been doing for hours. "You're beautiful. Just like your mother. *Mothers* if I'm being honest."

"Speaking of, I was hoping we could call Molina," I said. "I think it will be easier for her when we arrive at the palace if we've spoken first. And hopefully, it'll drag you out of this embarrassing slump."

Yael didn't get up, but she did scratch Juri's neck. "P'Ken, what do you think?"

P'Ken slammed her cane down on the floor, and I was sure to shoot her a pout and puppy dog eyes before she answered. Adults couldn't get enough of them.

"I believe that would be for the best," P'Ken said, almost smiling.

"All right then." Yael sat up and cracked her muscles. "I'm not up to making any decisions so sure, let's do this. P'Ken, some privacy please."

P'Ken did as she was told and went upstairs to her room, while Yael got up, seemingly cracking every muscle in her body. Even without her enhancements, she was probably still ridiculously strong. I'd never spent time in a gym, and I never would.

While Yael dialed Molina on her watch, I took her hand and clenched it, trying not to crush it again. "She'll love me, right?"

Yael did her best to clench my hand back. "You bet."

A few moments later, Molina's face appeared. It wasn't meeting her in person and being held in her arms, but it was still more than looking at Mother's photos. She was here. And I could talk to her.

"Hey, baby," Molina said, weakly smiling. "Is everything okay?"

Her eyes widened as she noticed me. I smiled back at her. "Oh. Hi."

I stood firmly with my hands clasped in front of me. She couldn't see how scared I was.

A princess didn't show fear.

"Hello, Mother," I said. "Is it all right for me to call you that?"

She hesitantly nodded. "Yes. Yes, that's all right."

She was more relaxed around me than I'd expected. Maybe she really didn't blame me for what I'd done.

"Moli, meet Kaya. Kaya, Moli." Yael put an arm around me. "I know you were planning on meeting in person, but we both really wanted to talk to you."

Molina's smile faded, replaced with a skeptical leer. "I ask again: Is everything okay?"

Yael laughed with pain in her voice. "Well. I kinda got

myself kicked out of the Order of the Banshee helping Layla."

"Oh no."

"Yeah, I'm in too much pain to even drink. It's real bad."

Molina's eyes softened. "I'm so sorry, baby. I'll do everything I can to make you feel better when you reach Cykeb." She gently smirked. "Things we can't talk about in front of Kaya."

"Hey, I'm old enough to hear about sex." I hung my head and pouted. "I just don't want to hear about you two having it."

The two of them laughed. I'd made Molina laugh. Thank the gods, I wasn't messing this up.

"How are things on your end?" Yael asked. "You keeping your cool?"

"Of course," she answered, expanding her lips into a full smile. "I was a Sunriser captain after all. I know how to stay in control of my emotions." She smiled directly into my eyes. "Kaybell's told you all about me. You wanna tell me about yourself?"

I giggled with glee as I puffed up my cheeks, blood rushing to my head. I'd been preparing what I was going to say if she asked me that for over a year, and I'd been editing my answer in my head all day.

"Words cannot express how sorry I am ," I began. "My aunts twisted me and made me think violence and death were the answers to my pain. But I swear by the heavens, I'm not going to be that person anymore. You may not have wanted me, but I am going to be everything you could ever want in a daughter. I'm smart, I'm strong, I'm well-mannered, and I just discovered how good it feels to help others. When I'm emperor, I'll use my power to help everyone. Just like I know you'd want me to." I swallowed. "I'd also love to learn about swords from you."

Molina bit down on her lip. It looked like she was going to

draw blood, but she relaxed her teeth before they broke through.

"I put many bad people away in prison when I was a Sunriser," she said. "I had to talk to a lot of them and get to know them to extract information. And I can tell just from seeing you here that you're not like them. You're a good girl who was misled into making some bad mistakes." She sniffled. "There's a part of me that wants to hate you. But I can't. I couldn't ever. The people truly responsible for my father's death are going to rot in a dungeon. And that has to be good enough for me. That has to be enough justice." She took a quick breath. "You sound wonderful. And I don't know if I'm going to be everything you've imagined me to be, but I'm going to try my best to be there for you."

I didn't want to cry anymore, more than enough tears had been spilled today, but I couldn't stop myself. My mission hadn't gone the way I'd planned. It had gone even better. After only having one incredible mother for so long, now, I was going to have three.

Yael wiped my tears with her thumb. "It sounds like you've worked some things out since this morning."

Molina raised her head. "I'm so glad you called. You weren't the only ones who needed a pick-me-up."

DEET DEET! DEET DEET! DEET DEET!

"You'll have to give me the details later," Yael said, turning off the beeping from her watch. "Sounds like we've got trouble." She smiled even wider than I had, with as much affection as Mother had ever looked at me with. "Losing the Order hurts me worse than anything has in a long time. But as long as I have you, even at long distance, that's all that matters. I love you, Moli."

Molina looked back at her with the same extreme devotion. "I love you, too. And I'm looking forward to loving you as I tell you all about swords, Kaya. Now go kick some ass."

Molina's image faded away as the call ended and the beeping from Yael's watch resumed. "She's perfect," I said.

"Yeah. She is." Yael wiggled her eyebrows. "Now let's go see who picked the wrong enemies."

CHAPTER 24: MOLINA

The last thing I thought I'd want tonight was to speak to Kaya. I'd imagined introducing myself to her, and listening to her introduce herself would bring out all my worst impulses and make me screw up for the umpteenth time.

It wasn't like that at all though. Looking into her big, cerulean eyes, and seeing that she unmistakably had my hair, nose, and lips, I was instantly transfixed. This was the girl who'd killed Father, but she was also unmistakably my daughter. I'd thought I didn't want to be a mother yet, but hearing her enthusiasm and witnessing her love and desire for affection, my heart changed directions. I wanted to watch her grow, help make her the better person she wanted to be, and teach her every last thing there was to know about swords.

Of course, if I wanted to be a part of her life, that meant I'd have to be willing to tolerate Kaybell. And I wasn't sure how to do that.

Making use of the sterile, barely touched royal gymnasium, I practiced my kata. None of Kaybell's swords met my standards, but training was still the best way to clear my head.

I'd grabbed the most adequate blade available and spent the past several hours in peace and solitude.

Yael was seemingly ready to make nice with Kaybell, despite the horrific torture she'd put her through. What she'd done to me was completely different, but was it worse? If Kay had turned out to be lying about everything and she and Kaya were evil monsters, the answer would be obvious. But Kay had truly changed, and only made one terrible choice in a moment of weakness, and Kaya was the victim of the true monsters in this family.

Maybe, so long as she understood what she did was wrong and learned from it like she had her past mistakes, I could forgive her. In time.

That left the matter of what I was going to do after Yael and Kaya arrived. I wanted to be a mother to Kaya as much as I wanted to stay with Yael, but neither of those paths would lead to filling the hole in my heart. How could I balance everything?

To try and balance my soul, I balanced myself in the air with my sword plunged into the floor, my legs held high, and my toes pointed. It had taken me years to get this right, and pulling it off always put me at ease.

The ear-piercing sound of Griffin and Marcos scream-ing "Professor!" at the top of their lungs from outside the gym threw me off balance, and with the same level of ease my heart had found, I fell over onto my face, bumping my forehead against the thankfully padded mat.

"Dammit," I groaned, rubbing my head as Griffin pushed Marcos into the gym. "What is it?"

The kids stood and sat over me, respectively, glaring at each other.

"Platyperson hacked my tablet and replaced all my photos with pictures of Jolla," Griffin declared. "Not only do they know how much I was hurt by this morning's events, but so many precious memories I'd captured are now lost. My first modeling championship, my array of fabulous bouquets…" He sniffed. "My prototype gentleman thief outfit."

"Posh boy's whining over nothing," Marcos said with zero sympathy. "It was a harmless prank, and I told him I could bring all his photos back whenever I want. Although I've seen that prototype costume, and he'd be better off without anyone else being able to see it."

"It has sentimental value, you unruly gremlin!"

"It was a gaudy mismatch that made you look even dumber than you are. And that's saying something."

I clenched my forehead and stood up as their bickering caused a ruckus in my ears. I couldn't take this any longer. These weren't my children, they were my students. Yael may have considered us one big, happy family, but I'd served on enough ships to know the difference between feeling like a family and really being one.

If these two kept going at it, I was going to lose my mind. Marcos could hate me if they wanted to, but I was putting a stop to it.

"By the gods, maybe I should propose to Prince Megz. I haven't spent too much time with him, but anything beats spending more time with you."

"Oh yeah, have fun getting the shit beaten out of you while you get fucked."

"I was joking!"

"Sorry, couldn't tell. You aren't wearing your clown costume.”

“Enough!” I shouted with the same great volume they’d been using. “By gods, that’s enough. Griffin, Marcos is only a bitchdick to you because they’re in love with you, and they’re emotionally constipated.”

That shut them up. Griffin continued to stare at Marcos, now wide-eyed, while Marcos directed their venom toward me.

“You’re dead, Professor,” Marcos growled.

“Wait,” Griffin said, knees trembling. “You mean she’s telling the truth?”

Marcos cast their eyes down and swore under their breath in at least four different languages.

“It seems like you two have a lot to talk about,” I said. “You should go do that. Elsewhere.”

Griffin continued to stare out into space, bewildered, while Marcos picked their head up and tapped their fingers against their chair’s armrests.

“You’ve had a long day,” they said. “I get that, and I feel for you. But that’s no excuse to break my trust.”

I picked up my sword and rested it on my shoulder. “And not being able to spit out your emotions isn’t an excuse to be a bully.”

Marcos shook their head as Griffin regained his senses and took hold of Marcos’s chair’s handles.

“This better not be a trick,” he said as he turned them around and walked back the way they’d come in.”

“Oh, this would be so much easier if it was.”

I sighed as they exited the gym. With them gone, I could get back to focusing on myself. I wasn’t a selfish person, but right now I needed to be my priority. I needed continued peace and solitude.

Kaybell didn't get that memo.

Mere moments after my students departed, Kay sauntered into the gym in a conservative black and silver nightgown, pursed lips mixed with a smirk on her face.

"Griffin and Jolla would have had the most adorable babies, but I think those two work better together."

I turned away from Kaybell as I resumed my kata. "I apologize for my outburst earlier. And I appreciate you not hesitating to punish your sisters."

Kaybell stepped toward me in her heeled slippers. "I didn't mind the outburst. It was deserved." A soothing, crackling feeling coursed through me as Kay wrapped her arms around me from behind, resting her head on my shoulder. "Captain Asparago would have had your head if you'd pulled that on her."

I halted my sword swings once again and sheathed the, in truth, completely inadequate and dull blade. "That's *General* Asparago, now."

"Different title, same hardass." I looked down at Kay's dainty hands on my waist. Yael's were strong and always on the move, while hers were delicate, but sturdy. "Yael called again earlier. She introduced me to Kaya."

"Did she?" Her grip tightened ever so slightly. "What did you think of her?"

I took Kay's soft hands and removed them from my sides as I turned around to look her in the eyes. The only difference between hers and Kaya's was that Kay had had the color changed.

"I don't know how I would have felt if I'd met who she was yesterday. But the girl I spoke to today is an angel."

"My thoughts exactly." Kay looked away from me, cringing as much as she'd ever let herself. "Did you mean what you said earlier about never wanting to see me again once you left Cykeb?"

I bobbed my head up and down a few times. "Yes. But I changed my mind." Kay looked back at me with wide eyes. "Don't get the wrong idea. I'm still fucking pissed at you. But I've forgiven you before and I'm forgiving Kaya now. And for her sake, we can't be enemies. So you get one more chance. No more."

"That's all I'll need," she said, softly laughing and grinning. "Thank you."

There were any number of ways Kay could betray me again. She could keep me from leaving Cykeb, she could have her army kill Yael so she'd have me all to herself, and with how physically strong she'd made herself, it wouldn't take any effort on her part to force herself on me again.

Maybe I was a fool to place my trust in her once again. I'd shown myself to be an idiot today already. But trust was nothing except educated faith. And there was no one more educated about Kaybell Bythora, and who more strongly wanted Kaybell Bythora to be a good person, than me.

"You know," Kay giggled. "I've thought about how this would all go for years. I imagined every possibility, or so I thought. And among them, there was one I was truly hoping would play out. A fantasy you can call it."

"Aren't we getting a little old for those?"

"Hush. I for one plan on celebrating my fourth consecutive 30th birthday next year." She choked up. "I imagined unveiling Kaya to the universe and allowing everyone to bask in her presence. You'd notice the resemblance between the two of you and you'd come to confront me about it, without Yael. I'd welcome you with open arms, explain to you the circumstances of her birth, and, over an extravagant meal, I'd introduce the two of you. She'd rush into your arms, you'd hold her, and you'd be as instantly in love and protective of her as I was."

She covered her eyes as her voice weakened. The hand she'd placed on her face trembled, while the other tightened around the silk fabric of her robe.

"You'd be torn between staying to help raise her, and returning to your wife," Kay continued. "But I'd convince you to stay. Even without catching up this past week, I knew you'd never be satisfied playing second fiddle as a thief. More a wife than anything else. So I'd offer you a job. The role of my chief advisor. Your heart changed mine, and it would continue to keep my conscience in check. To make sure I never gave into the nobles who hate me. To make sure I didn't go too far in the coming war. To make sure I didn't revert to who I used to be."

Kay removed her hand, revealing her now red and puffy eyes.

"You'd choose to stay, remaining in a long-distance relationship with Yael. But slowly, over time, you'd realize what a mistake you'd made. You'd see that your soulmate who you were destined to meet that day at academy orientation was right in front of you. You'd leave Yael, but remain the best of friends with her, while the two of us would be married. And we'd be the happy family Kaya deserves."

My face burned. It didn't take long for the heat to trickle down through my blood and flare up every other part of me. If we were at the pool instead of the gym, I'd have jumped into the deepest end, and if there was an ice bath set up, I'd go in head first.

"That's… certainly a fantasy."

Kaybell rubbed crust out of her eyes. "Yes. It is. Here in

reality, I do still love you, but I'd never want to come between you and Yael." Her vermillion lips formed a small smile. "But also here in reality, I'd like to offer you that job."

The soles of my feet burned worst of all, as if I was walking on hot coals. I had to keep stomping on them to keep the pain in control.

"The advisor job?"

She nodded. "What you've told me about how you've spent the last five years has only confirmed my suspicions. You're not happy. You're being wasted." She took my hands. For a moment, I thought they'd cool mine off, but they only further heated them up. "As Sunrisers, you were always one step ahead of me and, as such, it was my job to give you advice. Now it's time to return the favor. Together, we can win the coming war with as few casualties as possible, and unite the entire universe under the Cykebian flag. And with you to keep me in check, I won't rule like my father or Leon or any of my other ancestors. We will create a true paradise."

I hung my burning head and shook off the flames. "You have the wrong woman, Kay. I wasn't qualified to be a Sunriser, and I'm sure as Hell not qualified to be a royal advisor. I'm average on a good day, and an overly emotional fool on a bad one."

Kay pressed her forehead against mine. "Let me tell you something. I meant it when I said I couldn't think of anyone with better DNA to make Kaya from. That wasn't my decade-long crush talking, but the result of months of in-depth thought and research. You've surrounded yourself with so-called geniuses. Master thieves, master hackers, prodigies. If they have made you feel like all your hard work and training and dedication, and accomplishments all mean nothing, then let me say, as someone who grew up under the thumb of the biggest of all abusive bastards: you've found yourself in a toxic environment. And you need to get out."

I pulled back, still holding onto her hands. The flames grew cold.

"My students and my friends definitely all see me as beneath them. But not Yael. She sees me the same way you do. And I don't get it. How do you both see me from so far above?"

Kay pulled one of her hands away and brushed a stray hair out of my eyes. "Because you shine."

The flames transformed into the ice I'd craved, freezing me in place. This was it. I didn't have to go on a potentially fruitless search after all. My path to completion was right here. All I needed to do was say "yes". All I had to do was fully accept Kaybell back into my heart. See the woman I'd been inseparable from for a decade, who'd been fully prepared to sacrifice her life for me, who'd changed everything about her worldview because of me, and who saw my true value.

"Molina?" Kay asked, concerned by my petrification. "Are you alright? Should I call the doc—?"

I cut her off by gripping the sides of her head and planting a forceful kiss on her lips.

Thoughts fired through my head faster than lasers.

This is amazing! I'm garbage! I love you! I hate myself! Keep going! Stop! Stop now!

Don't do this! Please, gods, stop!

Just like last time, she tasted of meat and berries. But this time, the berries were more sweet and far less sour, and the meat was well-done.

Kay pushed me away, her whole body shaking in terror.

"I… I can't do this. We can't do this to Yael."

She's right! You can't do this to Yael! You love her!

She's wrong! She can give you the life you want! You love her too!

I pressed a finger against her lips and glared at her. "Shut up, take your clothes off, and let me see your flawless body."

Kaybell hesitantly shook her head. She knew this was as bad an idea as I did. But the heart couldn't deny what it wanted. In matters of love, the brain was powerless.

Kay tackled me to the cushioned floor and did things with her tongue beyond what Yael was capable of. As she disrobed, I worked to rip my pants off.

Now, there was only one thought in my head. I was the worst person in the universe. And I was okay with that.

CHAPTER 25: KAYA

"The five brave heroes return to Takatona Village, victorious over the demonically possessed giant worms who'd threatened to wipe it out. Tired, filthy, and caked in blood, but satisfied by the results of your work, you are greeted at the village's entrance by the dozens of people alive because of you, all of them cheering your names."

"Huzzah!"

Yael and her family owned a lot of tabletop games. More tabletop games than I knew existed. They'd seemed childish to me, but Yael assured me most of the ones she owned were specifically targeted toward older players. Dungeons and Dragons 392nd edition was one of them, and to my surprise, role-playing as Mela Hronslogdl, gnome rogue, was so much fun.

"Heroes, how can we ever repay you for your great deeds?" Yael asked, doing a freakishly accurate impersonation of a frail old man.

"No payment is necessary," Aarif, or, rather, Arjun Wudaar, dragonborn paladin, answered with extra bass in his voice. "Slaying monsters and helping the helpless is what we live for."

"Arjuuuuuuuun," P'Ken, AKA Victoria Dof, half-giant fighter, moaned in a baby voice. "We haven't gotten any gold in forever. I want some shiny gold!"

Shun, AKA Pena Selatrix, human wizard, sighed, not doing anything different with her voice. "I almost got eaten. We deserve at least a hot meal."

Our dungeon master smirked at me. "What say you, Mela?"

I crossed my arms, held my head high, and prepared to speak in the most gravelly voice I could manage. "These people owe us. I say we take advantage of that gratitude and enslave the population."

The rest of the party looked at me with wide eyes filled with fear and suspicion. Aarif's looked like a deers'.

"Crap, do we need to teach you that slavery is wrong, too?" he asked in his real voice.

"No, obviously slavery is wrong," I lied. I'd gathered from everything else I'd recently learned that it was as immoral as slaughtering innocents, but I'd spent the past year fantasizing about having slaves. They didn't need to know that though. "But this is a game, and we could use the free labor to provide us with a regular source of food, clothes, and supplies."

"Doesn't matter if it's a game," Aarif said. "Right, Yael?"

"Right, enslaving people is always wrong," she said. "But it is still an option for the party."

"We're heroes," Aarif said, half-way between his two voices. "We do what we do because it's right, and we definitely don't do things that are objectively evil."

"Oooh! I could have them mine gold for me!" Victoria

cheered.

"I'm ready to wrap things up for tonight, so whatever gets us out of here quickest," Shun said. "Sure, let's subjugate them."

"I draw my knives, get behind the village elder, and put my blades to his throat," I said eagerly. "Sir Arjun, tell them all how they can thank us."

Aarif desperately looked at each of us, Shun indifferent and P'Ken with gold in her eyes, before looking at Yael, who simply shrugged.

"Fine. We enslave the population."

"Huzzah!"

Layla laughed as she walked in from the kitchen, a particularly foul-smelling sandwich in her hands.

"I walk out of one session to grab a late dinner, and the party goes from lawful good to neutral evil. Amazing."

Aarif buried his face in his hands. "I've broken my oath. I'm a sham of a paladin."

Yael patted him on the back. "We can always reset things after Mela leaves the party."

"But the shame will never go away."

The horrid scent of Layla's meal only intensified as she sat down and bit into it. I leered at her. "What is in that sandwich?"

"Peanut butter, hazelnut, and potato chips," she answered, sickening my stomach. "Coach never let me eat these as a cheerleader, and P'Ken never let me eat them as her student, but now I'm free. I can make you one later if you want."

"Thank you, but I think I'll pass," I hissed.

Layla shoved her sandwich in Shun's face. "Hmm?"

Shun glared at Layla's abomination with the disgust it warranted. "I'll stick to yogurt."

Layla shrugged and stuffed the sandwich back in her face. "More for me."

Yael leaned back, kicked her feet up on the table, and looked at her watch. "All right, as soon as you're done eating, you three are heading to bed. We've got a big day tomorrow."

I nodded excitedly as I stood up. My stay on *Ricochet* had been more enjoyable than I ever could have imagined. Yael knew how to have a good time *and* thoroughly humiliate bounty hunters and pirates, Layla was the best friend I could have asked for, Juri was the best dog in the universe, and even Shun had stopped being so stand-offish; she was our party's quiet but loyal sorcerer.

In spite of all that, this could only ever have been a temporary arrangement, and returning to the palace was the only acceptable path for me. As nice as the dress P'Ken had made for me was, it was still only a single dress. I looked forward to never having to wear the same thing twice again.

"We're gonna miss you so much," Layla said, setting her sandwich down and hugging me. "Right, Shun?"

Shun joined us on our feet rolling her eyes. "I suppose you haven't been as annoying as certain other people Yael's had me live with."

"That's Shun for she's gonna miss you," Aarif followed up.

I hugged Layla back, holding back nearly all of my strength so I didn't break her spine. "I'll miss you all too. You're certainly better than my real aunts and uncle."

Yael snickered. "No need for everyone to get so sappy. This won't be goodbye for long. Now come on, get ready for bed. Aarif, grab *us* some beers."

"On it!"

As Layla and I pulled away from each other, we performed the secret handshake we'd come up with, consisting of flipping our hair, bumping our fists together, wrapping our pinky fingers around each other's, clapping our hands three times each, and flipping our hair again.

"Good night, everyone. And thank you again for everything."

"It was our pleasure," P'Ken said. "Except for the parts where you maimed us."

Aarif returned with an armful of beers for himself and the other adults and set them down on the table.

"Good night, Kaya," Yael said. "Pleasant dreams."

I was so lucky as to have ended up trying to kill this particular band of rogues. If Madame N'gwa had been the love of Molina's life, not only would that have been beyond gross, but she likely would have shamed me for all I'd done before killing me or selling me back to Mother for a price.

Madame N'gwa may have had the highest bounty and been the leader of the Order of the Banshee, but Yael was the best there was.

Returning to her room, I changed out of my dress into a nightgown P'Ken had loaned me.

It was two sizes too large, but for sleepwear, that was acceptable.

I took a teeth-cleaning capsule, sprayed my face with cleanser, and tied my hair back, before shutting the light and crawling into bed.

The past few nights, I'd struggled to get to sleep due to the cheap sheets and mattress, and pillows that weren't stuffed with fresh feathers daily. I'd gotten used to all of that by now, but something else kept me from entering the dreaming realm.

Yael said this wouldn't be goodbye for long, but I didn't want it to be goodbye at all. I had no desire to spend any time living at their crummy little school, but they should have all been jumping at the chance to live in the palace with me. I hadn't made any such invitation, but I doubted these peasants would be so polite as to wait for one.

It just made sense. With how much Molina had calmed down when we'd talked, she and Mother had probably made up by now, and that meant Mother had most likely made the job offer to her she'd talked about a few times. Molina would be staying with us, at least as a close ally, if not as an empress. She and Yael were in love, Mother wanted to befriend Yael, and Yael had changed my life, so it was logical for her to move in as well, and bring her friends and students with her.

Layla said they were like a family, and that there was a place for me in it. But we could all be one big family.

Yael was probably already a few beers deep, but I needed to speak with her forthwith. If I was going to be well-rested for my first proper meeting with Molina, we needed to discuss this tonight.

I crawled out of bed and went downstairs, hoping to find three barely conscious, barely functional adults. Instead, I found three passed out adults, surrounded by at least twenty beer bottles.

"It is a miracle you're all still alive," I hummed. I nudged Yael, trying to wake her up. "Yael, we need to talk."

"Blaaaaaaah," she moaned. "Not the vegetable forest. I hate vegetables."

I didn't want to, but she left me no choice. I placed my hand on her back and sent a mild electric shock through her nervous system.

"Uggggh," Yael groaned, her eyes opening a little. "Kaya, I thought we were past you trying to kill me."

I smirked. "If I wanted you dead, you'd be dead. You know that." I helped her sit up straight. "There's something I need to ask you."

She went through each part of her body, one by one, cracking her muscles. "Questions. I'm pretty dang good at answering those." She slurred all her words. I'd woken her up, but she still wasn't mentally present. "I'm less good at asking other people things. Can I try on you?"

If I was going to get to my point, I was going to have to deal with drunk Yael's whims. "You may."

"Cool cool." Yael reached out for another beer, but there were none left. She turned her head to me and hung her mouth open. "Is Moli gonna leave me?"

My heart skipped a beat. "What?"

Yael laughed, falling back over onto the table. "She's been so unhappy with me. Before, the problem was that I didn't see her as an equal. Now she's mad because she hasn't gotten to act as one." She slammed her fists down. "It's not my fault she can't keep up with me. No one can. Well, except maybe you and Layla. Not the point." She looked back up at me, her eyes drained. "She's been so happy working with your new and improved perfect mother. It was bad enough when I thought we'd have to fight through long-distance, but now I have someone to compete with. What if they're already together when we arrive on Cykeb?" She reached her arms out and rested her hands on my shoulders. "What if you end up getting what you wanted?"

I took her rough hands and gently moved them off of

me. Was this the real Yael I was talking to? Underneath all her quirks, strategies, muscles, bravado, and kindness, was she as messed up as everyone else? As much as I was? Was even Mother like this deep down?

"That's not what I want anymore," I said truthfully. "I want each and every one of us to get the happy ending we deserve. Mother herself has completely accepted that she never had Molina's heart, and she has no interest in stealing her from you. So whether you and everyone else move into the palace so you can remain with Molina as she takes on the role of Mother's advisor, or you and Molina both find places in your hearts for Mother..."

I trailed off as I tried to imagine the three of them together as a polycule. Yael didn't know the first thing about royal etiquette, she probably had no interest in political power, and I wasn't sure how much time she'd need to fully forgive Mother for what she'd done to her, but maybe they *could* somehow make it work.

"She won't leave you," I continued. "I've only known you a short time, but there's no way one of *my* mothers would be so foolish as to let someone as incredible as you go. It would be as if Gianni Afrozyan confessed that he was madly in love with me, and I pushed him off a cliff. It's simply implausible."

Yael laughed again, this time clutching me in her arms as she continued to do so. She kissed my cheek. "I'm so lucky I ended up with a daughter as awesome as you."

I clenched my eyes shut as tears formed in them. She saw me as her daughter. She actually saw me as her daughter. In spite of how we'd first met, she was willing to take me in as her own. She'd met a monster, and she'd risked everything to save them.

She'd changed my life. And I was going to be the perfect
daughter in exchange. "I love you," I said, hugging her back.

Yael hummed. "Love you too, kid. Love you too."

———

I sit on the pewter and diamond throne my ancestors
have sat on for generations. My power and authority is absolute.
I am Emperor Kaya Langstone Pavnick Bythora. The universe is
mine. And it is a utopia.

Every planet is a part of the Holy Cykebian Empire.
Poverty, crime, hunger, unemployment, discrimination, and all
forms of inequality have been dismantled, ended, and/or done
away with.

It is the anniversary of my ascension. Children from
across the stars, from every world, are lined up in the palace.
Each of them a prodigy, they bring me gifts that best speak to
their home world. There are all kinds of flowers, chocolates,
fruits, and luxuries. As they're handed to me, the children thank
me for giving them the best possible universe to grow up in.

The three greatest women in the universe besides myself,
the regents, stand beside me.

They whisper in my ears how proud they are. Of my
strength, of my mind, and of my heart.

Lady Layla is like the older sister I would have wanted if
she wouldn't have stood between me and the throne. Lady Shun,
Lady P'Ken, and her are among the most trusted voices in my
royal court. Whether I'm in need of advice or desire to play a
game, they're always there for me.

Uncle Megz stands as my army's general. Of course,
there are no wars, no large-scale conflicts at all, but he stands

ready in case anyone ever tries to disturb the peace I've achieved.

Aunts Jolla and Wink are here, too. It took them far longer than it did me, but they came to understand the severity of their past sins and changed for the better. They've happily embraced the new way of things.

Aarif isn't here. He isn't a part of my court. But he is the chief engineer of my flagship.

And he'll be coming with the rest of us to the leisure world of Pom-4. We need a vacation.

The scene shifts. We're on Pom-4, all on horseback. No. Unicornback. There are unicorns now.

We ride through a beautiful meadow with flawless green grass as the sun shines down on us. The sky is a brilliant orange. We are joined by all five members of EZ Street, who've all attained immortality and haven't aged a day since I was twelve. Jamal is particularly good with his unicorn.

Arriving at our picnic spot, the unicorns evaporate into sparkles, waiting to be called upon again. EZ Street performs a private concert for us, but mostly for me, as I munch on some of the fruits and chocolates I was gifted, along with my ox hearts, my favorite treat of all.

When they're done performing, they evaporate into sparkles as well. I'll call them again when it's time for bed.

Mother and I pour glasses of wine, while everyone else has a beer. Yael has changed and learned so much and become a proper royal, but she remains a functioning alcoholic. I wouldn't want her any other way.

Layla shows off her most recent, exquisite masterpieces on her tablet. With the universe at peace, art has never been more valuable. Molina and I enjoy a duel. She knows I long ago surpassed her, but she still has fun. This inspires Yael and Shun to spar. I still hate fighting, but watching other skilled fighters engage in combat is enjoyable.

The sun sets and the sky turns purple. The day couldn't get any more perfect. But then it does. Juri runs up to us. She's immortal as well. And she's part unicorn now.

She licks Aarif's face first. He's the least important member of my family, but he's still her favorite. I'd never forget the touching story of how he saved her. She licks Yael next. Then P'Ken. She greets the rest of us one by one, before she furiously licks my face.

I run my hands through her fur as I kiss her back. She's the best.

To think, my life could have gone completely differently if I'd been a more successful killer. I wouldn't have my family, in fact, most of them would be dead, I'd be a vicious, bloodthirsty monster, and the universe would be a darker place.

Mother and I may have been directly responsible for all the good we'd done, but none of it would have been possible without Yael. The nobody daughter of pickle people who didn't consider herself a hero had saved the universe.

And that was the coolest.

"Isn't she the coolest, Juri?" I asked.

Juri barked as her eyes glowed red and her unicorn horn disappeared. Then everyone else disappeared as the sky turned black. I could only begin to scream as Juri leaped onto my face and bore down on it.

I couldn't breathe. "Ahhhhhhhhh!"

I woke up in a cold sweat, screaming into my pillow, still unable to breathe. The pillow was being pressed down on my face and smothering me. A bounty hunter or pirate must have snuck aboard the ship.

I wanted to push my attacker off of me, but I couldn't move. I couldn't move at all, and I didn't understand why. My arms, legs, and weapons just weren't listening to me. I couldn't even sit up. Was there a drug powerful enough to shut me down completely?

"Yael!" I screamed, muffled by the pillow. "Yael! P'Ken! Layla! Shun!" I coughed heavily into the pillow. "Someone please help!"

No one came. Of course no one came, because no one could hear me. I tried moving my arms again, but nothing happened. With each passing second, my mind grew foggier and my screams grew more desperate.

This couldn't be happening. Not now. I'd just seen my future. The future that had to happen. I had to make it happen.

For my mothers, for my old family, for my new family, and for the universe, I couldn't die such a meaningless death, and especially not here and not now.

I screamed as loud as I could, praying to the gods that someone would hear me. Then everything turned black. Green text scrolled down by eyes.

REBOOTING

REBOOTING REBOOTING ADAPTION COMPLETE

A full power electric blast fired out of me as I came back to reality, still screaming at the top of my lungs. My attacker was blown back through the wall of the ship, as the pillow flew out of their hands, and my electricity made the lights flicker on and off.

Sitting up, I gasped for air. Thank the gods for Mother. She'd thought of everything when designing my cybernetic parts. Even if a drug was strong enough to affect my organic parts, my cybernetics would protect me. And if anything was capable of hurting me, of killing me, my body would always adapt before I kicked it. It would have been nice if I'd known I had that power before so I wasn't scared for my life, but she likely didn't want to scare me with the idea of anything being able to bring me so close to death.

I took the biggest, longest, breath I'd ever taken as I got out of bed. Torturing and killing innocents was wrong. But this bastard had just tried killing their princess. I was going to cut into them and make them scream so much louder than I had. I'd make them tell me how they were so deranged as to pointlessly murder a teenage girl in her bed.

I looked down onto the ship's first floor to find my attacker. And I immediately stepped back and looked away.

"No."

"What the Hell is going on?!" Yael shouted, running onto the scene.

"Is everyone ok?"

"The... the plan didn't work Yael," Shun twitched on the floor, paralyzed.

No. No, no, no, no, no. This couldn't be happening. This couldn't be real. This had to be a nightmare. Oh gods, no, no, no, no.

"Kaya!" Yael called out. "Kaya, what happened?"

I stepped forward and looked down over the banister. Still breathing heavily, and with tears and snot consuming my entire face, I popped out my katars.

"You promised."

CHAPTER 26: MOLINA

Kaybell was always peaceful in her sleep. At least, that was how it seemed from the four nights we'd spent together. Being able to sleep through the night in her strong arms, the strongest in the universe, without being woken up once, was refreshing.

After the passion driven, wild and primal experience that had been exploring each other's bodies on the floor of the gymnasium, I'd tensed up a little once we'd moved to the bedroom.

Partially because there was still a voice in the back of my head telling me to stop, and partially because, as it turned out, Megz wasn't the only member of this family who got off on hurting their sexual partners.

But as she helped me discover, a little bit of pain could mean a whole lot of pleasure.

When you were with the right person at least.

As Kay's eyes flickered open, she gently jostled her nude form against mine, the two of us only covered by a thin, fine, silk blanket. Once she was fully awake, she hummed and pulled my face into her chest. I'd never realized how impressive her breasts were before. How curvaceous her whole body was.

"Good morning," she whispered, nibbling on my ear.

"Good morning," I whispered back, taking in her warmth.

"It's a big day. Are you excited?"

"Yes. And nervous. I can't wait to meet Kaya, but saying goodbye to Yael will be the hardest thing I've ever done."

Kay pulled away from me, cringing, while still keeping me in her arms.

"What is it?"

She massaged my back as she relaxed her face. "These last few days are what I've dreamed of for so long. They've made me happier than I've ever been. But this has to stop."

"No, it doesn't," I assured her, flashing a smile. "Why would you say that?"

Kaybell took her hands off of me and pulled them into her chest. "After my actions led to losing you, I made a vow to be a better person. That didn't just mean caring more about commoners and ceasing to torture them for fun, but to change how I prioritized in different situations. I love you, and I want to be with you every moment for the rest of my life. But I'm not going to steal you from another woman. Not permanently."

"So what?" I raised an eyebrow. "You've just been borrowing me?"

She shook her head. "I've been making a mistake. One too good to resist, but a mistake nonetheless. When Yael arrives, we'll tell her that you've elected to remain here as my royal advisor, but we will mention nothing about what we've been doing, nor will our relationship continue in this form. I'm sorry. I can't hurt Yael like this. Not again."

I reached out and took her hands by force. Worry filled her eyes as I sneered at her, breathing through my nose.

"Fuck you. You think *I* want to hurt Yael? I'm her wife and I will always love her. But people change. Feelings change. And as much I love her… I love you more. And I'm choosing you." I shuffled closer to Kay as I helped her hands over to my chest. "You changed your whole life for me. That's something Yael was never able to do. You don't just see me as your equal; I'm able to act as one. We have a *daughter*. An amazing, beautiful daughter."

I paused to take a breath as Kaybell's blood red nails dug into my breasts. "For most of my life, my eyes were set on becoming supreme general of the Sunrisers. That was partially because I wanted to make Father proud, but it was also because I want to help as many people as possible. I want that *power*."

I pressed my lips against hers and allowed our tongues to dance as I tasted the ever-sweeter meat and berries. With a moan I pulled away.

"Don't make me your advisor," I said. "Make me your empress."

Kaybell shivered as her eyes popped open almost as much as Madame N'gwa's, and she hugged herself tightly.

"Molina, are you asking me what I think? Don't you think that's a bit fast?"

I shook my head, grinning. "We spent every day together for a decade and we have a damn daughter. I'd say we know each other pretty well." I ran my fingers through her short hair, almost as silky as the sheets we laid on. "Marry me."

Kay continued to shiver, but as she did so, her eyes withdrew, her lips curled up, and her head bobbed up and down. She sat up on her knees, and pulled me up to mine with one firm, genetically enhanced tug.

"Yes," she said. "Yes, I'll marry you."

Moving in perfect harmony, we gripped each other's heads and kissed passionately one more time.

I would never regret the time I spent married to Yael, and I could only hope she wouldn't hate me so much as to cut me out of her life, but this was where I belonged. This was who I was always meant to be.

It was destiny.

———

After breakfast, Kaybell adjourned to the throne room to hold court earlier in the day than usual. A great deal needed to be done this morning so that she'd be free when Yael, Kaya, and the others arrived. That left me with the opportunity to take care of a piece of unfinished business.

Dressed in a flowy, sparkling silver dress with matching heels, and wheeling a bag of luggage behind me, I stepped down into the dark depths of the palace's dungeon. Three armed guards stood in place, and with Galopire having been sent to a Sunriser prison to spend the next thirty years of his life, with no chance of early release, the only ones stuck behind a forcefield were Wink and Jolla.

They'd been down here less than a week, but they were already shells of their former selves. They were covered in filth and stank as bad as Juri's shit, and they were dressed in rags, rather than the fancy clothes they'd been born in. Most notably, the rank, unearned arrogance and belief they could do anything with zero consequences that defined them had abandoned their eyes. Their lives as they knew them were over, and they knew that.

At least, Jolla did. Noticing my entrance, Wink smirked at me and wiggled her fingers. "You're not who I was expecting," she said. "But I won't say no to a visitor."

I stepped in front of the forcefield. Wink sat up straight, while her sister was curled up into a ball at her side.

"That's all you have to say to me?"

"Kaya murdered your father, not us." She snickered. "Of course, we wouldn't have minded skinning both of you alive. No matter what jobs you held, you'd always be filthy commoners."

I clasped my hands behind my back and glared back at her, remaining stoic. "It's funny you say that, seeing as I'm to be the next empress, while you'll both be lucky if you aren't sentenced to death."

Wink curled her lower lip in disgust, while Jolla finally acknowledged my presence. "You and Sister are getting married?" the latter whimpered.

"That's right." I took a step closer to the forcefield, my heels banging against the stone floor. "And you're going to tell me why I should consider showing you mercy."

Wink cackled. "Mercy? We don't need your mercy. Sister is soft. She doesn't have it in her to punish us for long-tern, let alone kill us, and she knows she's committed far more "atrocities" than we could have ever hoped to. Or has the woman you plan on marrying not shared many stories of what *she* used to do to commoners?"

"I don't need to concern myself with a past she left behind. You had the chance to do the same, and you wasted it."

"*We* stuck to our family's traditions. *We* continued to pay our respects to the great Emperor Leon, the man responsible for all we have, instead of spitting on his grave. *We*—!"

I cut her off with my sword, bashing it against the force-field, and blowing it in half in the process, the bulk of the blade flying across the dungeon. Wink shrieked in response, clinging to the wall, while Jolla continued to whimper.

"If that was all you'd done, you probably wouldn't be here right now," I said with a sneer. "But you taught my daughter to think like you. You turned a ten-year-old girl into a mass-murdering sadist. Why?"

Wink struggled to stand, her legs shaking and her muscles likely atrophied. "We did it for her own good. An emperor of the Cykebian Empire needs to be strong. Kaybell's successor especially must make up for her weakness. We taught her the natural order of things so that she would rule over all with an iron fist, and not a gentle handshake. I for one regret nothing, and if your *current* wife hadn't corrupted her, things would have gone perfectly."

I shook my head, carefully breathing in and out so that I didn't lose my temper. "Her age meant nothing to you?"

"Your ignorance is frankly astounding."

"I'm not ignorant. I'm not stupid."

"But you are! So stupid! Members of our family have always been given our first torture kits on our fifth birthday. If anything, she was late the second she was born."

This culture was beyond perverse. I'd inadvertently served it for years, going after whatever criminals I was told to, while my superiors turned a blind eye to, or actually were, the greatest villains of all. Wink was right that the universe needed to be ruled with an iron fist. It was the only way the deep-seeded corruption would ever be crushed.

Jolla's whimpers turned to speech. "We're kids too.

Practically. We're only 18. On a lot of worlds outside the empire, we're far off from being considered adults. If what we've been taught is so wrong, why does Kaya get your sympathy and another chance, but not us?"

I turned my glare to the blue-haired bitch who'd broken Griffin's heart. "You had your chance, and you wasted it."

"A chance?!" she screeched. "What chance? We were barely older than Kaya is now when Sister had her change of heart. Our heartless father still made us do whatever he wanted every damn day, denying us any and all free will."

"And then, because of you, at only fifteen, we lost *both* of our parents," Wink spat. "And of course Kaybell was so busy getting accustomed to her new position, she barely had time for us, and just told us to "be better." Judge us if you wish, but don't you dare say as much effort was put into us as you're going to give to your precious, little daughter."

Perhaps they had a point. Maybe they were as much victims of their circumstances as Kaybell and Kaya. Maybe before I clenched my fist for the good of the universe, I needed to reach out my hand one more time.

"Guards, lower the forcefield." Wink grinned and Jolla gasped at the order, but the soldiers didn't move. "Perhaps you didn't hear me, but I'm to be your empress soon. It would be in your best interests to do as I say."

That got them to follow through on my command. Being a teacher could never compare to the true authority I'd once wielded, and the unlimited power I'd soon have.

"Thank you so much, Molina," Jolla breathed, Wink assisting her in standing up. "And… despite what Wink's said, I… I think I might have done some things wrong after all. And I'd like to make things right. Starting with Griffin."

"That's very sweet." I cracked my neck. "Faces against the wall." The twins' smiles disappeared in a flash. "What?"

"Guards, aim your blasters at their heads."

Without any question this time, they did as I commanded. "What do you think you're doing?!" Wink screamed.

Maybe they deserved mercy. Maybe they deserved another chance. Or maybe they deserved to pay.

"You were right. Kaybell doesn't have it in her to properly punish you. But I do." Jolla clung to her twin. "Molina, this isn't you."

"The only thing I was ever good for was being a soldier. If you think I've got a problem killing two monsters who would have skinned me alive while laughing when I first arrived on Cykeb, then you've sorely misjudged me. Face the wall."

Wink held Jolla's hand tightly as they finally listened to me. The guards lined up, ready to execute them on my word.

"I'm glad we misjudged you," Wink said, a slight bit of smug satisfaction still present. "You might actually be a good empress."

I unclenched my hands and raised one of my arms up, ignoring her. "Jolla, do you have any last words?"

Jolla sniffled, evidently facing death in tears. "Just... please tell Griffin I'm sorry." I swung my arm down, and the guards put lasers through their brains.

"No," I said as their corpses fell over. "Clean this up. The emperor never hears about this. If she asks, you have no idea what happened to the prisoners."

"Yes, Ms. Langstone," they said in unison, performing the Cykebian salute of jutting both of their elbows outward.

While they got busy, I had one more thing to do down here. At the far end of the dungeon was a furnace. Old emperors used to toss prisoners into them when they got bored with torture. I wouldn't be burning any bodies. Kaybell would easily be able to figure out what happened, but I had something else to dispose of.

Opening my luggage, I pulled out the leather outfits I'd worn for the past five years. I'd thought that it would be a good style choice to help me embrace chaos, and that Yael would find it sexy, but I was only half right. Chaos wasn't for me. I was a warrior of order. These clothes never suited me. So into the fire they went.

I stared into the flames as I watched my clothes burn to ash, and as I did so, I wondered if Father would approve of what I'd done.

Yes. Yes, he would have.

———————

Court was wrapping up as I arrived in the throne room. Built from the same pewter and diamond as the throne Kaybell was seated on at the far end of it, the room was entirely black and silver, with the only extra color present coming from the fancy tunics and dresses worn by the nobility. Both Cykebian flags and communication monitors lined the walls. It was a cold place, and it stank of death, countless people having been executed inside these four walls.

As the nobles filed out, Kaybell was assisted in standing up by her guards. Noticing me, the dour look on her face turned upside down.

"Excellent timing," she said, approaching me, two of her

guards remaining behind her. "Yael and Kaya should be arriving within the hour."

"I can't wait," I said, allowing my hands to flap freely. "This is the dawn of a new era."

"With you at my side, no one will be able to stop me." Kaybell leaned forward and pressed her lips against mine. It was a brief kiss, but a sweet one nonetheless. "But don't think we're getting married before I issue a more formal proposal. This morning was sweet, but not up to the standards of Emperor Kaybell Kose Bythora—"

"Daughter of Stephen and descendant of Leon, first emperor of Cykeb and founder of the Sunrisers, ruler of the Holy Cykebian Empire," I helped her finish.

Kaybell laughed like she didn't have the weight of all of humanity on her shoulders. "Shall we head to the docking port?"

A glimmer caught my eye. "You go on ahead. I have to find Marcos and Griffin. I'll be quick."

Kaybell nodded and kissed me on the cheek as she was escorted out of the throne room by her guards. The only ones still present were myself and a handful of elite soldiers. And with my relationship with Kay clear for them to see, none of them would stop me from doing what I had to.

One step at a time, with all the grace an empress required, I stepped across the hard floor, my heels clacking against it. I walked up the small staircase at the far end of the room, and I stared down at the throne right in front of me.

When an empress was around, a second, less grand, less ornate throne was brought out and positioned adjacent to the emperor's. Soon, that would be my throne. I would be the second most important person in the universe. But, even if it was just for a moment, I wanted to know what it was like to be #1.

I sat down on Kaybell's throne and crossed my legs. The chair was as rough as it was priceless, jagged bits jabbing against my rear-end. It was no wonder Kay looked so uncomfortable.

Still, from this position, in spite of the pain, one could do anything. Emperor Leon may have been a mad man, but his power really was equivalent to that of a god's. We were going to be able to shape reality as we saw fit. The universe our daughter grew up in would be perfect, and no harm would ever come to her.

Entropy is chaos. We are extropy.

"Professor, there you are," Griffin said, pushing Marcos into the throne room, saving me the trouble of rounding them up. "What are you doing?"

This was the first time I'd seen the two of them together, outside of a meal, since I'd revealed Marcos' secret to Griffin. Hopefully they'd finally embraced one another. True love took the mind to another level. I'd experienced it twice, now, so no one understood that better than me.

"Thinking about the future," I hummed. "Are you all set to return home?"

"*We* are," Marcos said. "It doesn't look like you are, though."

I smiled at the kids. "That's because I'm not going anywhere. I was planning on telling you at the same time as everyone else, but I've decided to remain on Cykeb. Kaybell and I are betrothed."

"What?!" they both screamed at the top of their lungs.

"This is surely a joke, right?" Griffin asked. "You're already happily married."

"I wish I was more shocked than I am," Marcos followed.

I shook my head. "Don't think for a second my heart still doesn't beat for Yael. Telling her what's happening, and seeing the look on her face, is going to kill a part of me. But this is where, and who, I'm meant to be. As much as I may hate myself for doing this, it's the only way I'll ever be happy."

Griffin was aghast, his eyes wide and soft and his mouth hanging open, while Marcos sneered and spat on the floor.

"But... you and Yael. You're perfect together. You're our professor."

"Not anymore," I said. "You're both always free to visit, however, especially if you'd like to do some sword training. And if being a gentleman thief doesn't work out, Griffin, I'd love to have you as a member of the court. You too, Marcos... if you've gotten together."

"We're working on it," they said in unison, neither of their expressions changing.

"Well, if this is really what you want..." Griffin choked up. "Then I suppose we can't stop you."

"Speak for yourself," Marcos snarled. "I warned you what would happen if you broke Yael's heart."

"I understand you're protective of her, but this is what's best for both of us. She hasn't been happy lately either. Ask her."

"I'm sorry, *Molina,* but I know for a fact that losing you will only send her spiraling," Griffin spoke up. "She'll be destroyed, and our training will never be completed."

"Glad we're on the same page, Posh Boy."

"Naturally, Platyperson."

I sighed internally. Why did they have to make this so difficult? It was already hard enough for me, and the only thing I was clinging to was the idea that Yael would still want to be a part of my life, and that she'd help us raise Kaya. I was hurting more than they could even imagine.

"What page exactly are you on?" I asked.

"The one where if you're the empress, then we're enemies of the empire," Marcos said.

"You were always my favorite teacher, but my honor as a noble insists that I stand by Yael," Griffin followed.

I wanted these two to grow up and live long, happy lives. I'd invested too much time and energy into them to want anything else, even if I did have a child of my own I now needed to prioritize. Griffin especially, I truly cared for. And if it was only him standing against me, then I'd just have one more nail driven into my heart.

But Marcos was a different story. They were possibly the greatest computer genius the universe had ever seen. With abilities like theirs, they could be a genuine threat to the empire, and everything I sought to build. I couldn't allow this to stand.

"Very well," I said, uncrossing my legs and rising from my seat. "Guards, seize these traitors!"

On my word, the remaining guards in the throne room swarmed around Griffin and Marcos, aiming their blasters at them before slamming them down against the floor and restraining them.

"Dammit, Molina, why are you doing this?!" Griffin cried out. "This isn't you."

"I wouldn't be so sure about that," Marcos grunted. "This might be the real her after all."

I took that as a compliment. "Take them to the dungeon. Give them time to discuss their relationship and rethink their priorities."

"Molina! Don't do this!" Griffin shouted at the top of

his lungs as he was dragged away.

"You're dead!" Marcos followed. "You hear me?! Yael's gonna kick your ass!"

A moment later, I was alone in the throne room. And as much as what I'd just been forced to do hurt, and how much I prayed Yael wouldn't choose to be my enemy again, there was one thought that superseded all others.

Who's average now?

CHAPTER 27: KAYA

It was all a lie.

All the laughs, all the lessons, all the time they'd spent with me. It was all to lower my guard. They'd tricked me and manipulated me to save their own pathetic lives. They'd taken advantage of me in my moment of weakness and tried to convince me that everything I knew was wrong.

No more. I knew who I was. And it was time for them to face the wrath of a Cykebian crown princess.

"Kaya, Shun, one of you tell me what's going on," Yael pleaded so desperately I almost bought her performance.

"Raaaaah!" I shouted, leaping off the upper level of the ship and diving down at the woman who'd dared to say she loved me.

I swung my katars wildly, not focused enough to concern myself with proper form. Yael dived and ducked out of the way of all my attacks, her breath heavy enough to warm my face.

"Come on! Use your special power! Fight back!"

"That's not happening," she grunted as I managed to leave a shallow cut on her stomach. "If you tell me what's wrong, we can talk things out."

"You'd like that, wouldn't you? Talk to me so you could brainwash me and make me feel like a monster again?!"

In one movement, I retracted one of my katars and crashed my fist against her face, sending her flying and hitting the ship's metal walls hard enough to cause an alarm to go off.

"It's… no use, Yael," Shun stuttered as she struggled to stand. "She's onto us."

Blood dripping out of her, Yael stood back up too. She turned her attention to Shun for a moment before looking upstairs, and back at me, a spark in her eyes.

"She tried to kill you," she said, managing to sound genuinely horrified. "Oh gods. Kaya, I am so sorry, but I had no idea she was going to do this."

"Liar!" I shouted, opening fire with laser blasts as Yael cartwheeled out of the way.

She was a damn good actress, I'd give her that. But a performance was all this was. Shun was her student. Why would she have attempted to assassinate me if not on her teacher's order?

"What the Hell is happening?"

Aarif, P'Ken, and Juri ran onto the scene, having been woken up by the battle. I didn't want to hurt the good doggie if I could avoid it, but Yael's most trusted allies definitely needed to die.

I raced toward them, ready to cut them into a million pieces, but Shun intercepted me, managing to tackle me to the floor.

"Sorry, you little demon, but it'll take more than one blast to put me out."

I could have easily thrown off her person on my own,

but instead, she was tackled off of me by Yael.

"Are you serious right now?" Shun asked as she and Yael rose up and began exchanging blows. If I wasn't so absolutely livid, I might have been impressed by their degree of martial prowess. "You're really gonna try and pin *your* plan off on me?"

"Shut up!" Yael cried.

This was my chance. While they were busy putting on this act, I could kill them both. I raised my hands and fired lasers at both of their heads.

But something caused me to misfire: A sudden thud.

Her cane-whip in hand, P'Ken approached me sternly and without fear.

"Kaya, you must stand down this instant. Throwing a temper tantrum is not the type of behavior a princess must express."

I pulled out my withdrawn katar as my blood boiled. "A temper tantrum? That's what you think is happening? You tried to murder me!"

P'Ken's face fell as mine was partially obscured by tears. It wasn't my fault I was crying.

They'd used me, and made me think they were my friends, my family. Of course having to kill them now hurt.

"P'Ken, switch partners," Yael said, knocking Shun aside. "I'll worry about Kaya, you take down Shun. She's a traitor!"

"I'm not buying it!" I declared once more, running toward Yael, while P'Ken did her part in this performance and attacked Shun with her whip.

Beating the crap out of the woman I'd almost considered a third mom was more fun than anything else I'd done in the past few days. Each punch, kick, slice, and blast filled me with relief.

Yet as clear as it was that she stood no chance against me like this, she still didn't use The True Adventurer. She thought playing nice and continuing to lie to me was a better option than using her ace. That was a fatal mistake.

With Yael underneath my foot, I turned to see how the other fight was faring. P'Ken was skilled with her weapon of choice, I'd seen that during our previous fight, but even with her superior training, she was no match for Shun's enhancements. In the brief time my attention was turned away from Yael, she was knocked out.

"You know what?" Shun asked, charging at me. "All of you can go to Hell!"

Shun dashed around me with more speed than I'd ever seen her move with in our previous fights. Had she been holding back? Why? Was she *ten times* dumber than Kenneth Roz?!

She landed a few blows to my face with her unexpected speed, but even though she also hit harder than she had before, she had to have been hurting herself more than me. The gap between us was too great for her surprises to save herself.

As she threw her next punch, I caught her fist. I caught her next one too. And the look of fear that appeared on her face was too delicious for words.

"One blast wouldn't put you down? How about a second?"

I loaded her up with so much electricity, her hair spiked up and her skin turned crispy. It wasn't enough to kill her though. Some of these peasants would get quick deaths, but hers I'd prolong as long as possible. I was having the time of my life, and I didn't want the fun to end.

"Kaya," Yael whimpered, her face black and blue, and her body cut and bruised all over. "Please don't do this. This isn't you."

Wiping my tears away, I grinned down at her, and picked her up by her hair. "Hey dungeon master. Rocks fall, everyone dies."

I threw her as hard as I could against the ceiling, setting off even more blaring alarms. Yael was down. P'Ken and Shun were unconscious. The engineer was too afraid to move, and he knew better than to send Juri in to die. That only left...

"Kaya!"

My stomach ached as I heard a voice come from upstairs. Layla's voice. Shun was the one who'd tried to kill me, Yael was the one who'd ordered her to do so, and P'Ken and Aarif would have known what she was planning.

But maybe, just maybe, my friend hadn't betrayed me.

"Kaya, look at me," she said softly as she walked down the steps. "I don't have any gas grenade this time, and I'm not stupid enough to try and fight you, nor would I ever want to. Let's just talk."

I looked all around me as the ship's alarms continued to drum on. None of the crew's fighters would be getting up anytime soon. I had time.

"Tell me you knew nothing about this," I pleaded, more tears running down my face. "Swear to me that unlike everyone else, you care about me. Tell me you're my sister!"

Arriving on the first floor, she looked at the barely breathing Yael before looking back at me, her whole body trembling. On the one hand, if she was really my friend, then she had nothing to worry about. On the other hand, everyone in the universe would soon be right to fear me.

Layla hesitantly stepped toward me. "I have no idea what's happened here. I only know what I've been hearing from my room. I believe that Shun tried to kill you, and for that she needs to pay. Much as it pains me, I'm also willing to believe that Yael gave the order. But I had no part in this at all. You're my EZ Sister, and I'm not gonna let anything happen to you."

I wanted to believe her. I wanted to believe her so badly. But with how much of a performance Yael and the others were putting on, I couldn't tell what was real and what was fake.

"She hates me," I spat, shivering. "She hates that Molina had a daughter with someone who wasn't her. She hates Mother and can't forgive her. And so she went through all of this to try and kill me in my sleep."

Layla hugged herself. "I'm sorry. That's…that's unforgivable. But are you sure that's what happened? If Yael's guilty, I will completely support you killing her. I am on your side, no matter what. Before you do that though, you should make sure you know the truth."

I shook my head, giggling through my tears. "Such a common way of thinking. But that's not who I am, and that's more clear to me than ever. I don't need evidence. I'm a princess. I'm a future emperor. And I'm free to kill and torture whoever I damn well feel like." I continued to giggle as I reached my hand out. "It's my turn to teach you, Layla. Join me. I'll make you a noble and help you understand the way of things. My dream for the future is dead, but you can still be my lady in waiting. What do you say?"

Layla shifted around uncomfortably, not looking back into my eyes. But then she did. Not only that but she smiled, and initiated our secret handshake. We flipped our hair, bumped our fists together, wrapped our pinky fingers around each other's, clapped our hands three times each, and flipped our hair again.

"So long as you don't mind me continuing to study my craft

and submitting to competitions, I'd love to be your lady in waiting."

"Of course not!" I cheered. "You know I love your art."

"Great. So let's kill Shun and continue on our way to Cykeb. But please, for me, give Yael, P'Ken, and Aarif a chance to regain your trust. If you still don't believe them after really talking to them, I'll happily stand by you as you tear them apart."

I clenched my fists. Why did she have to make this difficult? Why couldn't she just give me what I wanted? I knew what I knew, and even if I was wrong about any of them, they were still worthless peasants.

"I... I can't." My smile broke down. "What if you're lying to me right now? What if you don't care about me and you're only trying to minimize casualties?"

"No. That's not it at all. I'm not just your sister; I'm your big sister. And I need you to trust me."

I wanted to believe her. I wanted to keep her. I didn't want *all* of this to have been a lie. But she was being so difficult. Why couldn't she do what I said? She may have been older, but I was her superior. She should have known her place. And since she didn't, it fell to me to remind her.

"I'm sorry," I said, raising my hand, and putting a laser through her chest.

She fell over, unconscious, and if I was lucky, she'd survive and learn not to question me.

"Layla!" Aarif howled at the top of his lungs.

I giggled as I turned to the only one left standing. "Abase yourself, engineer. Amuse me enough, and I might keep you as a slave instead of killing you with the others."

He breathed heavily as his whole body tensed up. A fire lit up in his eyes that he couldn't hope to follow through on.

"You… you're such a stupid little brat," he breathed. "They all saw something in you, believed in you, and this is how you repay them?! Even I was starting to really like you. I could have been your cool uncle. But I guess the apple fell too close to the tree for that to happen."

"What do you think is gonna happen here?" I continued to laugh. "Emperor Leon claimed to be a god, but I have the *power* of one."

"Maybe so." He spat at the floor. "But I refuse to let you take my family from me! Juri, cripple!"

The adorable doggie's true self rose to the surface. She had glowing red eyes, razor sharp claws, and cannons that were as large as her entire body popping out of her. Damn this unruly vermin for making me fight her, when I only wanted to hug her now more than ever.

She fired gargantuan energy blasts at me, but compared to the miniature ones I could fire from my hands, they were pitiful. All they were successful in doing was pushing me back a couple inches.

When she noticed that wasn't working, she stopped firing and tackled me to the floor. Once again, she was harmless. Her claws tore up my nightgown, but they were unable to even break my skin. They tickled more than anything else. With as little strength as I figured I'd need to put her down without killing her, I struck her jaw, knocking her unconscious and sending her flying away from me.

"Juri," Aarif whispered, dropping to his knees, all his rage and bravado replaced by fear and desperation. "No."

"Hee hee hee." I got up, walked over to the smelly engineer, and picked him up by the neck, strangling the life out of him. Helping people may have felt better than I'd expected, but this was what I was born to do. His powerless whimpers fed me.

"Hey, Yael. Open your eyes. I want you to watch me squeeze your best friend's head off."

I must have broken half the bones in her body with how hard I'd thrown her before, but somehow, she still managed to push herself up and stand, the wounds in her torso having only grown wider.

"Put him down," she grunted. "Please don't make me hurt you."

"And how do you expect to do that? Even with your special power, you only got one lucky hit on me last time."

"Yeah, well, the thing about that is…" Her eyes sharpened. "I'm a quick study."

The next thing I knew, she drove her fist into my stomach. And the pain was unreal. "What?" I snarled, struggling to breath. "How?"

An agonizing kick to the back of my head knocked me down and shook my brain around my head. This made no sense. How was she hurting me? I was invincible. I was supposed to be invincible.

My cough intensified as I felt the thick, sticky blood drawn from the back of my head.

Looking up, Yael and Aarif were nowhere near me, standing on the other side of the ship. "I need you to take everyone onto a shuttle and get out of here," Yael said to him.

"What? No. I'm not leaving you."

"Layla and Juri are dying, and we need to know why Shun did all this. Take them all and get them to a hospital."

"But what about you?"

"Sorry. I can't abandon my baby."

The two hugged, tenderly embracing one another. They really thought they were the good guys here, fighting to stop an evil monster. But this was my story. I was the fairytale princess here. And I was the only one of us who'd get a happily ever after.

"Come back to us," the engineer said as he pulled away.

"I always do," she replied with a grin.

"Not a chance!" I shouted, opening fire on both of them.

In the split second between when my lasers escaped my hands and when they would have gone through their heads, the two disappeared.

Yael had gone from messing with my mind in the traditional way to doing it with her power. She'd gone from making me see multiple versions of her to manipulating my entire perception of reality. She was taking the lengths of how far you could push the idea of "Performing multiple actions at once" to their limit.

But how was she *hurting* me?

Yael appeared right in front of me, her arms not flying toward my face, but at her sides.

Everyone else was gone.

"All alone now, Kaya," she said. "It's just us."

I leaped back, away from her. "That's fine. I don't want Layla or Juri dead anyway. Let them get the treatment they need. Hunting the others should be fun."

"You don't believe that," she said. "That's not you talking, that's your aunts. Your aunts, who I remind you, are rotting in a dungeon."

"And with one puppy dog look at Mother, I'll get them out." I clanged my katars against each other, electrifying them.

"You shouldn't have betrayed me. You could have had everything!"

"I didn't betray you," she lied again. "I get what you must be thinking. Molina didn't choose Kaybell to be her wife, and so the idea that another mother didn't want to be a part of your family terrifies you. But I swear, being your mom is *all* I want."

"Stop lying!"

I fired a massive electric blast, disabling the alarms and other parts of the ship, including the lights, as Yael blinked out of existence again.

I gasped for air as she chopped my neck, before blinking away again. My coughing intensified as I pounded my stomach.

"How are you doing this?!"

From behind, Yael put me in a headlock. One from which I couldn't escape.

"I can make your mind think I'm doing anything. That includes hurting you. I may not be able to punch sense into you, but I can trick your brain into feeling pain. And lemme tell you Kaya, I know a thing or two about pain."

From the headlock, Yael flipped me around and threw me down onto the floor with a Canadian destroyer. Even knowing what she was doing, it was still like she'd broken my back, and I was only just able to stand up.

"You're an amazing kid," she said, backhanding me with her fist across my face. "This evil person who takes pleasure in pain and death isn't you." She backhanded me again.

Everything started spinning. "Come to Cykeb with me. We'll find Molina and Kaybell. We'll take care of you. And we'll raise you into the emperor you were born to be."

With a final kick to my jaw, I fell over again, and I couldn't get back up this time. I was drained. I couldn't take pain like this. How did anyone take pain like this?"

"You can stop… with the lies," I said, tears and snot now flowing uncontrollably. "I'm at your mercy. Get on with it and do what you wanted to from the start."

Yael bent down on the balls of her feet and smiled at me like nothing was wrong.

"I've never lied to you. Since that laser blew off your mask, I've only been looking out for you. If I gave Shun the order to kill you, you're right, I could finish it right now. But you know what I'm gonna do instead?"

As I braced myself for her to continue torturing me, she wrapped her arms around me.

Firm, but not too tight. And so warm.

"Give a hug to a kid who really needs one," she said, joining me in tears. "I am so, so sorry Shun did this. I don't know why she did it, but I promise you, I'll get to the bottom of it. And I'll make sure personally you never have to worry about her again. Okay?"

I pulled back a little and looked into her soft, wet, defeated eyes.

She wasn't lying. She meant it. She meant every word. She wasn't behind this. "Yael…"

"Shhh," she hummed, bringing my head into her chest. "It's okay."

She wanted to stand by me. She wanted to be my mother. She wanted us all to be happy. "I'm sorry."

"It's okay," she said, stroking my back. "It's all okay."

The bulk of my dream could still come true. Take away Shun, and the rest of it could still happen. There was just one problem.

I didn't want that anymore. "Guh!"

Yael panted and gasped as I drove my katar through her chest. I pulled it out and moved away as buckets of blood poured out of her.

"I'm sorry," I repeated, continuing to cry. "The girl you love isn't me. The girl you tried to make me think I was isn't me. And you'd never accept the real me." I fell over onto my hands and knees. "I'm so sorry!"

Maybe it would have been nice to create a utopia where every last person in the universe lived a blissful life without hardship. But deep down, I knew that wasn't the universe I wanted to create. I liked hurting others, and killing, and making those around me suffer. I wanted only the elite to thrive, and for everyone else to live in fear and desperation, and to tremble at the sound of my name.

Yes. That sounded much better. The only downside was it was a universe Yael could never be a part of.

I tilted my head up. Yael laughed with a smile spread across her face, even as she bled out.

"Quit... apologizing, would you?" She laughed even harder. "Didn't I promise I'd always forgive you?" She was completely covered in blood, but I didn't care. I raced back into her arms one last time. "I hope you and Moli are happy. Man... we could have had such an awesome story."

I waited for her to continue, but nothing else came out of her mouth. Those were the last words she spoke, as the light left her eyes.

Yael Pavnick was dead.

And all I could do was scream.